Death
on
the Green

Also by Catie Murphy

Dead in Dublin

Death on the Green

on the

A Dublin Driver Mystery

CATIE MURPHY

KENSINGTON BOOKS
www.kensingtonbooks.com

KENSINGTON BOOKS are published by

Kensington Publishing Corp.
119 West 40th Street
New York, NY 10018

All Kensington titles, imprints, and distributed lines are available at special quantity discounts for bulk purchases for sales promotion, premiums, fund-raising, educational, or institutional use.

Special book excerpts or customized printings can also be created to fit specific needs. For details, write or phone the office of the Kensington Sales Manager: Attn.: Sales Department. Kensington Publishing Corp., 119 West 40th Street, New York, NY 10018. Phone: 1-800-221-2647.

Kensington and the K logo Reg. U.S. Pat. & TM Off.

First Printing: October 2020
ISBN-13: 978-1-4967-2420-5
ISBN-10: 1-4967-2420-8

ISBN-13: 978-1-4967-2421-2 (ebook)
ISBN-10: 1-4967-2421-6 (ebook)

10 9 8 7 6 5 4 3 2 1

Printed in the United States of America

This is for the Lady Writers' Club: Susan, Ruth, and Sarah,
who help me so, so much with this series.

Acknowledgments

Writing is frequently rife with the conviction that one Cannot Do This, regardless of how many times one *has* done it successfully. In the midst of one such crisis, my Lady Writers came through for me with a brainstorming session that really helped me get my feet under myself again, so I'd like to offer a particular thanks to Susan Connolly and Sarah Rees Brennan for talking me off a (metaphorical) cliff whilst walking home on a blustery Dublin night. This book, and this series, is much better for your insights, and you, along with Ruth Long, have gone beyond the call of duty in making sure I've got my Irish idioms right. Thank you all so much.

I've very much enjoyed working with editor Elizabeth May, and remain ridiculously thrilled with the Kensington art department, and cover illustrator, Anne Wertheim, for the bright, charming, funny covers for these books. Also, props to Lorraine Freeney, the back cover copy writer for *Death on the Green*, because I laughed all the way through reading the copy. It's just amazing. <3

And, as usual, all honors are due to my family for helping me carve out space to write in, and to the War Room for making sure I used that time well. You're all the best!

Pronunciation Guide

Irish names will often trip up English-speaking readers because we try to map English letter sounds and combinations onto a language never intended to use them. The trickier names in *Death on the Green* are pronounced as follows:

Cillian = Kill-ee-an
Fionnuala / Fionn = Finn-OO-luh / Finn
Niamh = Neev
Aibhilín Ní Gallachóir = Evelyn Nee Gallaher
Howth = Hoath
Saoirse = Sersha

CHAPTER ONE

Lou MacDonald lay face down in the hazard pond, his pink shirt billowing and puffing with air as the water dragged him under.

A baffled silence rolled over the little group who crested the small hill to find him there. They were mostly fans, men and women who had braved a soft, not-quite-raining September morning for the chance to watch aging PGA champion Martin Walsh play a casual game across the green. The soft-voiced, good-natured murmuring that had come with watching a world-class golfer—even one past his prime—couldn't stand up to the shock of a death on the green. The entire gathering stood rigid, no one able to even imagine what they should do.

Goosebumps shivered over Megan Malone's spine and arms. She didn't even *belong* there, really: she was just Martin Walsh's employee, hired to drive him around for the ten days he was in Dublin. She knew almost nothing about golf, but Martin had invited her to walk along the course after dropping off his wife, Heather, at *her* golf course, farther north on the little flat island in Dublin Bay. Megan, always preferring to go for a walk than sit idly in the car for hours at a time, had come along willingly. She felt her black-and-white chauffeur's uniform marked her as the help, but as far as Walsh's fans were concerned, being in his employ meant she belonged to some secret league they couldn't hope to aspire to. They kept a respectful distance. His caddie, a man half again as large as Walsh himself, was pleasant, especially after Megan offered to help lug clubs. That got her into his good books, but he'd turned down the offer, and since his job was being at Walsh's side, he didn't have much else to say to her. So Megan had trailed along with the group, watching them from the outside rather than being a part of it. Not that she minded. Getting a glimpse of people's lives from the outside was part of why she loved her job as a driver.

Usually, though, those glimpses didn't end with a dead man floating in the middle of one of Ireland's trickiest water hazards.

Lou MacDonald, a big, friendly man, had been less impressed than the fans, and more open than the caddies. He'd chatted Megan up at the clubhouse, fascinated to hear how an American had come to be driving limousines and town cars in Ireland. The short version, she'd told him, was that she had citizenship through her grandfather, so they couldn't keep her out. He'd laughed and she'd offered to tell him the long version as they walked around the greens, but MacDonald waved her off with a promise that he might join the group on the last few holes, if the weather warmed up a little. Otherwise, he was more content to sit with a tumbler of whiskey than tromp across the damp greens on a misty Irish morning.

It seemed absolutely impossible that he could be drowned in a pond at the fifteenth, when they'd left him in the cozy clubhouse less than two hours earlier. And yet there he was, sinking lower into the pond while everyone stared in dismay.

Megan finally jolted toward the water, jumping the low, overhanging bank into the pond with her knees well bent, to keep from landing hard in unexpected shallows. Freezing water splashed up as she landed deeper than she expected, soaking her all the way to her bra. She straightened, gasping, and lurched forward, struggling through hip-deep reeds that were nearly invisible from the surface. She heard splashing behind her, as if her actions had shaken the others into motion. Someone was on a mobile, calling for help, but Megan reached Lou's prone form and turned him over, fearing it was too late. His face was flaccid and his skin cold to the touch. She checked for a pulse anyway, found none, and still lowered her ear to his chest, just in case she might catch some last, promising thump of his heart.

Martin sloshed to her side, his face a grimace of distress. "He's—he can't be—" Like Megan, he felt for a pulse, checking Lou's wrist, though unlike Megan, he dropped the dead man's hand almost instantly, looking queasy. He wasn't a large man, was Martin Walsh, but neither was he so small that he couldn't hit a golf ball what looked like miles, to Megan's untrained eyes. He was fit, dressed for casual warmth on the course, and trembling like a frightened animal. The whites of his eyes glared around their brown pupils, and his lips were already going blue. "It hasn't been an hour since we left him! He can't be this cold!"

"It's the water." Irish lakes might be pretty nearly at their warmest in mid-September, but the pond still had a bone-chilling heaviness. It had already penetrated Megan's thigh muscles and was draining the heat from her core. Standing waist-deep in numbing wetness, she felt the muck on the bottom of the pond seeping over her shoes and slowly offering a false sense of warmth. She gnawed her lower lip, staring at Lou's body, then made the decision and seized his arm, wading back toward the shore.

"Megan, what are you doing? What are you doing?" Martin splashed after her, wake from his movement rolling ahead of them both. "He's dead! Shouldn't we leave the body where it is for the police?"

"He might not be dead. Cold-water shock can slow the metabolism way down. I want to try CPR, but it's a lot easier on shore. Get something warm. Take everybody's coats. There's a—" She got to shallower water and had to turn, grab Lou by the armpits, and drag him the rest of the way to land.

Lou MacDonald hadn't been a small man in life. Now, weighed down by pond water and the boneless relaxation of unconsciousness, Megan would have sworn he weighed about a quarter ton. Her foot slipped on the overhanging pond lip, sandy soil breaking off to splash into the water, and she nearly lost her grip on the body. Teeth bared and breath short with concentration, she tried again, taking a large, awkward step back and straining to haul Lou up. She staggered, back aching, heart pounding so hard it blurred her vision, and shook her head, although whether she was saying *no, I can't do it,* or *no, I won't fail,* even she didn't know.

Martin, nearly green with horror, grabbed the dead man's legs and heaved him upward as Megan scrambled backward with the bulk of his weight. A second heave got him all the way onto shore. Martin all but ran from the water as Megan fell onto her bum, then righted herself to hands and knees so she could turn Lou's head to the side. She fished in his mouth with a finger, pulling his tongue straight so it wouldn't choke him. Water dribbled from his mouth and Megan heard Martin throwing up on the grass a few feet away.

"Here." One of the onlookers came forward with his coat. Other people came with him, offering help in increasingly loud, chaotic tones, until a matronly-sounding woman snapped, "Put them on top of each other on the ground and smooth them out. You and you, help this woman move the body onto the coats." Even in the midst of a crisis, a tiny spark of humor blossomed in Megan's chest when everyone fell in to helping, unable to deny the Irish Mammy Voice. A few seconds later, Lou had been moved to the pile of coats. Megan crawled on them too, putting weight on his sternum in hopes of forcing water from his lungs. The coats were enough warmer than the damp ground that she became aware, very abruptly, of just how cold *she* was.

Someone with a floral scent and long, polished fingernails touched Megan's shoulder and spoke quietly. "Let me get this wet coat off you."

Megan, still trying to force water from Lou's lungs, nodded. Between one push and the next, the woman stripped away Megan's chauffeur's jacket, then dropped a warm, puffy winter coat over her shoulders. A violent shiver started in Megan's gut and shuddered its way out. She shoved her arms through the coat's sleeves, wishing she dared stop to strip her wet shirt from beneath the coat, but except for that first mouthful, no water had come out of Lou yet. Megan didn't want to risk a hesitation that could cost the man his life.

It felt like forever, although it surely wasn't really more than a minute or two before someone said, "There's no water coming out."

Megan snarled, "I *know*," and only then, slowly, upon hearing someone else say it, began to realize what that actually *meant.*

Lou had only expelled a mouthful of water, and that when she'd turned his head. She hadn't been able to force any more water out of him since, although she was both strong and trained to do that sort of thing correctly. Suddenly spent, she fell back from Lou's body, only then seeing that blood had pooled beneath his head, staining the light blue lining of someone's coat.

Megan clenched her teeth and reached into her inner chest pocket for her phone. For a heartbeat she panicked: the phone wasn't there. But then, neither was the pocket, because she was wearing somebody else's warm winter coat, not her black uniform jacket. She looked around at a couple of dozen, maybe more, worried, frightened people surrounding her and the body. One of them was the nail-polished woman who'd taken her jacket and still held it, clutched against her chest. Megan waved her hand and the woman startled, hugged it closer as she looked around as if wondering what Megan wanted, then visibly realized she was *holding* what Megan wanted. She handed the jacket back, and even in the grey morning light, even with the fabric black and hiding water well, Megan could see that, despite her splashing entrance to the pond, it wasn't wet much past the ribs. Her phone was probably safe. She still breathed a sigh of relief when the phone turned on without complaint. Megan closed her eyes as she touched the name she needed and put the phone to her ear.

"Detective Bourke? This is Megan Malone. I've just found a dead body."

CHAPTER TWO

The Royal Dublin Golf Club, at some eight kilometres—five miles—northeast of Pearse Street Garda Station, was not, strictly speaking, Detective Paul Bourke's jurisdiction. On the other hand, it was Bourke whom Megan had met three months earlier when she'd become entangled in an investigation after one of her clients had been murdered, making him the only police officer she knew well. Or at all, really. And she didn't know who was responsible for policing Bull Island, off Dublin's coast, anyway, so Bourke was as good a choice as any.

He arrived at the golf club less than half an hour after Megan called. There were other gardaí on the scene by then, presumably called in by himself and, also presumably, from the precinct Megan should have called in the first place. Either way, he was the first plain-clothes offi-

cer to arrive, the sharply cut lines of his skinny suit somewhat spoiled by calf-high green wellies that kept the
damp off his feet. He wore a trench coat over the suit and
came striding across the green like a badly shod Doctor
Who, with the wind rifling his sandy red hair. Upon his
arrival, he said, "Ms. Malone," with a note of incredulity.

Megan turned her hands up helplessly. "I know. I don't
know how this happened again." For a few seconds they
fell silent, their eyes meeting, as Megan remembered,
vividly, how Elizabeth Darr had died at her feet under
suspicious circumstances just a few months earlier. Bourke,
clearly remembering the same thing, sighed heavily, and
Megan spread her hands again. "I didn't even know the
victim this time. Does that count for anything?"

Bourke, sourly, said, "Not really. You said on the phone
you thought it was a murder. Why?"

"There was no water in his lungs." Megan looked toward where paramedics had taken MacDonald's body
into an ambulance, which had left thick, deep tracks across
the golf course green. "I thought there was a chance he
could still be alive and in cold-water shock, so I dragged
him out and tried to expel the water from his lungs and
stomach, but nothing came up. I know how to do CPR
correctly," she said with a glance back at Bourke, who
nodded. He'd been there in the aftermath of her doing
CPR on Elizabeth Darr. "If there'd been water in his chest
to dislodge, I'd have managed it," Megan went on with
confidence. "There wasn't. So he died before he went in
the water. And there's a wound on the back of his head, so
either he smashed his skull against something before
falling face-first into a pond he hadn't been planning to
go near, or somebody killed him."

Bourke's eyebrows, so blond they were nearly invisible, rose to wrinkle his forehead. "And how is it you know he'd no intention of going to the pond?"

"Mr. Walsh introduced me to him at the clubhouse before we came out onto the green. When we left he said he'd far rather stay in the warmth with his whiskey."

"So you *did* know him."

"I met him once, two hours ago," Megan argued, then glanced at the sky as if the thick cloud cover might part, reveal the sun, and, with it, the time. "Three hours ago now, I guess. Anyway I didn't *know* him."

"What was he like?" Bourke had taken a notepad with a dark purple cover from his trench coat pocket. The one he'd used for Elizabeth Darr's investigation had been dark green. Megan wondered if he had a new one for every investigation, and if it meant he had to carry several around at once. He wrote quickly as she spoke, loops and stops visible in the action of his hand.

"He seemed nice enough. Friendly in that I'll-talk-to-anybody way the Irish have." Megan pursed her lips, having forgotten momentarily that she was speaking to an Irish-born person, but Bourke only smiled briefly at the stereotype and gestured for her to continue. "He was the sort to have a tumbler of whiskey in hand before noon, but he didn't come across as drunk, and he didn't toss back a whole glass of booze while we talked, or anything. I'm not even sure he drank any at all. He wanted to know how I'd come to be driving in Ireland, and that was about it. We only talked for a few minutes. He said he might join us on the back nine if the weather cleared up." She cast another dubious look at the sky. "I did have somebody say to me, 'It *is* clear, the clouds are very high . . .' right after I moved here, and I think she was half serious, but they were a lot higher and thinner than this. *I* wouldn't have called this cleared up. Still, he obviously decided to go for a walk. Or someone did a *Weekend at Bernie's* with him."

Bourke took this flood of information stoically. "Any idea what his relationship to Martin Walsh is?"

Megan made an I-don't-know face. "They obviously knew each other pretty well. They're about the same age, I'd say? Midforties? Not much older than you and me anyway. Martin is still trying to win a last PGA Tour, so he can't be *that* old."

"Martin Walsh is forty-eight," Bourke said in a tone that suggested he couldn't believe Megan didn't know that.

"Forgive me for not being up on Irish golf prodigies," Megan replied, amused. "I knew who he was, isn't that enough?"

"Next you'll be telling me you've only the faintest notion who Katie Taylor or Conor McGregor are," Bourke muttered beneath the sound of Megan's laugh.

"No, I know them. Look, Detective, I know this probably isn't your usual beat, so thanks for coming out when I called."

"I can't imagine explaining to the chief why I got a personal call about a murder and didn't come to have a look, so no worries. I'd best get to it." Despite his words, Bourke lingered a moment. "How are the puppies?"

A smile split Megan's face. "They're grand. Dip is bigger than Thong—"

Bourke looked pained, and Megan fought down a laugh. She had, in the midst of Elizabeth Darr's murder investigation, acquired a Jack Russell terrier who had just given birth to two puppies. The boy's brown face looked like it had been dipped in chocolate, so Megan called him Dip and, as she now had it on good authority because she had a weird sense of humor, she had dubbed his sister Thong, making them a *diphthong*. No one else thought it was funny, and Megan's friend Fionnuala, who had promised to adopt Thong, also swore the little girl puppy would be renamed something more appropriate. Bourke clearly agreed with Fionn's sentiments, although he his own self had dropped by to woo Mama Dog a few times, showing little interest in her offspring.

"—and they're both pretty thoroughly weaned," Megan finished, still smiling broadly. "Fionn's supposed to bring Thong home this weekend, I think. I hope so. My boss gives me the stink eye every time she sees me. I'm not supposed to have dogs in the apartment."

"Sure and that'll teach you to rent a flat from your employer." Bourke, with a nod, went to interview people.

Megan said, "As if that makes sense," under her breath, and then, as if it needed a defense, added, "It was a good deal!" aloud before muttering, "It's not like I *knew* I was going to end up with puppies when I rented the place," to herself.

Detective Bourke was a long time talking with Martin Walsh. The ambulance drove away, and several terrified-looking young people driving golf carts arrived, keeping their distance from the witnesses to the aftermath of Lou MacDonald's death. Megan, shivering with cold, sidled toward Bourke and Walsh under the guise of being responsible for taking the golfer home, but mostly she just wanted to listen in. Once she was close enough to hear, she stamped up and down a short path behind Bourke, trying to stay out of his sight and hoping to warm her muddy feet and half-frozen thighs. She did have a pair of survival blankets in the boot of her town car, but going to get them would mean abandoning Walsh and, more to the point, abandoning any hope of overhearing his conversation with Detective Bourke.

Martin, wrapped in a woman's long wool coat to keep some of the cold off him, looked a wreck, and kept glancing toward the ambulance tracks. His pale hair collected mist until the beads pulled it down over his round face, making him look like a particularly dim-witted, shaggy-haired sheep. "Everybody liked Lou," he said for the fourth time that Megan had heard. "He wasn't the sort to make enemies. He didn't have time for that rubbish. If you didn't like him, that was on you. He'd never make a fuss about it. I've known him since I was twelve, and I only ever saw him get into a fight once."

"What happened then?" This was apparently new even to Bourke, who began writing again. Megan stood in place and stomped her feet on the squishy grass, listening.

"Ah, we were out at a pub like, and some wee gobshite came after one of our mates, a Nigerian fella. The gobshite called him a word I wouldn't want to repeat, and Lou stood up and asked him if he'd care to say that again. The wee gobshite threw a punch, and it was like in the movies so, where a wee little man hits a big one and the big one barely turns his head? That was Lou. I'd never seen him so surprised. He was six three like, and built like a barrel back then, though he'd taken some of the weight off these last few years. No one *punches* a man like that, especially not a wee gobshite. So Lou hit him back, just the once, but that's all it took. The wee gobshite fell down, and we went back to drinking while his lads dragged him out of there. But that was most of thirty years ago, and you couldn't even call it a fight like."

"He golfed?" Bourke asked with a nod, as if it all tied together.

Martin, shivering in his borrowed wool coat, shrugged. "When we were lads, ah, with the shoulders on him, you'd have never seen the ball again, if only he could hit it. But his wife golfed, and he took it up to spend time with her. He was never so competitive as I, but he might have been a better golfer, once he got into the game with Kim. We were making a run at the Ryder Cup wild-card selection together this year." Pain shattered across Martin's face, and, compounded by the cold, nearly turned to tears. "I guess it's only me now."

Detective Bourke looked around at Megan, who apparently hadn't gone unnoticed after all, at the gathered entourage who were still being spoken to by uniformed gardaí, and finally back to Martin Walsh. "You and Ms. Malone had best get to the clubhouse and warm up. I'll need to talk to you more there, but there's nothing that has to be discussed in the wind and mist and cold, especially with you wet all over."

Megan blurted, "Oh, thank God," and scurried, with Walsh, to one of the golf carts, which had been abandoned by its driver some time ago. The kid came running back, though, and dragged a heavy wool blanket over the front seat, offering it to them.

"Would you want a hot toddy or coffee waiting for you?" he asked in concern. "I can radio ahead for it."

"Jesus, yes," Walsh blurted. "As stiff a coffee as they've got." He huddled under the blanket. Megan nodded at the driver, who looked glad to have something to do, and radioed in their request as they tucked themselves under the blanket. "There's a washer and dryer at the clubhouse," Walsh told Megan through chattering teeth. "They'll get us sorted."

Megan, shivering uncontrollably, still giggled. "I don't think I'll pass muster for the dress code in my underwear, Mr. Walsh."

Walsh, dryly, said, "I think they'll make an exception this once. Look, lad"—this was to the golf cart driver—"has anybody got robes or slippers up there? I know it's not a hotel, but—"

"They'll bring clothes in from the Pro Shop, sir," the driver said, quickly enough that it had clearly already been discussed amongst the staff. "We weren't sure how many people were wet, or needed clothes, but they'll have shirts and shorts, at least." He gave a worried glance over his shoulder at them. "I don't know that there are any slacks, or anything tailored for you, ma'am . . ."

"If the club can see past an ill-fitted polo shirt and shorts just this once, I'll get by," Megan promised. The driver gave her a relieved smile, and for the remainder of the short drive to the clubhouse, everyone was content to ride in silence.

Under the dull afternoon light, the clubhouse's red-slate roof looked nearly black, but its clean, bright white walls silhouetted distraught staff as they came running out to meet the golf cart. Some bore towels, others, the promised Irish coffee, and still others appeared to be there for the craic—the fun of it—so they could later tell everyone the story as they'd seen it firsthand. Megan accepted a towel—warm from a heated towel rack—gratefully, and heard one of the male members of staff murmuring, ". . . this way, and I'll bring you to the showers so you can warm up," to Walsh.

Megan took a delicious, warm slurp of whiskey-laden coffee and stepped toward the boy talking about showers, only to receive a look of uncertainty. "You said showers. I'm freezing."

"Ah, uh, well, I'm afraid—you see, we have no facilities for women's showers here, ma'am."

A bubble of heat that had nothing whatsoever to do with the coffee bloomed in Megan's stomach. "I'm sorry?"

"No, no need to be sorry, ma'am, we just do—"

"I'm sorry," Megan said again, this time much more sharply. "You misunderstood. That wasn't an apology. That was a polite expression of disbelief. What do you mean, you have no facilities for women's showers here?"

"It's—well, the clubhouse is—the club is—that is to say, the membership—" The young man faltered and looked desperately around at his coworkers, none of whom seemed inclined to rescue him. His gaze finally came back to Megan, but he didn't finish what he had to say, only opened and closed his mouth like a gasping fish. Megan, feeling a ferocious smile tighten her face, just waited, and when the boy didn't speak, she said, clearly and precisely, "I'm sorry, I just don't understand what you mean. You're going to have to explain it to me in small, exact words."

"The Royal Dublin doesn't allow ladies as members," the boy finally whispered. "So there are no facilities for women on the grounds."

Megan, fairly sparkling with rage, smiled until the young man took a step backward. "Excellent," she said when he moved. "You may lead us to the men's facilities, then."

"What?" The youth, naturally pale to begin with, went ghostly white. "What? No, ma'am, I'm afraid—"

"Kid," Megan said through the teeth of her smile, "the only reason I am not ripping you personally to shreds is because you are not yourself responsible for a no-doubt-centuries-old, reprehensible rule. That said, you are one hundred percent responsible for opting to work at a facility where women are apparently considered not even as important as second-class citizens, but instead are not worthy of thinking about at *all*." Her gaze raked all of the staff, many of whom looked away uncomfortably. Megan growled, "That goes for *all* of you," before bringing her attention back to the luckless lad who had chosen this hill to die on. "I assure you that I have *no* intention of simply drying off and taking however long it takes to warm up naturally when there are showers available. If any of the I-hesitate-to-use-the-word-'gentlemen' at this club have a problem with that, I invite them to take their antiquated, sexist, misogynistic views up with the management."

Flushed with fury, she stalked past the kid, fully intending to find the showers herself. He made an alarmed sound and ran ahead of her, pretending he still had control of the situation, and Martin Walsh, chortling, followed on behind.

CHAPTER THREE

"**L**ou would have liked you," Walsh told her, once they were both showered—privately, Walsh having given Megan the run of the place before taking his own—dressed, and dried. "He thought the bylaws forbidding women members were despicable."

"*Lou* thought?" Megan had the opportunity to be glad that even in the modern era, many Irish men ran to the small side: the Pro Shop had found a pair of khaki slacks and a nice, dark green polo shirt that fit her pretty well, all things considered. Her hair, up in a French twist, had a lot of damp in it, but not quite enough to undo and let dry, so despite the circumstances, she felt well presented. Everything but her feet, at least, which were clad in socks whose stripes matched both her shirt and slacks, but unshod. "What do *you* think?"

They'd found shoes, along with everything else, to fit

Martin, who was dressed almost identically to Megan. He was about five nine, already inches taller than Megan, but the way he stood suddenly suggested he was taking advantage of the extra half inch of height his shoes granted him. "I don't know, I think there's something grand about hewing to the old ways. There aren't so many spaces where men can be men without women clucking over them anymore."

"Right." Megan barely managed to keep it under her breath, remembering at the last moment that for the moment, she was effectively Walsh's employee. "Nowhere like most boardrooms, or government offices, or most widely respected sports, for that matter, or . . ."

Walsh obviously heard her anyway and gave her a sidelong wink that seemed at odds with his friend's death only hours earlier. "Like I said, Lou would have fancied you." He opened the locker room door, holding it for her, and Megan accepted the gesture as gracefully as she could. An agitated staff member—not the same young man as before—appeared with an ornate, doily-lined silver tray—and Megan bet the doily was real linen, not paper—upon which two magnificently cream-topped Irish coffees sat.

Megan reached for hers eagerly, wrapping her hands around the hot glass and hissing with pleasure as it reddened her palms. Walsh took his, too, and the twitchy waiter said, "This way, please."

They were escorted through high-ceilinged halls, dark wainscoting changing to bright as they were led into a bar that looked, to Megan's eye, as if the décor had come straight out of the 1970s. Judging from the condition of the orange-and-blue-plaid chairs, though, it was almost certainly modern retro. Grey light spilled heavily through enormous windows on one side of the bar, making glimmers of brightness on the dark brown tables and the wood of a large, partitioned bar. Megan and Walsh were brought to seats well away from the windows, not, Megan thought, for their warmth, but more to try to discreetly hide the fact that a fox was amongst the hounds, as it were.

It didn't last: Detective Bourke came striding in just as Megan finished her coffee. Walsh stood, concern cutting lines around his mouth and deepening shadows under his eyes. "Detective Bourke. Do you know what happened yet?"

"I'm afraid not." Bourke sat, one long leg crossed over the other and his notebook resting on the chair's orange arm. His wellies looked even more incongruous in a setting that encouraged his well-fitted suit. "Are you two warmed up? Nice shirt, Megan."

Megan wrinkled her nose and the detective flashed a smile. A professional, polite smile, sadly, rather than the occasional disarming grin that took him from pleasant to breathtaking. "The color is good on you," he said with all evident sincerity, then opened his notebook. "Mr. Walsh, can you give me a few minutes with Ms. Malone? I prefer to take statements alone, if I can."

"Another coffee is calling me." Walsh rose and went to the bar, where he looked as grateful for the second Irish coffee as Megan had been for the first.

Bourke followed her longing gaze. "Need another?"

"Desperately, but I'm on the clock. I shouldn't have even had the one I did. At least they didn't make it the way Ruth Negga does." At Bourke's quizzical look, Megan grinned. "It's one of those spend-a-minute-with-a-star kinds of videos. Look it up, it's brilliant."

"It can't be bad if it involves her own self and whiskey," Bourke allowed. "So, what happened out there?"

Megan threw her head back against the chair's cushions. "I've no idea. Lou said he might meet us on the back nine, which . . ." She raised her hands to the sky, indicating she was only repeating what she'd been told. ". . . which *apparently* isn't *actually* a 'back nine' here because it's an out-and-back course, which I guess means you turn around halfway so you don't end up on the other end of the island and have to hoof it back three miles to the clubhouse when you're done with your game."

She lifted her head to see what Bourke made of all that. He'd lowered his chin to give her a look that would have been well suited to a librarian glaring over the top of her glasses. Megan muttered, "Look, I don't know anything about golf, okay? This is all news to me. I'd been wondering why a man who didn't want to be bothered coming out with us in the mist would meet us on the back half of the course. But the out-and-back thing means he was going to meet us at the fifteenth hole, or something. Not a long walk, in other words."

The detective's expression cleared and he made a note. Megan craned her neck to look at his page, but even if the glimpse she got had been enough to read anything, his upside-down—from her point of view—handwriting was indecipherable. "So I never saw him again until he was face down in a pond. That crack he took on his head? I didn't even notice it until the blood stained the coat he was lying on. There wasn't a lot of visible blood in the water, or anything. His face had gone pinkish, so I thought he'd drowned, but now I think the blood must have had a few minutes to pool in his face? His hands were a little pink, too, but I thought that was the cold water, not lividity."

"It probably was. Lividity doesn't generally set in for a few hours, even if the body is in extreme conditions, like five-degree pond water."

"Fi—oh." Megan shook her head. "I've lived here for over two years and I still think Celsius is a lousy system for temperatures. I just think if you can viably say it's twenty-two *and a* half degrees, you've got too much variable in there. Anyway, that's pretty cold, that's like forty, forty-one degrees Fahrenheit. Cold enough, anyway. And he wasn't in the pond very long. He couldn't have been. Mr. Walsh wasn't playing with anyone, so we didn't really take very long at any given hole, even with the grandstanding and glad-handing."

Bourke's pale eyebrows rose in invitation for Megan to continue. She snuggled down into the chair, wishing she had a blanket, and smirked. "He was putting on a good show for his fans, talking up his plan, shaking hands, then making a big deal of sending everybody back a few steps while," and she deepened her voice, "the champion lined up his shot." Bourke's smile flashed again, and she went on in her normal tones. "There weren't enough people to really be in any kind of danger, I don't think. Not unless he let go of the club, or hit a ball backward. But he wanted room to work with, and it added to the mystique of it all. You know, the lone hero silhouetted on the green hills, making the game-changing swing, all that."

"I thought you weren't into golf."

"I'm not, but I love human nature, and I can totally see a dramatic story when it's being played out in front of me. Anyway, so call it about six minutes a hole? And we were on our way back when we found him. That's just barely an hour between leaving the clubhouse and finding Mr. MacDonald in the water hazard. He'd been in the water long enough to get cold, but *I* was in the water long enough to get cold, and I still had blood flowing through my veins. So, if I was in there three minutes, he might have been in there thirty? We were at the fifteenth hole, so he had to have time to walk that far, get clobbered, fall in the pond, and die. I guess he had to leave the clubhouse pretty early, even if he knew the straightest path across the green to us."

"You've been thinking about this." Bourke sounded very faintly amused, and Megan spread her hands.

"Of course I have been. It's not every day you come across a dead body." At Bourke's expression, she grimaced. "Or every month, either, I guess. I mean, maybe *you* do."

"But it's my job. Did you see anything noteworthy while you were out this morning? Aside from a dead man," Bourke said before Megan could go there. "Any uncomfortable behavior from the ensemble? A sullen caddie?"

"Those are very leading questions, Detective. Are you supposed to ask things like that?"

"No, which is a problem with interviewing someone you know and whom you suppose is not responsible for the incident. So were there?"

Megan shook her head. "I talked with the caddie for a minute while we were setting out. He was pretty formal, but nice. I didn't know part of their job was walking ahead of the golfer to find out where the ball had actually landed, but he only did that for a couple of holes this morning before Mr. Walsh said it was silly to put him to the trouble when it was just himself playing and no one coming up behind us." Megan smiled, amused. "I could tell the caddie didn't really think much of that. Like Walsh was trying to make himself a man of the people, right? To impress the ladies, I guess. It worked, too."

"Oh?"

"Oh, you know. You've gone out with Niamh a couple of times, right? You know how people get around celebrities. If they do anything vaguely normal, people get all fluttery about it."

A smile pulled at the corner of Bourke's mouth. "I didn't expect to find myself trending when somebody snapped a picture of her buying a smoothie and then wanted to know who the bloke was, so I suppose I do."

"It was a good picture, though."

Bourke looked faintly horrified. "You saw it?"

"You *were* trending." Megan grinned broadly. She'd accidentally mortified both Bourke and her friend, rising film star Niamh O'Sullivan, on a phone call a few months earlier. They'd recovered from their embarrassment enough to date, which not-so-secretly delighted Megan. "All you needed was Dip or Thong and you'd have been a perfect family portrait."

"We're getting off-topic," Bourke said firmly. "Please relate your experience on the green this morning, Ms. Malone." He managed to combine a light note with absolute seriousness in his tone. Megan sat up, gathering herself, and closed her eyes to help herself recall the morning.

"I was a little distance away from most of the crowd for most of the walk," she admitted. "Closer to the caddie than the fans. The fans definitely thought I belonged with Walsh. One woman even sidled up to ask me if I'd been with Mr. Walsh long. I mean, she must know he's married, right? But I don't know, maybe that didn't matter to her. She looked pretty thrilled when I said I was only his driver. Which I would have thought obvious, because . . ." She gestured at her clothes, then, remembering she was no longer in her chauffeur's uniform, opened her eyes and shrugged expressively.

Bourke met the wordless commentary with a brief nod, and Megan continued, her gaze now focused out the windows. They had a splendid view of the green, and she imagined that on a sunny day, it was truly glorious. Even today, with the heavy mist and thick clouds, it had a certain deep quietness that offered a feeling of serenity at odds with knowing a man had just died out there.

"I think Martin shook everybody's hand at least once. He was right in there, enjoying being the celebrity. One of the women—not Fingernails—"

Bourke lifted his pen a few centimetres, questioning. Megan said, "The woman I talked to, the one who lent me her coat, had great fingernails. An inch long, pointy, with coral and gold sparkle shellac." She glanced at her own hands, at nails kept short, tidy, and polished with unobtrusive, clear varnish. "I'd love to do that, but I'd live in terror of breaking them every five minutes. Anyway, a different woman asked Martin if he could help her with her backswing. She was obviously angling to get into a clinch with him right there on the field, but he put her off charmingly and played alone. It's something, watching him. Even if I don't know anything about golf, I was obviously watching a master. He played the whole front nine—is that what they call it?—under par, except for a couple of bad shots early on that put him at only par for the hole." Megan rolled her eyes. " 'Bad shots.' As if I could have done it at all. But I could tell he wasn't pleased about them. He stood there for a minute looking after the ball, then came back and talked to them about a slice or a hook or something before we went on. Somebody—a guy—asked about a shot like them from some competition a few years ago, and he was polite, but kind of cranky about it. Later, I heard somebody say that had been the beginning of the end for his pro career, at least in any meaningful way."

Megan looked toward the bar and the second Irish coffee Martin had more than a little longingly, then sighed and turned her attention back to Bourke. "He and the caddie went a little ways ahead then, and I kind of hung back to eavesdrop. They all knew everything about him, and the guy who'd asked about the competition said a shoulder injury had opened him up to the slice. Somebody else said she knew he'd gone to physical therapy and it had mostly helped, but sometimes, especially on a cool morning like today, when he hadn't warmed up enough it came back to haunt him. I would hate to be famous," she said, almost mystified. "Can you imagine living your whole life with strangers knowing that much about you?"

"Some people want that," Bourke replied. "What happened next?"

"I don't remember any more bad shots after about the fourth hole, so it all kind of got samey-samey. A load of people tromping along going 'oooh' and 'aaaah,' and Walsh eating it up with a spoon and sparkling those big brown eyes at the ladies. And then we came over the hill at the fifteenth hole and saw MacDonald in the pond, and everybody froze for a second. I thought Walsh was going to pass out. I went into the water and decided there was a chance he was just in cold-water shock—I hadn't seen the head injury—and pulled him out. Martin helped, but it made him throw up. And when I realized MacDonald hadn't drowned . . ." Megan spread her hands. "I called you."

Bourke closed his notebook and sighed unprofessionally. "That's pretty nearly what everyone's said like. The course has been closed down and we've lads on the bridge and the causeway, so no one's left the island, at least. I'll be interviewing everyone on the grounds, but so far, the stories of all the people who were with you corroborate."

"Are those of us who have been interviewed allowed to leave?" Megan glanced toward the window again, then looked for a clock. "Mr. Walsh has an actual game tomorrow, if he's up for it, and I have to go get his wife from St. Anne's."

"The hospital?" Bourke looked startled.

"No, the golf course! The other golf course!"

"Oh." Bourke shook himself. "That makes more sense so. The hospital closed when I was a kid."

"Just because you look like the Doctor doesn't mean you can time travel, Detective."

Pure delight spread over Bourke's face. "Do I now?"

"Well, I thought so, in that outfit. The boots really kind of sealed it for me. So can we go? Although if my uniform isn't dry, I can't drive anywhere. Orla would skin me alive." Megan made a face and then made a gesture that threw the concern away. "She's going to anyway. She was half-convinced I'm a curse on the Leprechaun Limousine Service name after the business with Elizabeth Darr, and this isn't going to help. I'm surprised she hasn't called to give out to me already."

"Give it another hour," Bourke said, not at all helpfully. "She'll hear about it by then. And I think you can go, but don't leave the country."

Megan stood up, smiling. "If I left mid-job, Orla would fire me anyway, so I'll probably stick around. Besides, I've got to walk the dogs."

"Good to know the power of An Garda Síochána is less compelling than the threat of an ill-tempered, inner-city lass in her sixties and the power of puppy bladders," Bourke said dryly. He stood, too, offering his hand for Megan to shake. "Tell your wee creatures hello for me."

"I will, and Mama Dog, too." Megan shook the detective's hand, then looked around in search of someone who could tell her where her uniform had gotten to. She'd just caught a staff member's eye when the main doors burst open and Heather Walsh ran in crying, "Martin! Where's Martin? Oh my God, is my husband dead?"

CHAPTER FOUR

Heather Walsh collapsed in a wailing heap in front of the open doors, making, Megan thought, a nicely cinematic picture. Mist and clouds billowed in the background, the whites and greys contrasting with the dark doors. Heather, drenched with that same mist—it weighed and darkened the strands of her honey-colored hair to brown, and made a cream-colored polo shirt cling as well as knitted cotton could—looked fragile and helpless in their framing. Deceptively fragile: Megan knew perfectly well that the rangy young woman had the physical strength to drive a golf ball three hundred metres down the course. Her cheeks were flushed and her legs, bare beneath a black golfing skort, were as muddy as her shoes, as if she'd run all the way from St. Anne's, two miles up the island. Her heaving cries broke through the rush of noise as men ran to her side, shouting reassurances. Megan took a couple of prudent steps backward, keeping out of the surge, and bumped into Paul Bourke.

He caught her so she wouldn't stumble, and met her eyes with lifted eyebrows that implied both a trace of personal amusement and a great deal of professional interest in the ruckus unfolding around Heather. Megan allowed herself the very faintest smile in return and enjoyed the warmth of his arm around her middle for a moment as their mutual attention was drawn back to the performance before them.

For a few seconds, Heather was entirely engulfed by the crowd, but as Martin, who had sprung from his bar stool, tried to push his way through to his wife, the crowd parted to make a corridor—a funnel, Megan thought— that opened up to allow him a path. Heather sat at the base of that funnel, looking improbably tiny because everyone around her was on their feet. Like a small, helpless creature, she lifted a gaze torn between disbelief and hope until she saw her husband. A cry burst from her throat and her expression crumbled into agony as she scrambled forward to crash into Martin's arms. He fell to his knees as he caught her, and their gut-wrenching sobs briefly silenced all other sound in the clubhouse.

Later, Megan thought it was truly astonishing that no one took out their mobile to record the heart-rending scene, but just then, even she only dragged in a breath that shook with reflected emotion. The club members slowly closed ranks around the bereft couple again, as if protecting them from the outside world's view, although none of them spoke. Megan heard Martin's murmur clearly as he explained that Lou had died, that he hadn't called because he knew she was playing and didn't imagine she'd hear about it until he had a chance to tell her. Heather blurted something unintelligible. Through the gaps between legs and shoulders, Megan saw Martin shift, searching for his phone, then heard his low curse. Like Megan, he had not only changed clothes entirely, but had been carrying his phone, probably in a hip pocket. He wouldn't have been able to answer Heather's calls if he'd wanted to. His apology filtered through the crowd, and then he helped her to her feet. Solemn men parted again, allowing them to move slowly toward the bar, their heads bowed toward one another's.

Megan rocked back on her heels, half taken in by the theatrics and half feeling like she was watching a stage play. To her surprise, she found that Paul Bourke's hand still rested, lightly, on the small of her back, and her heart gave a sudden emphatic *thump*. "You're nice and warm."

"Mum always said I was a furnace, even though I was skinny. You're still chilled."

"It'd help if they closed the doors." Someone did as Megan spoke, the ambient warmth rising considerably as soon as the breeze passed. Bourke dropped his hand, and a little surge of disappointment ran through Megan. So did the impulse to kick her own ankle, as she knew perfectly well he was seeing her friend Niamh at least casually, and she herself had had a handful of nicely successful dates with Jelena from the gym. "Still," she said out loud to herself, and when Bourke looked askance, felt her face heat and shook her head. "Nothing. That was quite a thing," she said with a nod toward the Walshes, who were now locked in an embrace beside the bar, Heather's face buried in Martin's shoulder. "I wonder if I should interrupt."

"Find your uniform first," Bourke suggested. "Give them a few minutes to calm down."

"You're a wise man, Detective Bourke."

"That I am. Go on so. And Megan?" He spoke just loudly enough to make her turn back quizzically before searching for her uniform.

One of his brilliant smiles slid across his face, lighting his eyes. "Do try not to get involved in any more murders."

The youth she'd scolded earlier eventually brought Megan her newly dried chauffeur's uniform. Once back in the suit, she approached Martin and Heather Walsh at the bar.

A little to her surprise, they were both more sober than not. Martin's second Irish coffee remained half full, and although a crystal whiskey tumbler sat next to it, the amber liquid looked barely touched. Martin saw her glance go to the drinks and a look of bitter acknowledgment swept his face. "My best mate's dead and I can't even drown my sorrows for fear of the hangover losing me a wild card slot tomorrow."

"I'm sorry, Mr. Walsh. Is there anyone you'd like me to call?"

"Oh, they're already ringing Heather's phone because mine's banjanxed. She had to turn it off." Heather Walsh's mouth tightened in grieved acknowledgment, and she put her hand on Martin's arm as he said, "What kind of man turns away his bereaved friends so it won't upset his game?"

The recrimination in Walsh's voice ran deeply enough that Megan caught the bartender's eye and, with a couple of pointed glances and a small gesture of one hand, asked, without words, if Walsh had drunk more than she thought he had. The bartender shook his head, flickering two fingers up, and then shrugged. Surprised for the second time, Megan schooled her expression.

"I know I only spoke to him for a few minutes, Mr. Walsh, but your friend seemed like the kind of person who would—" Megan broke off with a breath of laughter. "Honestly, he seemed like the kind of person who would probably want you to play the game brilliantly and then break down on national TV so everyone would really appreciate what a terrific guy he was."

Martin Walsh gave a startled, sharp laugh that lurched between hilarity and hysteria before settling into a wheeze that had him wiping his eyes. "You sized him up, all right. God, he'd love that!"

"Well, then, I suppose that's the kind of man who puts off bereaved friends for a day," Megan said gently. "You're from Westport, aren't you, Mr. Walsh? Will I call any family over to be with you? Mrs. Walsh?"

"My family is all in America." Heather had a naturally low, smoky voice that now broke over the roughness in her throat caused by her earlier sobs. "And Lou—we've called his daughter. Someone's driving her over from Westport." She took a shuddering breath. "She's destroyed. I don't know what we're going to do, how we're going to—I don't think I can play on Thursday, Marty."

"Of course you can." Walsh's tenor changed, becoming supportive. "He'd want you to, love. You know how good he thought you were. He wouldn't want to be the reason you didn't play."

"He wouldn't want to be dead either!" A gut-wrenching cry tore from Heather's chest, and she swiped her arm over eyes suddenly flooded with tears. She blurted, "Sorry," at Megan, who shook her head helplessly, murmuring, "No, it's fine. It's fine. Come on, why don't I get you two back to the hotel?"

She guided the Walshes out the doors, her breath

catching at the sea-borne mist's cool contrast to the warm clubhouse. The sky had brightened over the past hour or so, white now instead of heavy grey, but clouds still hung low over the island. It left the mainland, only a few hundred metres away, feeling distant. Someone closed their car door with the dull, hollow *pop* that wet air could carry. Then excited, insufficiently hushed voices made it clear that the story of Lou MacDonald's death was spreading. Megan put herself between the Walshes and the gawkers, hurrying them to her Lincoln Continental. The faint, dark green Leprechaun Limos emblem embossed on its door caught the light as she held the door for them, and faded again as she closed it behind them.

Martin Walsh didn't seem to notice the onlookers, Megan's efforts in getting the Walshes out of the public eye, or even Heather as she buckled in beside him. He sat heavily and staring out the tinted side window until Megan got in the driver's seat, then said, "Lou was the only family I got on with besides Heather. And God, he hated my first wives."

"Wives?" Megan winced, having not meant to say that out loud.

Heather gave a short laugh. "I'm number three."

Megan offered a brief smile in the rearview mirror. "Three's a lucky number."

"That's what I tell myself." Heather wiped her hand across her eyes again, then took Martin's hand as he turned a wan smile on her and said, "You *are* my luck. My first wife died," he said to Megan. "My second . . . Americans call it rebounding, don't they? It wasn't a good relationship. I'd given up on love until I met Heather."

Megan swallowed the impulse to say *good lord* and managed, "I'm sorry to hear that" instead. "I'm glad you and Heather found each other." Martin shrugged with the stiffness of a man who couldn't do anything about the past, and Megan decided it was probably an excellent time to end the conversation, before she said something unforgivably insensitive about middle-aged men and young wives. Heather, similarly disinclined to talk, leaned her head against Martin's shoulder, and he pressed his lips against her hair. Megan turned her full attention to the road, pulling out of the club's parking lot and down the short drive leading to the road off the island.

Bull Island's southern end stretched straight across Dublin Bay, a kilometre-long border that, to Megan's astonishment, was literally unnatural: the North Bull Wall had been built two centuries earlier to deal with ship-grounding silt building up on the River Liffey's bottom. In less than two hundred years, the low, flat Bull Island had grown up from that wall, and now curved five kilometres—almost three miles—along the Dublin coast. The "wall" itself wasn't what Megan had imagined either: instead of being tall and perpendicular like a building wall, it was huge chunks of immense rocks and concrete shored and piled up at an angle, and upon which the road appeared to have been built. She kind of wondered whether it had been wide enough for a road when finished in the 1820s, or if the island's swift expansion had given them the earth they needed to make a road on.

Either way, the intervening centuries had created a space that was equal parts golf course, sand dune, and marshy wildlife preserve. Seals, geese, hedgehogs, and a half-dozen endangered bird species made their homes there, and there were signs proudly proclaiming it the only biosphere reserve entirely within a capital city's limits. It all sounded cool enough that Megan was vaguely

embarrassed to have only barely known it existed prior to
driving the Walshes out there. She looked forward to the
better weather tomorrow so she could get out and explore
while her client worked.

Right now there were cars parked all along the wall
road up until the point, about a kilometre from the mainland, at which vehicles were forbidden. Beyond that lay a
beach on the northern side and entry points into the sea
along the wall for swimmers. Even in the chilly, misty
September afternoon, they were out there, along with
kitesurfers and kite fliers out in the water or on the beach.

A long section of the single-lane, wooden bridge leading onto the island was built on the wall, too. Megan
couldn't quite believe people were allowed to drive on
the bridge, which right now stretched away from the island into thick fog, as if putting its best atmospheric foot
forward for her benefit. Most of the island's traffic went
through a newer causeway farther north, but the old
bridge—which replaced an even older bridge a century
ago—remained the easiest way to get to the Royal Dublin
Golf Course, the first of the two on the island. Driving on
it felt, to Megan, like a step out of time; like if a highway-
man, or a coach and four, were to come along on it, that
would be perfectly natural.

That sensation wasn't hurt any by the hotel the Walshes had booked for their stay. Barely two miles from the
island's golf courses, the Clontarf Castle Hotel had made
Megan laugh out loud when she drove up to it the first
time. Like almost any castle hotel, it had modern addi-
tions, but there was no denying that a significant chunk of
the massive stone edifice was a straight up nineteenth-
century castle. As far as Megan was concerned, its loom-
ing towers and dramatic bay windows cried out for

Gothic romances. She allowed that they were probably in short supply, but there was no point in being an American immigrant to Ireland if she couldn't cling to the romantic potential of centuries-old architecture. She drove into the castle's parking lot, killing the engine and taking a moment to watch the little leprechaun dashboard figure do a dance with an epic background.

"I own a house in Dublin," Martin said suddenly from the back seat. "Haven't lived in it in years. Not here enough. Silly to leave it sitting empty for me when I can rent it out. And nobody brings dinner to my door at home."

"I would," Heather protested, although she followed it with a tinny laugh. "Well, sometimes. Once in a while. Maybe. Although I don't really like to cook."

"You do your best work on the green." Martin kissed her hair again.

"Room service alone justifies staying in a hotel," Megan said. "Although I guess that's kind of what take-away is, only for houses instead of hotels." She got out, opened the door for the Walshes, and earned a small smile from Martin.

"I never thought of it that way." He climbed out of the car, straightening his borrowed clothes, and turned to offer Heather a hand. She accepted, looking weary as she stood and smoothed her skort over her bottom. She was a solid two inches taller than Martin, and Megan glanced at their feet to see who had the shoe advantage. Martin did: his leather golfing Oxfords had a half-inch heel, and she wore flat white runners that she probably hadn't been golfing in. "Tee time is at ten tomorrow, Ms. Malone. Can you collect us at half eight?"

"I can." Megan dipped her hand into her coat pocket, coming out with Leprechaun Limo business cards. "I know you have our contact information, but please call and let Orla know if you need anything. I'll take care of it. You've both had a hell of a day."

Martin took the card, furrows plowing across his forehead as he looked from it to Megan. "Have I? You're the one who had the presence of mind to go into the water, to try to save Lou."

"Thank you for that. Thank you for trying." Heather spoke too sharply and her face crumpled with dismay.

Megan, tentatively, touched her upper arm with understanding. "You're welcome. I did twenty years in the Army. A lot of my training is to run toward trouble, not away from it. I'm sorry I couldn't . . ." Megan trailed off, but Martin nodded.

"Me too. Thank you, Ms. Malone. We'll see you tomorrow." He went into the hotel, leaning on Heather with the posture of a man who had been hit unexpectedly and thought another blow might be coming. Megan exhaled heavily and leaned against the Lincoln's passenger door, eyes closed as she tilted her face up to the misty sky. Raindrops splattered her cheeks, and she opened her eyes, offended, to say, "*Really?*" to the uncaring clouds.

Another raindrop splatted right into her eye. Megan blurted, "Augh!" loudly enough to draw attention from other people in the parking lot, one of whom then gave a sympathetic smirk. She wiped the back of her hand over her eyes, grimaced back, and, still blinking to get her eyes feeling right again, crawled back into the car as the skies dropped a deluge of enormous raindrops across the windshield. Megan could hear shrieks of dismay as hotel patrons ran for its safety, and flicked the headlights on as she drove out of the car park to work her way back across Dublin city centre in the storm.

CHAPTER FIVE

The ten-kilometre drive—six miles—took nearly an hour in the late afternoon traffic. Edging along through the city paid off, though, as a triumphant rainbow spanned the clearing skies when Megan turned down Merrion Square East, bordering the St Stephen's Green park. All along the sidewalks, people stopped to pull their phones out and take pictures, and even Megan risked taking one when she paused at a long traffic light. Rain splattered again outside, and a host of umbrellas and hoods went up, although a really remarkable number of people had neither, and just hunched their shoulders against the weather.

Every time that happened, Megan was reminded of her friend Kate from down the country explaining that you could tell German and American tourists in Ireland because they were the ones with brollies and raincoats. The native Irish, Kate claimed, were the people hiding in shop doors or using newspapers to cover their heads, all the while glaring at the sky, as if in some ten thousand years of inhabiting the small, northerly European island, *nothing like this had ever happened before,* and it was therefore a great and shocking betrayal. And just like every other time Megan thought about that, she laughed, because it had such a great grain of truth to it. But judging from the number of snap photographers, they didn't take the rainbows for granted either, and it seemed fair enough to Megan that if you never became inured to rainbows, you could equally never become inured to the rain.

She was still chortling about it twenty minutes later when she pulled into the Leprechaun Limo garage beneath the finally fading rainbow. The garage and the parking lot behind it ran a couple of hundred feet back from the main street, surprising Megan every single time with their depth. She perpetually expected it to be shallow, only twelve or fifteen feet deep, like the cramped company offices that sat cheek by jowl with the garage. A lot of Dublin shops and homes were like that, the result of decades or even centuries of expansion into what had once been gardens or thoroughfares. Not much in Dublin went *up*: it all went *back*.

A car was parked over one of the pits that let mechanics get beneath the vehicles to work on them. Another had just been driven through the big, rattling doors at the back into the ten-vehicle covered car park that protected most of the Leprechaun fleet when it wasn't in use. One window and a door looked in from the office to the garage, but they were both closed off: Orla didn't think clients needed to see the sausages being made, as it were. Otherwise, the walls were blind, pressed against the buildings next door to them. Big, overhead lights had recently been replaced with LED bulbs, and Megan still wasn't used to their intensity, although the detailers said it helped them get the cars cleaner. There were a couple of them working now, and a mechanic in the pit. One of the drivers, Cillian, whose shift usually ran so diametrically opposed to Megan that she rarely saw him, kept walking in and out of the garage as she parked, looking at the sky and then coming into the building, then doing it again. Megan called, "Are you looking for the pot of gold?"

"I am so, and it should be in here! I'm going to start a trust fund for Dervla with it." Cillian Walsh looked as though he'd been purpose-built to fit Hollywood's idea of a strapping young Irish man, with black hair, bright blue eyes, and shoulders that filled out his chauffeur's uniform very nicely. Dervla was his three-month-old niece, and he couldn't have doted on her more if she'd been his own. "The leprechauns must have hidden it here, what with the place being named for them and all, but I can't find it." Cillian ducked inside as a gust of wind blew rain in from nowhere, and bumped shoulders with Megan. "What's the story?"

"You wouldn't believe me if I told you."

"Don't tell me you've got another dead client," Cillian said cheerfully. Megan wrinkled her face, half her teeth exposed in a lip-curling contortion, and Cillian's jaw fell open. "You never! Jaysus, Megan, who now? Jaysus, not me own cousin, Martin Walsh!"

"Martin Walsh is *not* your cousin!" someone bellowed from across the garage.

Cillian shouted, "Leave me my dreams and my claims to fame!" back, while almost hopping with agitation at Megan. "Tell me it's not Walsh. I've laid a wager at Ladbrokes on him being a Ryder Cup wild card pick!"

"No, he's fine. He's . . ." Megan slumped suddenly, the drama of the day finally hitting her. "It was an old friend of his, Lou MacDonald. He died in one of the water holes. It probably wasn't an accident."

Dismay crashed across Cillian's face. "I had a tenner on MacDonald, too! I wonder if I can get over and cancel the bet before they know he's dead—"

Megan said, "Cillian!" in an only half-joking tone of scolding shock, and the office door crashed open at the same moment to allow Orla Keegan's outraged, "*Who* is dead?" to roll thunderously across the garage.

The entire Leprechaun Limousine Service staff tried to cram into the offices behind Orla and Megan. Orla Keegan might have been barely over five feet tall, but she still, somehow, managed to throw them all out on their ear. Megan was willing to bet that they all remained crowded against the door, those ears pressed to it in hopes of hearing what was going on after Orla slammed it in their faces. She turned on Megan, a ferociously cold, blue look in her eyes. "*Who died?*"

"Nobody you know," Megan promised. "Or maybe you do, I don't know, but they weren't a *client*." The garage door into the office suite opened behind the reception desk, so Megan stepped past the desk and around it, avoiding a low, brochure-covered table to sit in one of the expensive, soft leather chairs that sat beneath a large window overlooking the street. Autumn sunshine spilled in the window right then, warming the leather, and Megan gave a contented little sigh of comfort before straightening up under Orla's glare. Her boss made her feel like a guilty teenager most of the time, despite the fact that Megan knew perfectly well she was a model employee. "I was following Mr. Walsh around the golf course and we found one his friends dead in a water hazard."

"And you didn't think to call me."

"With all due respect, I don't think there's anything you could have done. What were you going to do, ma'am, come out and take the limo away from me? I know you're concerned about the company's reputation, but it's not like *I'm* going around murdering people."

Orla's rattlesnake glare sharpened, and Megan groaned. "Well, I'm not. I promise, I had every intention of telling you what was going on as soon as I got back to the garage. Which I'm doing now."

"I don't see how I can trust you to drive a client like Martin Walsh if this kind of thing is going to happen around you."

"It didn't happen around me! It just happened! And you can't cancel my contract with the Walshes, for heaven's sake. If you think me being adjacent to a death or two is a problem, imagine what'll happen if you start canceling high-profile clients!"

"Who said anything about canceling? I'll assign Cillian as his driver."

Megan pressed her lips shut on another protest. One of the reasons Orla had hired *her,* an American driver whose commercial Irish license she'd had to help pay for, was because Megan was happy to take early morning shifts. Cillian had never met a lie-in he didn't like, and vastly preferred driving the clients whose business took them out late at night rather than early in the day. Several of the other drivers worked strictly nine-to-five shifts so they could be home with their families, and Orla knew all that. Arguing with her would only get her back up, and *not* arguing meant Orla would work it all out herself.

Aggravated color stained the other woman's cheeks in response to Megan's silence. Orla had learned her hair and makeup techniques in the eighties and never updated either; the flush of color didn't go well with her glittering blue eyeshadow. Megan, trying not to be aggravating, said, "Mr. Walsh did say he'd see me tomorrow, so I don't think he objects to me continuing to drive him. And I'd like to be there to support them if they need it, ma'am. I wasn't friends with Mr. MacDonald, but I went through the discovery with Mr. Walsh, and that's a pretty shocking event. I think we might have bonded a little." She didn't think that at all, but it sounded reassuring.

Orla thinned her lips. "You're *ma'am*ing me to make me feel like I've control of this nonsense."

A flicker of a smile danced over Megan's face. "Yes, ma'am." Orla's mouth flattened even more, and Megan's smile grew. "What you *do* have control over is whether the contract is canceled. I'd like to think you wouldn't want Leprechaun Limos to get a reputation for running from a tough job. And it's not really a tough job. It's just had an unfortunate turn of events."

"And why," Orla said, "would a nice American girl—"

"Woman," Megan said under her breath.

"—want to keep hanging out where a murder's taken place?"

Megan, straight-faced, said, "It's not about the murder, Orla. It's about doing my job well." She waited a beat or two, then admitted, "And also I totally want to know what happened, and if you kick me off the job I'll have to wait for the official report, which you *know* won't be as good as whatever dirt I can dish up. I mean, you want to be Johnny-on-the-spot with all the latest gossip, don't you?"

"Ah, so now you're only thinking of me." Humor had finally crept into Orla's eyes. Megan had seen her charm clients, but that charisma was saved for when she wanted something. In fact, Megan had been charmed by Orla herself when she'd first moved to Dublin; the other woman's spark and humor had convinced Megan to drive for her. The fact that it all dried up into ruthless business pragmatics as soon as Orla got what she wanted told Megan a lot about her, a little too late. It was nice to see some hint of humanity still in there, since mostly the term "old battle-ax" could have been coined for Orla specifically.

"Don't tell me you didn't get a lot of mileage out of knowing details about the whole Darr investigation," Megan warned. "I bet with the sentencing coming up soon you're going to be the inside woman for information again, and you can't tell me that's bad for business. No publicity is bad publicity, right?"

Orla tipped her head in concession, then pointed a sharp-nailed finger at Megan. "If you learn anything good, I hear it first!"

"You'll hear it," Megan promised, and amended, *but not necessarily first*, to herself.

"And you keep our name out of it!"

"I honestly don't know why anyone would mention the company, but I'll make sure of it." Megan thought there was less chance of keeping *that* promise than the first, if someone decided to care who was driving Martin Walsh around. Still, Orla's gimlet stare relaxed and, judging the moment right, Megan made her escape from the office.

*   *   *

Cillian caught her eye as she slipped out, and Megan made an exaggeration of sneaking away. He cast a smirk toward Orla in the office, and Megan scurried down the street, caught between amusement and disgust with her own behavior. Orla Keegan didn't actually scare her—not much did, after a tour in Iraq—but she certainly bowed and scraped to the short-tempered Irishwoman. It was partly that Orla was both Megan's boss and her landlord, but more that there were half a dozen other immigrants working for the company. All of them treated Orla with obvious deference. They didn't necessarily have Megan's advantages—Irish citizenship, English as a first language—and Megan had noticed that if she back talked, the rest of them got a little tense. More, she'd noticed that if Orla wanted someone to work a particularly awful shift, or clean up after a job that had turned gross—usually teenagers sicking up in a car after their debs—she never went to any of the English speakers first. Since all the other English speakers were Irish-born, Megan didn't know if they were aware, or cared, about that, but she was, and did, so she'd stayed late a couple of times to help on some of those nasty cleaning jobs. Orla had made it clear she wouldn't pay her for that time, and Megan had never pushed it. She just did her best to help out, and tried not to rock the boat for the others.

Besides, she'd rocked it enough for herself. That dour line of thought turned to a smile as she anticipated the greeting, and the source of the boat-rocking, within her apartment. She unlocked the street-level door and took the stairs two at a time to her second floor flat. *First* floor, she reminded herself for the hundredth time. Two and a half years in Ireland and she still hadn't adapted to the fact that they didn't consider the ground floor to be the first floor of a building. You had to go up a flight of stairs to get to the first floor in Ireland. Anyway, whether it was the first or second floor, there were puppies and an increasingly lazy mama dog waiting on the other side of her apartment door. She pushed it open to a rush of wiggles and Dip, the larger of the two pups, making a break for the outside world.

Megan scooped him up and rubbed her nose against his. "No, you don't, you little monster. Besides, even if you did, there's another door down there, and you're never going to be tall enough to open it on your own." She scooted Thong back inside with her feet, got the door closed behind her, and sank down, wrinkling her face to accept puppy kisses of greeting. The two little dogs had gone from barely a palmful to small armsful, but unless there was some crossbreeding hidden in their genetics, they would never be more than about a foot tall. Their mama, although she'd proven chipless—unwanted and uncared for—was a purebred Jack Russell, and she barely came to Megan's calf.

She, more dignified than the puppies, came to lean on Megan's shin and accept rubs while her offspring became increasingly squirmy. Megan, in what she had come to realize was a fruitless ritual, said, "I'm not keeping you," to all three of them, then plunked down on her butt so the puppies could climb on her more easily. A small, scratchy foot immediately went up her nose and, eyes watering, Megan put Dip back on the floor. "Ow. I'm *not* keeping you if you're going to do that to me."

Had they been any bigger, she never would have convinced Orla to let her keep them, extra pet deposit put down or not. Animals were strictly forbidden, according to Megan's lease, and Orla did not have a meltable heart of gold behind her steely gaze. She could, however, be paid off, and Megan was out nine hundred quid—three hundred for each dog, which was both outrageous and beyond the letter of the law—as well as an affidavit promising a deep professional clean of the apartment when she moved out. An actual affidavit: Orla had made her get it notarized and everything. On Megan's own dime, of course. Or, rather, on her own ten cent piece, because they didn't technically have dimes in Ireland, and had nothing like quarters at all.

Megan picked Thong up, kissed the top of her head, and said, "I miss quarters" into the short, fluffy fur. "Okay, who wants to go for a walk?"

Even Mama Dog hopped into action at that, although Megan stopped to grab an apple before herding the three animals out the door. She'd always thought puppies required long walks and lots of exercise, but it turned out they couldn't take more than a ten- or fifteen-minute walk at once at their tender age. It was, Megan had discovered, exactly enough time to take her to any one of half a dozen takeaway restaurants. Her meal planning, since becoming a dog parent, had gone out the window. On the other hand, the falafel guys knew her order by heart now. So did the kofta place, and two different Indian restaurants, and the regular staff at the chipper knew she didn't like vinegar on her French fries, but that the puppies did. That probably counted for something, although not for enough, as far as the dogs were concerned. Megan had looked it up, and cooked potatoes weren't *bad* for dogs, but they weren't great for them, either, so they were never allowed more than one fry each.

They got samosas and the spiciest lamb karahi Megan

could handle and stopped for a pint of milk on the way home. Once there, Megan spread her feast at her kitchen table and ate with three sets of tragic brown eyes watching every motion with patient hope. "Oo wldnt lkk igh," she promised the dogs. "Igsh shoo shhaishy." They would, though, like the rice and naan, and she didn't share those with them either. Finally, full to the gills, she leaned back in her chair—a dangerous proposition, as the slender legs were prone to tipping her over backward—and surveyed her domain through half-lidded eyes.

It had been a fine little apartment before the dogs moved in, but she thought it had become friendlier in the months since. Homier. The window that her tiny dining table sat under overlooked Rathmines Road, one of Dublin's busiest thoroughfares. Megan could just, if she craned her neck right, see the copper-domed church that dominated this section of the city through the window. The sadly neglected kitchen was functional, if somewhat scattered with dog food right now, as keeping meals in bowls were not among Dip and Thong's strong suits.

The other half of the open space made up her living room, with a couch and a comfortable chair, and a television that she resentfully paid the licensing fee for. Beyond that lay an en-suite bedroom where she could see a pair of jeans dangling over the end of the bed. She didn't usually leave clothes out, or her bed unmade, or dog food on the floor, for that matter.

"You kids are bad influences," she told the puppies, who scooted closer with their attention entirely on the leftover naan. Megan chuckled and tilted the chair back down so she could scritch them, then filled a two-litre water bottle from the tap and went to stretch out on the couch with her computer balanced on her lap. Dip tried to climb up on the couch with her and fell off enough times that she took pity and lifted him, whereupon Thong lay down on her foot and whined pathetically. Mama came over and lay down with Thong, and, peace established, Megan web searched Martin Walsh and Lou MacDonald.

A minute later, her phone buzzed. She pulled it out of her back pocket, glanced at the caller name, and put it to her ear, saying, "Hey, Nee."

"I'm looking at your ear, Megan."

"Oh." Megan pulled the phone away again to smile sheepishly at Niamh's image on the video call. *Vone* call, Niamh called it: *video phone*. The terrible thing was, Megan had started using the ridiculous term. "Hey, babe. What are you doing, calling me from California? Aren't you on set? Isn't it . . ." She glanced at the time. "Eleven a.m. there. Never mind, that's not an unreasonable time to call. What's up?"

"What's the story," Niamh corrected. "How will I ever get you sounding properly Irish if you won't pick up the lingo?"

Megan made a face and Niamh laughed, proving the worth of video calls all by itself. Niamh O'Sullivan's laugh would have, in Megan's opinion, made her famous one day even if no one had ever come to appreciate her broader skills as a performer. Her star had already been on the rise when Megan met her, and it had recently gone meteoric. Afro-Caribbean and Irish in heritage, her brown skin, kinky curled black hair, and broad Kerry accent had made her one of the actors breaking down international ideas of what being and looking Irish meant. Right now, her hair fluffed around a gaudily colored headband and backed enormous gold loop earrings, and her on-point makeup glittered green and gold around her eyes in flawless 1970s fashion. Nee could make the look work any day of the week and twice on Sundays, but wore it now for a film laden with enough big names that Megan had nearly hyperventilated as Niamh dropped them. "All right, all right, what's *the story*?" Megan demanded, and Niamh's brown eyes sparkled.

"What's this I hear about you getting involved in another murder?"

"What?! That was in the middle of the night your time! Who told you?"

Niamh, gleefully, said, "So it's *true*? It's all over RTÉ. They're saying Martin Walsh had something to do with it and won't talk to the press. What's the story, Meg?!"

"You're watching local Irish news in California?" Megan asked, surprised.

"Sure I've got the RTÉ Player." Niamh sounded a little offended. "Why wouldn't I? So what happened?"

"Walsh didn't have anything to do with it, but it was a friend of his and they were supposed to be in a game tomorrow for a Ryder Cup wild card, so I'm sure the media *is* all over it."

"It's never Lou MacDonald?" At Megan's nod, Niamh gasped. "What a shame, he was so lovely! I knew his wife," she said before Megan could ask. "She died in a car wreck a long while back, when I was only doing local theatre and commercials. The two of them had bad luck with wives. Martin and Lou, not Lou and his wife. Martin's been married two or three times. One divorce, one died—"

"One beheaded?" Megan asked dryly. Niamh startled, then laughed again, the bright sound pealing across the phone's speakers.

"God, I hope not."

"Me too, since I'm driving the third wife around with him. She golfs, too."

"Does she?" Niamh sounded supremely uninterested. "Martin must be devastated. He and Lou were thick as thieves. Kimberly—Lou's wife—used to say theirs was the only long-term relationship Martin had ever managed."

"He seemed all right," Megan said dubiously. "Upset, but not wrecked."

"But he would, wouldn't he. An Irishman of his generation—"

"He's *my* generation, Niamh."

Niamh passed it off with a wave. "You're American, and a woman, and not Catholic. Repression is the default emotional state of the Irish male born before 1980."

"You understand that that statement coming from someone in your costume seems really bizarre?"

Niamh glanced down at herself and burst out laughing. "And you've only seen the hair. Wait, take a look." She lifted the phone up high so Megan could see that she wore a green, long-sleeved, mostly unbuttoned, flowery blouse tied just beneath her breasts, and hip-hugging jeans with a leather belt nearly as wide as her arm. "And check out the shoes." The phone swung down to show off platform sandals with chunky heels big enough to knock somebody out with. "So speaking as a blast from the past, I can promise I'm not wrong about the repressed state of the average Irish man," Niamh said as she brought the phone back up again.

"Are we talking repressed or *repressed*? I mean, if Lou was his only successful long-term relationship . . ."

"Oh. Huh. I don't think so? I never got a hint of it, but

then again, I might not. Either way, even if he's being stoic, he'll probably need a friend, Megan."

"Or at least a driver he can't get rid of?"

"He's a golfer. I'd guess he's got a lot of drivers."

"Oh my God, you did *not*." Megan actually hung up in laughing horror, and a few seconds later got a text: **I did too, and you love me for it. I've got to go wear the face off your favorite Chris now, so I'm not calling back, but keep me posted.**

Dear God, Megan texted back, **keep *me* posted! And pics or it didn't happen!**

Niamh sent back kissy-faces and Megan, grinning, spent the rest of the evening trying to get the internet to tell her if anybody thought Martin Walsh and Lou Mac-Donald had been lovers.

CHAPTER SIX

Despite Rule 34—a decades-old internet "rule" that if a thing existed, there was a sexualized version of it available online—Megan couldn't even find real-person fan fiction suggesting the two golfers had been lovers, although she stayed up *much* too late looking. At ten, her usual bedtime—because she was old and boring, as she usually informed her younger friends who wanted to *leave* to go out dancing at that hour—the puppies, who were better trained than she was, stretched, wiggled, and trotted over to their bed to sleep. Mama Dog gave her a scathing look at eleven and went to join the puppies, and Megan, guiltily, tiptoed past them at about one in the morning to fall into bed herself.

The alarm went off at ten to six anyway, and through long habit developed in military service, Megan rolled out of bed and into her gym clothes before her brain could wake up enough to object. Her apartment lay across the road from one of the few gyms in Dublin that opened at six a.m., and even the splash of rain that hit her as she ran across the street didn't quite wake her all the way up. She got into the gym and onto a treadmill, where she could move without thinking for half an hour. The Irish were not, generally speaking, early risers, and there were still only a handful of people in the gym by the time she staggered off the treadmill, sweaty but awake.

To her disappointment, Jelena of the heart-shaped face and aquamarine eyes wasn't there that morning. Megan kept the free weights lower than she might have without the other woman there to spot her, but got enough of a workout that her arms were trembling and her legs felt numb as she tripped back home forty-five minutes later. She had to be in Clontarf, six miles across town, by eight thirty, and it was already seven fifteen, which was cutting it close with morning traffic. She took the world's fastest shower, brought the puppies on the world's shortest walk, and slid into the Continental at half seven, which earned her a warning look from Orla, who seemed to be at the garage 24/7. Megan caroled, "I'll make it" out the window with more confidence than she felt, and gave the dashboard leprechaun a rub for good luck toward picking Martin Walsh up on time.

The leprechaun must have done his trick, because she pulled into the rain-glistened hotel parking lot with two minutes to spare. Megan had just decided to risk running into the restaurant to get a cup of coffee when Martin appeared, wearing a long mackintosh raincoat and carrying a golf umbrella that dripped rain from its ribs. He looked dapper and incredibly Irish in argyle socks shown off by khaki, knee-length golfing trousers, a subtle green and gold jumper that matched both the socks and the colors of his saddle shoes, and a tweed flat cap. The whole ensemble should have been garish, but the colors were just muted enough to make it work. Megan got out of the car, looking beyond him for Heather, but he shook his head. "She'll be there by tee time, but she didn't feel up to the media before the game."

"I guess I can't blame her. You're looking good, Mr. Walsh." Megan took his umbrella and opened the door for him.

He gave her a brief smile in response, but up close, she could see that the cap helped disguise the hollowness of his bloodshot eyes, and that the jumper's color did his haggard skin tones a favor. As he got into the car, she noticed someone had hand embroidered a small, dusky green shamrock onto the back of the cap and outlined it with dull gold thread. The understated effect was hardly noticeable against the brown-green tweed wool, but Megan bet it showed up beautifully on TV. A lot of effort had clearly been put into Martin Walsh's branding, and today it gave him something to hide behind. She shook rain off the umbrella, tucked it into the boot, and eyed the scrolling traffic report on her phone as she got back into the car. "Shouldn't take us more than ten or fifteen minutes to get there."

Martin nodded. Megan glanced at him a couple of times in the rearview mirror, trying to gauge his state of mind as they drove. The third time, he caught her eye and offered another shallow smile. "Go ahead, you can ask."

"How are you *doing*?" She put a subtle emphasis on the second word, as if she'd asked the question before and gotten a rote response, but now had the privacy to pursue the reality instead of the polite fiction.

"Quite terribly." Walsh turned his gaze out the window. "I told the hotel not to put any calls through last night, but there were nearly thirty messages waiting for me this morning, and that didn't include my mobile. Even my ex-wife called."

Divorced, beheaded, died, popped into Megan's head, and she bit her tongue to keep from asking which wife it had been. The divorced one, obviously, rather than the one who had died. "Pardon me for asking, but have you eaten anything?"

Martin chuckled, a low sound with more weariness than humor in it. "That's what Jennifer wanted to know, too. Among other things. I have. A full Irish, the same thing I always have on a game day. It didn't taste like much," he admitted to the window, "but I suppose superstition made me eat it. The weather's good for me today. I'm only little, compared to some of the lads out there these days. It means I haven't the height for those long drives some of them do, but I don't sink into the earth on a wet day like today, either, and I've practiced in the rain all me life."

"I never thought of that."

Walsh's smile flickered. "The rain can throw off some of the best golfers in the world. Lou, now, he was like me. Played in the rain all his life. Knew how to deal with sinking an extra centimetre or two into the green. And the island's a sandbar, so the ground can be soft. It's all to my advantage today. Lou would have been happier in the sun, because of the size of him. We were like Laurel and Hardy, we were. Laurel and Hardy, sinking in the quicksand." He fell silent a moment. "I have to get that wild card position. For him."

"I know." Rain splattered the right side of the car as

they drove down the old wooden bridge linking Bull Island to the mainland. A proper line of traffic followed them, cars already parked along the island's southern wall and a few hardy kitesurfers out on the water in their wet suits, taking advantage of the gusts. "Will the wind affect you?"

"Not as badly as some of the others. Ireland wasn't so windy when I was growing up, but the past decade and more I've been playing in worse than this whenever I lived here."

"You lived in America awhile?"

"Long enough to go native." Walsh dropped into an American accent so completely that Megan gave a startled laugh that he looked sadly pleased at before returning to his own accent. "I have to concentrate to do it now, but when I was playing in the States I had to concentrate to keep the Irish. Susan used to make me practice. She said it was part of my branding."

"Susan?"

"My first wife. She died very young."

"I'm sorry." Megan hesitated. "Was it she who embroidered the cap?" Another spatter of rain left fat splotches of water on the side of the car, but a sudden bolt of sun broke through the clouds as Megan turned up the drive toward the golf club. Martin, half-seen in the back seat, took his flat cap off and turned it around to look at the shamrock.

"It was." He sounded almost surprised. "I've been wearing it so long I almost forget about that. No, if it hadn't been for Susan, I'd never have made anything of myself. She had all the ideas on what I needed to do, how I needed to present myself. She used to make me watch Irish actors being interviewed on American television.

Some of them laid the Irish on so thick *I* could hardly understand them, but if you listen to them here, back home, they sound nothing like that at all. It's what she wanted me to do. Lou was better at it, though. People liked him."

"Did he live in America, too?"

"Less than I did." Martin made no move to get out when Megan parked the car. "He had the charm; I had the drive. And I had Susan, who made something of that drive. When she died I suppose I had to keep going for her. An homage, and a way to move forward. Will you walk the course with me?"

A twinge of surprise sparked through Megan before she translated the phrase from Irish to American English. To her ears, it sounded like a request, as if Martin needed her support, but living in Ireland had slowly taught her that he really meant *do you want to walk the course?* "Oh! I—could? I was thinking of going for a hike around the island, though. Although I don't know, the weather is changeable. Maybe I just want to hide in the car, or the clubhouse, and let everyone else get wet. On the other hand, it's not like I'll get many chances to watch professional athletes that up close and personal."

"Golfers aren't the most impressive professional athletes to watch. We just walk around green fields and hit a ball."

Megan laughed. "I suppose, but I don't know, tell that to the millions of people who tune in to golf games around the world. I mean, granted, it's not like the obvious appeal of swimming or gymnastics, where they don't wear very many clothes. But people watch chess matches, too, and golfing at least involves dramatic posing, which chess usually doesn't."

Martin chuckled, and by then Megan had pretty well

talked herself into going with him. She exited the car to get his umbrella and escort him toward the clubhouse. All the other vehicles in the club parking lot were either hired cars like hers, expensive private ones, or media trucks, and dozens of people swirled around in organized chaos. Megan wielded the brolly like a shield, making a space to get them through. Even so, before they reached the front doors, a swarm descended on them: some media, some event organizers, and a handful of faces she recognized as being part of Walsh's regular entourage. One, the good-natured caddie who had turned down Megan's offer of help the day before, nodded to her in greeting. Together, they tried to fend off the media, but a strong-shouldered woman in an RTÉ Sports jacket, her dark hair swept in a tidy twist, turned sideways, and stepped right into Megan and Martin's personal space. A man lifted his camera over his head behind her, filming the sequence. Megan, recognizing the woman, jolted in dismay as she realized that despite her promises to Orla, she and her Leprechaun Limos uniform were likely to end up on the six o'clock news in proximity to Martin Walsh and Lou MacDonald's murder investigation.

"Martin," the dark-haired woman said with pleasant familiarity.

Walsh said, "Aibhilín," with a sigh, and the sportscaster, taking that as permission, dropped the friendly veneer and put a microphone in his face. "Mr. Walsh, the sporting community has been devastated to hear of the death yesterday of Lou MacDonald under suspicious circumstances. RTÉ understands that you, Lou's best friend, were the one to discover the body. Would you like to comment?"

"I would not," Walsh said, more gently than Megan

expected, but his voice trembled. "I've had a hard night, Aibhilín, and I've a game to play now, one that I expected my oldest friend to be playing alongside of me. I'd like to do me best in his honor, and to do that I can only look forward for the next few hours. Please excuse me."

A push came from behind, propelling them toward the clubhouse. Megan looked over her shoulder to see the big caddie had moved behind them. He clearly intended to get them through the clubhouse door even if he had to lift them up and carry them in himself. Aibhilín Ní Gallachóir called, "Does that mean you'll be available for an interview after the game, Martin?" as they were swept past her.

Megan barely got the umbrella closed before they were rushed through the door, and a supercilious Anglo-Irish accent said, "I'm very sorry about that, Mr. Walsh. Obviously we wish to keep the media from haranguing you, but we also simply can't ban them from the premises, given . . ."

The speaker—an angular, balding man with thin features and an obviously expensive suit—made a small, elegant gesture encompassing the entire, high-profile game about to take place at the club. The caddie guiding them into the clubhouse stopped short. Walsh shook his head and waved off the well-suited man's apology. "Not your fault, Ollie. Aibhilín's an all-right sort, just doing her job. I'll talk to her later and make her the darling of the newscast."

From what Megan knew about Aibhilín Ní Gallachóir, she didn't need much help in that department anyway. She was athletic, fit, bold, and had broken her way into the male-dominated sports room years before Megan had arrived in Ireland. She could disarm even the toughest rugby captains with either her encyclopedic knowledge of sports or a flash of an admittedly brilliant smile. To Megan's mind, she was a fixture of Irish sports, even if it had taken her months to realize the name written *Aibhilín Ní Gallachóir* in print was the same as the one pronounced *Evelyn Nee Gallaher* that Megan had heard spoken most evenings when she listened to the news.

"Mmm-hnn." The nasally tenor accent appeared to agree with Megan, to whom Oliver's gaze now turned. "And you are?"

"This is my driver for the week, Megan Malone. Megan, this is Oliver Collins, the general manager of the club." A smirk hurried across Walsh's face. "He'd be the one you'd want to speak to about the club bylaws."

Collins's eyelashes fluttered in a visual stutter as he looked at Megan. The extremity of flutter nearly hid a flash of other almost imperceptible expressions: the flaring of his nostrils, the tension around his lips, a pinch of his shoulders. Megan felt similar reactions flood her own face and posture, and wasn't at all surprised to hear that he knew who she was from his, "Ah. The lady who objected to club rules older than the founding of this country."

Megan stuck her hand out for a shake and offered her toothiest smile. "That's me. Given that the Constitution, which dates from the founding of this country, has been amended dramatically to improve equality and human rights just in the past few years, Mr. Collins, I think that the club could do with considering a few amendments of its own, yes."

"I'll mention it to the Committee." Collins managed to pronounce the word with a capital *C*, and shook Megan's hand with his fingertips, as if afraid to sully himself with her germs. A bustle of activity took place behind them, and Collins's entire demeanor changed, distaste replaced with delight. Megan and Walsh both turned to look, the caddie, who still stood behind them, stepping out of the way. Walsh, in a wealth of understatement, said, "Ah," while excitement charged through Megan until she had to clench her teeth on a squeal.

There were always a handful of athletes in any sport who rose into the common consciousness, whether people followed the particular sport or not. This one—taller, darker, and more charismatic even at a remove than Megan had expected—had gone through the entire hero's cycle, rising from obscurity, conquering the world, falling from grace, and rebuilding a career. Megan, who mostly thought of herself as inured to celebrity, clutched Martin's forearm and hissed, "I didn't know he'd be here!" like an overwrought teenager.

Collins minced off to greet the new arrival as a wicked smile darted across Walsh's face. "I told you you'd want to walk the course with me."

"But—I mean—doesn't that mean you're, uh—" Megan broke off, flustered, looked at the caddie, whose eyebrows rose, then shrugged and said to Walsh, "No offense, but doesn't this mean you're not going to win?"

"I don't have to win. I have to shoot—" Martin took a breath, judged his audience, and obviously cut the gritty details out of his explanation. "There's a cumulative score kept over a season. I have to shoot beneath a certain par to keep my overall score low enough to be a candidate. The selection is then made by the team captain, who—" He nodded to a swarthy, broad-shouldered man talking to a gaggle of reporters on the other side of the room. "Is Victor Fabron, this year. He thinks I'm a cockerel and would've chosen Lou over me, but my numbers are better and—" A grimace passed over his face, and Megan nodded, wondering if sympathy votes were a thing in golf tournament placements.

Walsh looked down, mouth crumpled in a sneer as he tried to compose himself again. After a moment he raised his head again in an abrupt motion, like sharp actions could recalibrate his emotions, and exhaled hard to say, "And I wouldn't have expected to see Fabron here today. He's not playing. I'd say it's a matter of watching me under pressure, up close and personal, now. Besides, yer man there is American, so he wouldn't be contending for the European wild cards anyway. So as I said, it's not about winning."

"Did any of these people dislike Lou?"

"More of them dislike me, but I can't imagine anyone knocking Lou on the head and pushing him into a pond to keep me from playing. They'd have done it to me instead, and kept Lou with them."

Megan inhaled to speak, then closed her mouth on the question, nodding instead. Martin didn't seem to notice. His caddie did, and cast a curious look her way, but also said, "We have to get going, Mr. Walsh."

"Yes, right. Could you make sure Ms. Malone's name is on my guest list, Anthony? I think Ollie will go out of his way to throw her off the grounds if she's not."

"I will." The big caddie smiled at Megan, pointed her at a set of doors leading to the green, said, "Wait there," and disappeared with Martin Walsh.

CHAPTER SEVEN

A few minutes later the caddie came back with a lanyard for Meg, her name printed on it properly, not just hand-written. She commented, and he rolled his eyes. "It'd never look professional and slick, hand-written, and Collins won't have that. He'd as soon throw you out on your ar—em, your ear, so you've got to look the part."

"Thanks." Megan slung the lanyard around her neck and put her hand out. "Megan Malone."

"Anthony Doyle. Friends call me Anto."

Megan's eyebrows went up. "Mr. Walsh calls you Anthony."

"Mr. Walsh pays the bills," Anto said diplomatically. Megan laughed.

"Right, I get you. Look, uh—" She stood on tiptoe, peering past Anto's shoulder and through the crowd. Most of the golfers had gone off the same way Walsh had, leaving the clubhouse full of caddies, coaches, and, Megan suspected, people who were simply hangers-on. They spoke to each other in low voices, and Megan didn't think she imagined that many of their gazes followed Martin Walsh, or that his name was on a lot of lips. So was Lou MacDonald's, all in a low buzz that she couldn't quite make out. Megan wavered, wanting to eavesdrop and wanting just as much to talk with Martin's caddie. "Do you have to go right now? I don't know how any of this works."

"Not just yet. They go out in groups of four, and Mr. Walsh drew a late tee time."

"Oh yeah?" Megan settled back down, arms folded across her chest and her chin tilted up at Anto curiously. "Is that good or bad?"

"For Mr. Walsh, it's good. He likes to know how everyone else is doing. The weather's gone softer, too, and he likes that, too."

"Yeah, he mentioned he had a lot of practice in the rain." Megan glanced past the slowly thinning crowd to the enormous windows. The morning was brighter than the day before, but mist collected on the windows and blew in soft, visible gusts over the low green. "Have you known Mr. Walsh a long time?"

"Long enough." Anto's tone made Megan snicker and step closer, dropping her voice conspiratorially.

"That bad, eh?"

"He can be a right charmer when he wants to be," Anto said, diplomatic once more. "Must be. Three women have married him."

"But?"

Anto gave her a side-eyed look. "Ye's know we'd get in trouble for gossiping about our employer."

"Only if we get caught."

The big man laughed quietly. "Fair enough. All I can say is, whatever happened out there, somebody must have had it in for Lou, because if the two of them had been together, I'd have expected Mr. Walsh to be the dead man."

"So you don't think somebody went after MacDonald to rattle Walsh?"

"Mr. Walsh has ice water running in his veins. He placed in the US Open the day after his second wife served him the divorce papers, and played his best year while his first wife was in the hospital with cancer."

"Jeez." Megan looked off where the competitors had gone, as if there might be a sign of Walsh's coldness following him. "Really, though? He seemed upset yesterday and looked pretty haggard this morning."

"All I'm saying is that I've walked alongside the man for some fifteen years and I'd say he knows how to put on a performance. He might have been different before his first wife got sick," Anto allowed. "I didn't know him then. But by the time she was dying . . ." He shook his head. "Ice water."

"But something rattled him, didn't it? He's trying to stage a comeback, right? Or go out in a blaze of glory, at least?"

"Injury. He bollixed his shoulder eight years ago or so, after his divorce. Doesn't matter how cool you are if your arm cramps and sends your swing short. And the truth is, Mr. Walsh isn't careful with his money, not that you heard it from me. He's got nothing to retire on but his name and winning personality. He needs today to go well. Even if he doesn't make the Cup team, it's one of the qualifying games for the Open. And it's part of a new initiative like, as one of the first tournaments men and women are both competing in."

"There's an entire world going on here I don't know about," Megan said, mystified. "I read up on professional golfing when the Walshes hired the company to drive them, because I like to be able to ask the clients a couple of questions to get them talking about what they love, but I'm not even swimming on the surface. I'm skating on it. Or maybe flying above it. I kind of knew men and women didn't compete together, but don't pro golfers get paid a lot?"

"Sure, if they're winning, or even placing. Mr. Walsh was never a headliner like, but he did well enough to be making seven or eight figures a year, and that stands a man well in the PGA's retirement fund. And maybe he saved up when Susan Walsh was still alive, but he spent it after she died, and his second divorce cost the earth. I know he cashed out what retirement he had then, thinking he'd do well enough to refill the well, but the shoulder injury held him back. He's old enough now, for a golfer, so this is his last chance to get on the Tour. He's either got to make it or marry money, and I wouldn't want to be facing another expensive divorce in hopes of finding a rich wife."

Megan's eyebrows shot up. "Or *did* he marry money?"

The caddie gave a knowledgeable tilt of his head. "If Heather Walsh has a fortune hidden away, it's well hidden. She wins a lot, but I'd say she's been shouldering a lot of Mr. Walsh's debts."

"Hnh. So Ireland's favorite is broke, desperate for a win, and just happens to have been in competition with his best buddy. Do you think he did it?"

"I'm not saying he *wouldn't* have, but—" Anto stopped

suddenly, like he was hearing himself for the first time. "Ah, I don't know so. I don't think Martin Walsh is a nice man, but he and Lou were like brothers. And we were all right there, watching him all morning, so I don't see how he could have done him a harm."

"Yeah, that's true. Tell me about them, though. Childhood friends or something?"

"From primary school. Lou stood up for Mr. Walsh's weddings, every one of them, and vice versa. Mr. Walsh is godfather to Lou's daughter, and if he'd had any himself, Lou would have been their godfather."

"That's right." Megan looked around, as if she could magically locate Lou MacDonald's offspring. "I forgot there was a daughter. How old is she? Is she all right, do you know?"

"I wouldn't be, if it was me own da lying dead in the morgue. Are you working with that guard detective? He had a lot of questions yesterday, too."

"Hah. No. I'm just really nosy, and I'd only just met Lou, you know? And it's kind of the second time this year somebody I knew got murdered."

"Get away outta that!"

Megan laughed. "No, it's true, I'm not joking. You remember that food critic who got killed in June?"

"That was never you!"

"Not killing her, it wasn't!"

A sudden shuffle of movement drove people toward the doors. Anto jerked his head, guiding Megan in the right direction, and for a few mystifying moments she was battered by media, fans, entourages—people who generally seemed to know the flow of things, and were comfortable flattening those who didn't, in other words. Without Anto's broad wake to follow in, Megan would not only have been lost, but crushed. The sensation set her teeth on edge and she pushed down the impulse to throw an elbow or two in order to open up some space around herself. Anto glanced over his shoulder at her and raised a concerned eyebrow. Megan muttered, "I'm fine," then repeated it loudly enough for him to hear, adding, "I don't much like crowds."

"Me either, which is probably why you drive cars and I walk around an open green all day long."

Megan grinned. "Probably." The crowd eased as they got through the bottleneck of the doors and the cool, misty air washed away her tension. Or maybe the wind blew it away: it came up in gusts that whipped around the northerly Howth peninsula and drove straight down the island, then changed dramatically and swept in from the south straight off the Irish Sea. "Holy moly. They can play *golf* in this?"

"Some of them better than others. And it's soft land—you know the island's really just a sandbar? Only a couple hundred years old?" At Megan's nod, he went on. "Soft land, a nicely shaped course, but it's the wind and the weather that makes it a challenge, even for golfers at this level. Some days it's the nicest walk in the world, out and back again hitting a ball around, and other days—" He opened his arms, encompassing the changeable skies—there were blocks of blue now, with rainbows fading in and out of the high clouds—and smiled. "Other days it's a wonder the ball doesn't come flying back on the wind. Today's one of those days. The golfing will be grand so."

"If you say s—whoa." Megan, stepping out from behind Anto's bulk, finally got a good look at the course. She'd thought Walsh's little entourage had made a nice blot on the green the day before, but hundreds of people lined the hills and hollows now, like Gandalf with the Riders at Helm's Deep. "Wow. How do they play without hitting anybody?"

"Sometimes they don't. It's one of the sport's dark secrets. There's loads of fans been hit, some of them really badly."

"No kidding?" Megan's eyebrows rose as she sought the golfers heading out for the first hole. "So somebody could have killed Lou MacDonald with a golf ball?"

"You didn't hear me say it."

"No, I literally didn't. Did you mention that to Detective Bourke yesterday?"

Anto shook his head. "Didn't even occur to me. It was never Walsh anyway. He never lost a ball. I'd know, for all that he was being a man of the people and collecting them himself. It would have taken a slice that even you would have known didn't send the ball in the right direction."

"Right, so it wasn't Walsh, but it might narrow down the suspects to the other golfers yesterday morning. Do you know who was playing?"

"Em, let's see, it was Donál Cunningham, he's a big lad who could hit a driver down half the course, but he and Lou got on, and besides he had his boys with him and I'd say he's never a man to go killing someone in front of his own sons."

Megan burbled with amusement. "How about not in front of them?"

Although he'd implied it with his phrasing, Anto still looked shocked. "I wouldn't think so, no."

"Right. So not Donál." Megan tried not to smile. "Who else?"

"I saw the Connolly brothers in the clubhouse after.

Now they'd have taken a shot at Mr. Walsh, no doubt
about it, but never Lou. People liked Lou."

"Well, someone didn't. Anybody else?"

"Not that I recall so. Not who'd be out on the course,
at least. There were a few like Lou who were laid up with
injuries or too lazy to go out in the rain. John Ryan like,
though he'll stoop and move a worm from his path on the
green, so I'd say he's not the murdering type. We'll wait
here so, Mr. Walsh isn't out for another hour almost."
Anto moved them into the lee of the clubhouse, where a
covered set of clubs with Walsh's shamrock emblazoned
on them sat. Megan looked askance at it, and Anto
shrugged. "I could carry them around in his wake all
morning, or I can set them up early before he arrives and
be ready to fall in when he walks out ready to play. Then
I'm as fresh as he is."

"And less liable to be annoyed by hanging out with
him too long?" Megan murmured. Anto's eyebrows flickered up in agreement. She folded her arms under her
breasts, gazing through the mist—it had come up again,
turning the rainbows grey—and made a face. "He got
under my skin yesterday by saying he liked the club's
rules about no women allowed, but aside from that, he's
been pretty charming, especially since his best friend just
died. It's a big aside, though."

"Maya Angelou said when someone shows you who
they are, believe them the first time." Anto produced a sly
smile at Megan's look of total astonishment. "You never
thought I was the poetry type, did you? You haven't much
faith in Ireland."

"She's not an Irish poet!"

"We've a fair few splendid ones, but most of them
aren't," Anto pointed out. "Irish, I mean. Still, watch your-

self with Mr. Walsh. I wouldn't say he'd do you a harm, but he wouldn't go out of his way to stop one, either."

"What about his wife? Heather?"

As if taking the idea perfectly seriously, Anto, solemnly, said, "I'm sure she couldn't hit a driver from St. Anne's all the way to the Royal Dublin to kill Lou with." Humor danced around his face as Megan blew a quiet raspberry, and he shook his head. "No, Heather's not the type to hurt someone. I've not known her as long—they've been married three years now—but she's quiet. Passionate, but all of it's focused. Dedicated, even. I'm surprised she's with a man like Wals—Mr. Walsh, to tell the truth."

"Why's that?"

"She's a good golfer. Maybe better than he is. An athlete like that doesn't need to hitch her wagon to someone else's star." Anto nodded toward the course, where the first golfers had begun their round. They both fell silent a few minutes, watching the sport's star athlete hit the ball with an elegance that even Megan could recognize, despite knowing nothing about golf. She let out a low whistle and Anto smiled, bright and open. "He's something, isn't he? He's got the height on him, too, that makes him look all the more impressive. I'd say there are few enough professional games where men and women play together, but she'd hold her own with all but himself and the likes of him."

"Really." Megan tucked her chin, impressed. "So maybe Martin hitched himself to *her* star."

Anto pulled his jaw. "Could be, at that, although I wouldn't say he'd handle that well. He doesn't like to be outshone."

Megan puffed her cheeks. "He doesn't like to be outshone, but he's not a top-tier golfer, and he played with his best friend who was his equal? Except that's wrong, because he *is* a top-tier golfer or he wouldn't be vying for a spot on the Ryder Cup team. So he's not . . . elite? Would that be the word? He's not the sort of golfer Heather couldn't keep up with?"

"Let me put it this way," Anto said. "Heather Walsh golfed with Lou MacDonald for fun, not her own husband. Lou, he didn't have that need to win, and he might have been a better golfer because of it. He loved the game and played it well enough to compete in the Tour, but winning it, being a household name, a world champion? That didn't matter to him. I don't know that there are many like him at this level, just playing for the love of the game."

"What about Heather?" Megan asked, idly curious. "Does she have to win, or does she love the game?"

"Some of both. I said she's passionate, and it's true. She wants to win something fierce, but she's happiest when she's out there with a club in her hand, no matter what the weather or the competition. It doesn't hurt her to lose the way it does Mr. Walsh. I'd say his identity is tied up in the win, but hers is in the game."

"What do people like that do when they can't play anymore? Or compete?"

Anto smiled briefly. "Some of them become caddies."

"Really?" Megan lifted her eyebrows at him. "Is that your story?"

"It is. I never loved anything as much as golf, but I wasn't good enough to play with those lads. Still, I couldn't give it up, and so here I am, walking the greens and advising my betters. I should have taken up with the ladies, though. I was never going to find anyone to love more than the game, working with the lads."

Megan, eternally optimistic, said, "There's time yet," and Anto chuckled.

"No, I'd say my heart's given over for good. All right, here's Mr. Walsh and his group." Anto collected Walsh's golf bag and stepped forward as Martin exited the club-house with a small group of other golfers. The crowd still lingering nearby murmured and nodded with satisfaction at their appearance, and Walsh took a moment to shake hands and speak familiarly to a few of the gathered fans.

He was just breaking away from them, looking pleased with his interactions, when a tall, red-headed young woman broke through the crowd. She stalked past the other golfers and stopped dead in front of Martin Walsh. "You son of a *bitch*."

The sound of her slap silenced everyone on the green, and into the quiet, Anto whispered, "That's Saoirse Mac-Donald."

CHAPTER EIGHT

Saoirse MacDonald towered over Martin Walsh, an easy six feet in height, and in the moment of their confrontation Megan had no doubt she could take the golfer in a fight. Evidently, loads of other people thought so, too, as they pulled her away from Martin, who stood, stunned, with one hand over the blossoming crimson mark on his cheek. Saoirse made no effort to rebuff the people pulling her away until they'd moved her several feet back. Then she threw them off with the confidence of a prize-fighter shrugging off a satin robe. She had her father's broad shoulders and wore a coral shell top that looked too cold for the weather, but certainly allowed her the freedom to deliver a good slap. It was French-tucked into jeans and looked smart; when Megan tried the half-tuck, she always felt like it looked like she'd made a mistake getting dressed. Color burned high in Saoirse's cheeks, her breath coming in heaves, like she'd run a race, and although an excited babble had replaced the silence, no one tried to get between her and Martin Walsh.

Heather Walsh, her color as high as Saoirse's, pushed through the crowd from the other direction with an outraged, "What the *hell*, Saoirse?!"

Saoirse spat, "Ask *him*," and spun away to stride back toward the clubhouse. The onlookers parted as if they were afraid she'd go after them next, and closed behind her again to turn their attention, as one, to the Walshes.

Heather had run to Martin's side and embraced him while the RTÉ sportscaster moved in like a shark scenting blood. Beyond them, Megan could see the other golfers Martin was supposed to tee off with, looking increasingly . . . teed off, as it were. But like everyone else, her attention was drawn back to the little drama unfolding, now on camera. Heather was in tears. Martin had developed the stoic expression of a man who couldn't imagine what the problem was, but understood he had to get through it. Aibhilín Ní Gallachóir got into the Walshes' personal space, demanding, "What was that about, Martin? Has bad blood developed between you and Saoirse MacDonald?"

"Don't be ridiculous, Aibhilín," Martin replied quietly. "The poor girl has just lost her father. Her emotions are out of control, and who can blame her? Please, I know this is—" A pained smile wrecked his features. "It's what you would call *compelling drama*, isn't it, Aibhilín? A human-interest story, playing out on the green. Dead parents, grieving children, shell-shocked friends. I know the news cycle could hardly ask for anything more, but my wife and I could use some privacy, and my group are waiting for me so they can begin the game. It's unfair that all of this turmoil should affect them. I wouldn't want to be the man who puts their game off, and God knows Lou wouldn't have wanted that either. Please, excuse me." His arm around Heather's shoulders, he began making his way toward the rest of his quartet, whose sour expressions became tempered with sullen appreciation as the gist of Martin's speech filtered back to them. Anto shot Megan an apologetic look and hurried after his employer, with Aibhilín shouting, "Mr. Walsh! Mr. Walsh!" after them.

When they didn't turn back, the reporter—not facing the camera—bared her teeth. As quickly as the expression came, it was gone again, her face pleasantly enthusiastic about the fracas that had just taken place as she turned back to the camera. "In the wake of golfer Lou MacDonald's death, today's game has taken a deeply personal turn here at the Royal Dublin. MacDonald's daughter, Saoirse, is in attendance and clearly bearing strong feelings toward her father's best friend and long-time competitor, Martin Walsh. We'll be speaking with all of the tournament participants later today, and hope to bring you an exclusive with some of those most affected by this terrible tragedy." She held her smiling pose until the cameraman indicated he was done filming. Then the smile fell away and she barked, "Somebody keep an eye on the Walshes. Don't let them get away after the game without me talking to them. I'm going to find Saoirse."

Megan, torn between the opportunity to watch Martin—and, more interestingly, the others—in action, and the chance to get to Saoirse before Aibhilín did, slipped through the crowd, heading back to the clubhouse ahead of the sportscaster. She'd nearly ducked inside when she caught a glimpse of red hair off to the north, and abruptly cut in that direction, following in Saoirse's wake.

Double-timing it in Saoirse's wake, really. The red-headed woman had about six inches more leg than Megan did, and anger drove her stride. When she was within shouting distance, Megan called, "Ms. MacDonald?" and saw a flash of outrage on the other woman's face as she glanced over her shoulder. "I'm sorry," Megan called. "It's just that Aibhilín Ní Gallachóir is after you and I thought you might want to . . . duck."

Saoirse's gaze flickered beyond Megan, back to her again, then forward as she found a rise in the dunes to position herself behind. A little to Megan's surprise, she paused, waiting for Megan to catch up, though her tone was ungracious as she said, "Who are you? What do you care if the news is pestering me?"

Up close, without her height and hair as her most obvious characteristics, Saoirse MacDonald looked younger than Megan had expected. She wasn't more than in her early twenties, though her strength of action earlier had made Megan imagine she was probably around thirty. "I'm—nobody," Megan said with a crooked smile. "I mean, my name is Megan Malone, and I'm driving the Walshes around, but I'm not anybody who wants a soundbite or an interview or anything. I just thought you probably didn't want to talk to Aibhilín and wanted to warn you she was looking for you."

"Why? Does Martin want you to convince me he's not a total shite? Well, you can tell him he is, and I'll never change my mind on that."

Megan raised her hands as if catching the onslaught of words. "Mr. Walsh doesn't want me to do anything. He didn't send me. I just wanted to help."

Saoirse gave her a perfectly filthy scowl. "You're American."

"Yeah, from Texas. I've lived here about two and a half years now. I drive a limo and I—" Megan hesitated. "I know I don't have any real connection to you, but I was the one who went into the water to try to get your dad out, yesterday. I just wanted to check on you, I guess. I'm sorry I was too late to help."

"Oh." All of Saoirse's fire ran out of her and she sank to the ground, arms wrapped around her knees and head lowered against them. Her butt brushed the damp, grassy sand, but didn't land in it. Megan didn't think *she* could squat like that for more than a few seconds without her legs going numb, but Saoirse remained there for a whole minute or two before raising her gaze past the dunes to the grey, foamy sea. "They told me that Martin and an American woman had gone in after him," she said dully. "I didn't know it was you. Sorry."

"There's no reason you should. I just . . . I wanted to say how sorry I was. I met your dad for about two minutes yesterday morning and thought he was funny."

"He was." Saoirse pressed her lips together, staring at the sea. "Tell me what happened."

"Um. Okay. Do you want to—if Aibhilín doesn't find you in the clubhouse, she's going to start looking around the island. Do you want to walk so she doesn't catch up?"

"Yeah, that's a good idea." Saoirse rose and began a ground-eating pace that cut through the lower paths of the dunes, parallel with the beach and, perhaps, keeping her red hair from being a visible flag that Aibhilín could follow easily. Megan scurried to catch up, and Saoirse slowed when she realized Megan just wasn't as fast as she was. "The police told me what happened, but . . ."

"Mr. Walsh was golfing on his own yesterday morning and—"

Saoirse snorted. "I doubt that."

"Well, without any other golfers. He had a lot of admirers. And your dad said he might meet us to walk back to the clubhouse." As she spoke, Megan realized someone could easily have overheard Lou's plans and taken advantage of them, although from what she could tell, the man had been very well-liked. "The next time we saw him, though—we came over a hill and found him in the pond." She sighed. "We all froze for a few seconds. I don't . . . I don't think it was long enough to make a difference, or . . . or soon enough. But when I unfroze I ran into the water, and Mr. Walsh came in after me."

"Hah! Here and the story that's gotten around is that Martin went in first. I should have known better." Saoirse scrambled up a small hill and jumped down its other side, catching her balance on tall, yellow and green seagrass. Her feet made deep divots in a patch of sand, and her arrival offended a scattering of sea birds that flung themselves into the air and resettled again several metres down the beach. "What happened?"

"I couldn't find a pulse," Megan said. "But then I thought maybe cold-water shock might have dropped his metabolism, so I pulled him out with Mr. Walsh's help. It wasn't until after he was on the ground that I realized he'd been hit on the head, too. I don't . . . I don't think I could have done anything more to help him. I'm so sorry."

"The police said he didn't drown. The crack on his

head killed him, for all that it didn't look like much. And they asked me a hundred different ways who might have killed him, and the only answer I have is Martin Walsh."

Megan watched sand collect around the sole seams of her shoes as they walked down the beach. "And he's got an airtight alibi, because there were about fifteen of us with him at the time. Why do you think it might have been Mr. Walsh, though? I thought they were best friends."

Saoirse shifted her shoulders, tension visible in the awkward motion. "Da's gotten loads better the past couple years. He was always good enough, like? But he'd gotten to where he threatened Martin's standing, and Martin couldn't handle that. He was forever trying to bollix Da's game. He even got his caddie giving Da bad advice."

"Anto?" Megan asked, astonished. "He doesn't even seem to like Mr. Walsh."

"No, never Anto. He's a good sort, although he can't dislike Martin that much. You don't spend years caddying for a man you don't like. Your caddie is closer to you than anybody except maybe your wife, and given how many of *them* Martin's had, I'd say Anto was closer to him than that. They had a deal. You know the usual rates caddies get?"

"Not a clue."

"Around a couple grand a week, and ten percent of a big purse. Anthony gets twenty percent, though, if Martin wins."

"Twe—why?!"

"Because Martin's shite with money and Anto comes along to caddy anyway. Da said Anthony bankrolled Martin through most of his injured years. It wasn't Anto, though. He only caddies for Martin when he's in Ireland. It was his other man, in the States. And Da wouldn't hear a word against him either, thought he was the salt of the earth, even when it was plain as day that he was sending Da's shots up through the rough or telling him to go around when Da's strength was in a drive." Saoirse bent to pick up a small stone and pitch it viciously at the water. It hardly splashed in the surf, but a seagull dived after it, just in case. "Da got a new caddie about three years ago—"

"The same time Martin and Heather got married?"

"About that. And his game's been getting better ever since. He had Martin over a barrel in this game, and Martin knew it. He'd have done anything to keep Da out." Just like that, Saoirse fell to the sand, sobs wracking her body so harshly they sounded like screams. Megan, shocked but feeling like she shouldn't be, put a tentative hand on the young woman's shoulder, and wasn't surprised when Saoirse shook her off. Red hair sheeted around her face and shoulders, blocking Megan's view of her expression, but she could see Saoirse's big hands clutching and releasing the sand in helpless spasms as she cried. Then, as unexpectedly as she'd fallen, she vomited, a horrible short sound that made Megan crouch and put her arms around her shoulders after all.

Saoirse MacDonald, it turned out, weighed a ton. She leaned on Megan like a giant dog who thought it belonged in someone's lap: all elbows and knees and, in this case, snot and sobs. Megan grunted quietly, leaning back into the bigger woman so she wouldn't end up on her butt in the sand. Saoirse turned in to her, wrapped her arms around Megan's torso, and cried helplessly. Megan got an arm arranged so she could stroke Saoirse's hair, and stared over her head at the green hills and hollows of the nearby golf course.

They didn't look like they held secrets and rivalries worth killing over, but she supposed most places didn't. And while she might not really think of golf as a sport where passions ran deep, she'd seen enough clips of temperamental golfers and emotional displays to know that it was her own imagination that lacked, not the devotion people had to the game. Someone—probably someone on the green right now—had wanted Lou MacDonald out of the way enough to kill him, and although it seemed impossible, the current favorite for the job was her client.

Which didn't matter right now, with a grieving child— an adult child, perhaps, but still a child—in her arms. Megan sighed and hugged Saoirse's head against her shoulder, provoking a fresh bout of choking sobs from the young woman. Finally, Saoirse shivered hard, tears giving way to exhaustion and, with it, cold. Megan said, "Come on" gently. "Let's walk, so you warm up. Do you want to go back to the clubhouse?"

"God, no! That woman will be there."

"Aibhilín? Yeah, probably. Okay. Come on. On your feet, hon." She disentangled herself and pulled Saoirse to her feet, although the redhead was so much taller than Megan she had to back up several steps to do it. Once Saoirse was up and wiping her face on hands reddened with cold, Megan asked, "Can I call someone for you?" cautiously.

Saoirse shook her head hard. "No. My mam died when I was a kid and my last boyfriend—" Her face crumpled. "It turned out I was the bit on the side and he got married to somebody else."

"Oh, God, I'm sorry."

"It's just not fair," Saoirse wailed. "All of this shite just isn't *fair*."

"I know." Megan tucked her arm into Saoirse's, drawing her along the beach. The mist had been blown away, or burned off, while they'd crouched in the dune's lee, and the waters around the low island were beginning to reflect a deep, burnished blue. "My mom always told me that life isn't fair, and she's right. It's not fair or unfair. It just is."

"But it feels so unfair!"

Megan breathed a smile at the tiny balls of sand kicked up before their feet, rolling forward to make thin lines that were obliterated with the next step. "One of my favorite comics is a kid complaining that he understands that life isn't fair, but objects to it never being unfair in his *favor*. It is, though, all the time. We just call it luck, and don't think of it as life being unfair in our favor."

Saoirse gave her a look almost as filthy as the one she'd bestowed with their first exchange. "Don't tell me you're one of those New Agey types who think everything happens for a reason and that there's some great cosmic plan."

"Not at all. And I know that this is all terrible, horrible, rotten luck, and it's not fair, and it's not right, and nothing's going to make it right. I just like that comic strip."

"I'll find the son of a bitch who did this and *make* it right," Saoirse snarled.

Megan inhaled, then stopped herself, knowing it was unlikely that Saoirse could carry out that threat, and that reason in the face of impotent rage was rarely welcome. Instead she said, "I'll help you find them, if I can."

"Like you'll be better at it than the guards?" Saoirse laughed bitterly.

"No, but at least you won't feel alone."

The poor girl's expression caved again, and Megan studied the changing light on the horizon while she tried to get ahold of herself. The Howth peninsula curved halfway around the island, both ahead of and off to the right of them, the deep green of summer still coloring its low hills. It made the water between them rich with shadows, though the blue faded as the sea opened up and reached toward Britain. "I grew up in Austin," Megan said aloud, hoping to help Saoirse recover by giving her something to listen to. "Galveston was probably the nearest proper beach, and it was a couple hundred miles away. I've been all over the world now—I was in the military— but I still think just seeing a huge body of water like this is kind of mind-blowing. And the wind is crazy."

Saoirse snuffled loudly, wiping her nose on her hand. Her voice broke dreadfully when she spoke, but she was obviously trying to sound normal. "Da says—said—" She choked again, then rushed through—"said that the wind wasn't so bad when he was growing up, that it's the changing climate that's pushed all the hurricane winds farther north and lashing the island. Ireland, I mean, not Bull Island."

"Right, I followed."

A quick nod conveyed Saoirse's gratitude at Megan's understanding. They'd stopped walking again, the wind lashing copper hairs into Saoirse's face. She brushed them away, only to have them fly back as she gestured around her. "*This* island, though—I spent a lot of time here growing up. Mam loved golfing and got Da into it. I think Martin hated that. *He* couldn't get his best mate into the sport, but a bird had. His words," she added swiftly, at Megan's elevated eyebrows. "Anyway, the birds, that's what I was going to say. It's a wildlife refuge, with a load of deadly birds—"

Megan couldn't stop the laugh that broke free. Saoirse broke off, offended, and Megan laughed again. "I'm sorry. I'm sorry. It's one of those 'separated by a common language' things. I know 'deadly' means 'really excellent' here, but to me, it sounds like the island is teeming with killer geese and terns."

Genuine amusement shone in Saoirse's eyes for a moment. "Don't knock them. Those terns may be little, but they be fierce." She looked along the shore, searching for one of the pretty, black-capped white birds, but there were none along the water. "Well, they're not so common here anyway. It's the curlews you have to watch out for." She made a long, curving, hooked beak with her fingers, and Megan smiled.

"Is that what those ones are? I thought maybe they were a kind of sandpiper. I know nothing about birds," she said hastily, but Saoirse looked pleased.

"No, you're right, curlews are the same family. And they won't come diving for your eyes or anything. They're bug-eaters, or shrimp, or whatever they can dig up in the mud. I know too much about them. I'm sorry, I'll stop."

"Please don't. I love hearing people talk about things they know a lot about. It's one of the reasons I chauffeur. I get to hear the most interesting things."

A shy, hopeful smile crept over Saoirse's face. "Okay. If you're sure. This is my job, and I get excited about it, so I'm never sure when I'm talking too much."

"Oh! So you're not following in the family footsteps?"

"I golf for fun, and it's really useful to be good at it when I need to talk businessmen into something. As long as I'm not *too* good at it, you know?"

Megan rolled her eyes as broadly as she could, and Saoirse smiled again. "You *do* know. So what I do is environmental planning. You know—do you know the Donnybrook expansion project?" At Megan's headshake, she said, "Okay, so, see, there's a field over next to St. Anne's Park that developers wanted to build a load of new houses on." She pointed to the west, across the width of Bull Island. "It's just right over there, on the mainland. You could see it if we were on a rise. And God knows Dublin needs more housing, but it's basically in the middle of GAA fields and disruptive to the community use of the park, but also their wastewater plans were to put a big pipe through the field and drain it into the sea on the northwest side of Bull Island."

"I'm not an environmental planner, but that sounds like a terrible idea anyway."

"It is, and it's worse than you think, because so many of the birds here are threatened species, and it would detrimentally affect the whole island. They tried to rush the proposal through, and the community fought back, and I . . ." Saoirse faltered suddenly, embarrassed. "Helped. I was their expert. I sóund like I'm putting on airs."

"Not at all, and that's terrific work you're doing. Wildlife reserves need passionate advocates."

Saoirse's smile went wet again. "Da was really proud of me, but I'd never have done it if I hadn't been half-raised on this island, with all its wildlife. It's kind of a plain little bar of sand, but I love it. I'm getting—I was getting—a degree in environmental law, too. What I've got, what I do, it's grown out of a wildlife management program, but I want to take it farther."

"You *were* getting?"

"I don't know now, with Da. . . ." Tears flooded Saoirse's brown eyes and she wiped them away. "Thank you," she said hoarsely. "For just talking to me like a person, instead trying to be solicitous or wanting something from me. I know it's barely been a day, but it's still nice to have that instead of people walking on glass around me."

"You're welcome," Megan said guiltily, too aware that she *had* grilled the young woman about her father and his relationships. "I really do like hearing about what people love. And I think you should keep pursuing that law degree. I think your father would like that."

"Now what is it that Lou MacDonald would like?" asked a cheerful voice behind them. Saoirse's expression shuttered, and they both turned to find Aibhilín Ní Gallachóir a few steps behind them, her microphone thrust at Saoirse's face.

CHAPTER NINE

Saoirse recoiled, driving an arm out to create a physical barrier between herself and the sportscaster. The heel of her hand hit Aibhilín's microphone, and Megan saw a glint of triumph in the reporter's eye. She stepped between them, aware she made a laughable obstacle: Aibhilín had at least four inches on her and Saoirse stood an easy half foot taller than Megan did. Still, smaller or not, the fact that Megan intervened certainly got Aibhilín's attention, and her triumph shifted to wariness. "And you are?"

"Not going to let you intrude on a young woman's grief," Megan replied icily. The other women might have nearly half a foot of height on her, but she had half a decade—or considerably more—on them, and a whole career's worth of facing down belligerent people who wanted to get through her. "I understand you've got a

story, Ms.—I'm sorry, do I say the Ní when I'm addressing you directly like this? Is it Ms. Ní Gallachóir or just
Ms. Gallachóir? I probably say it, don't I? It's like the O
in O'Sullivan, right? Only—I'm not clear on this. Does
the *Ní* indicate it's a maiden name? Because it means
something like *daughter of Gallachóir*, right? So—I'm
sorry, I don't know if you're married, it's none of my
business to know—but if you were to take your partner's
surname, would it be done to keep Ní Gallachóir as your
professional name? And then—I've kind of got the idea
from somewhere that whatever the family name might
be, if the mom is more famous than the dad, there's some
kind of linguistic trick that will end up calling the kids
children of herself like, is that right? I admit, if I were in
your shoes, given the groundbreaking sports work you've
done over the past several years, it would kind of get up
my nose if my kids ended up with my partner's surname.
You'd have to move into international celebrity status to
outshine the Ní Gallachóir name in Ireland, wouldn't
you?"

She delivered the entire query in her thickest Texan accent, gleefully watching Ní Gallachóir's eyes bulge
slightly and the quick breaths she drew in hopes of inter-
rupting the onslaught of questions and commentary, until
the woman's broad shoulders dropped in resignation and
she just waited it out. By that time Megan could hear that
Saoirse's breathing had steadied, having overcome the
shock of Aibhilín's intrusion on her life.

Aibhilín waited a heartbeat or two when Megan wrapped
up, eyeing her guileless gaze of interest suspiciously before saying, "It is Ms. Ní Gallachóir so, yes, and I am
married, and use Ní Gallachóir professionally and privately. *Who* are you?" She sounded as if the question was

a last-ditch, desperate attempt to retrieve a piece of information she would never get.

"This is Megan Malone," Saoirse said in a shaking voice. "She's the one who found my da's body yesterday."

Sheer avarice lit Ní Gallachóir's eyes. Megan, all too aware she was kitted out in her chauffeur's uniform, thought, *Orla is going to kill me*, and braced herself as Aibhilín put the microphone in *her* face and said, "Tell us about the moment of discovery, Ms. Malone," as if she'd been aware of Megan's role in the whole story all along.

"There's an ongoing police investigation, Ms. Ní Gallachóir," Megan said politely. "I think I probably shouldn't comment to the press."

"Of course, but how did you happen to be there?" Ní Gallachóir's gaze raked Megan's crisp black-and-white outfit before giving Megan a razor smile. "After all, that's not anyone's usual golfing outfit!"

"Oh, I don't know, Ms. Ní Gallachóir, you see people in all kinds of crazy get-ups these days." Knowing Aibhilín would find out anyway, and seeing an opportunity, Megan added, "I'm a privately hired driver, and I need to get Ms. MacDonald back now, so if you'll excuse us, Ms. Ní Gallachóir, and thank you for your time." She gestured for Saoirse to precede her and moved between the RTÉ team and the bereaved young woman. Aibhilín Ní Gallachóir developed the slow smirk of someone who realized she'd been put on the back foot, but she didn't chase after them as they headed north along the beach again.

Once they were out of earshot, Saoirse whispered,

"I don't know how you did that, but I don't think she liked it."

"You wouldn't believe how far *brash American* goes in this country," Megan muttered back. "One time I completely shocked all my friends because a waiter asked if everything was okay, and I said no, we'd asked for dessert menus twenty minutes earlier and hadn't gotten them yet."

Saoirse went so white that freckles Megan hadn't noticed before stood out on her cheeks. "You didn't!"

"That's what they said! He ran off to get the menus and I looked at my friends and they were all doing what you're doing now!"

"We're *Irish*," Saoirse said in not-entirely-joking horror. "We don't *do* that!"

"See? Brash American. Look, are you all right? I meant to keep you away from her and she ended up hunting you down anyway."

"You kept me from having to say anything. Or from risking saying anything. She would have pressed and pressed about why I slapped Martin until I snapped."

It took a concerted effort, but Megan didn't ask why she *had* slapped Martin. After a few seconds, Saoirse glanced sideways at her and blurted a tearful laugh. "You look like you're going to burst."

"It's not my business," Megan said firmly.

Saoirse gave another blurty laugh. "Do you have kids? I bet you're really good at getting them to tell you things, if you do."

"No, I don't. I was really gung ho career-oriented when I got out of high school, and I never really stopped to consider them."

"Do you regret that?" Saoirse sounded suddenly wistful. "I've never been keen on the idea of kids, but people tell me I'm young, and I'll change my mind."

A spark of irritation flew through Megan. "How old were you when you decided you wanted to work with the birds on this island?"

"Eight, although Da said I'd lie on the dunes for hours when I was littler, watching them, and that I'd tell him all about their habits when he got done with his games. But I don't think I knew you could birdwatch for a living when I was that little."

"So you've wanted to do that your whole life and never changed your mind?"

"That's right."

"I'd say if you can be sure of that since you were a child, you can probably trust yourself about not wanting kids, too." Megan shrugged. "I mean, sure, you might change your mind, and that's fine. People do, all the time. But I think that's often about circumstances, not just an inevitable thing that happens to women as they age. Because you notice how people who say things like that don't usually seem to say it to men?"

"I had," Saoirse replied sourly. "And here's Ireland thinking it's gotten so progressive."

"It's not just Ireland," Megan assured her.

"Martin had it coming," Saoirse said, quietly and unexpectedly. "I still think he had a hand in it somehow, but even if he didn't, he had it coming."

"How come?"

Saoirse shook her head. "For being a son of a bitch all his life. For not liking my mam. For coming back when she was dead, and going back to how things were. For telling Da to keep competing in Mam's memory, when he probably would have stopped after she died otherwise. If he hadn't done that, Da would be alive right now." Grief stormed through her again, driving her to her knees in the sand. Megan, protectively, looked down the beach to see if Aibhilín was down there filming Saoirse's private heartbreak, but the sportscaster and her cameraman had disappeared from view. Sighing with sympathy, Megan crouched beside the mourning redhead and put a comforting hand on her back.

Dealing with death, injury, and bereavement had been expected as an Army medic. It had been a part of Megan's life she'd been glad to put behind her. If someone had told her she'd end up supporting the recently bereaved in her job as a limo driver, she probably wouldn't have believed them. Even when she drove people to funerals, it was her job to be as circumspect as possible in those circumstances, hardly there, not trying to help ease the client's pain. This was twice, though, that she'd found herself in the center of someone else's emotional maelstrom.

And this time she was almost certain to end up on the news. Without meaning to, Megan let slip a sort of ugly little snort of laughter that made Saoirse lift a tear-stained face in confused curiosity. "I'm sorry," Megan said, meaning it. "I was just thinking how completely mental my boss is going to be when she hears I dragged the company name into this."

Saoirse snuffled. "You what? How?"

"Well, Aibhilín Ní Gallachóir might not be an investigative reporter, but I bet she'll be able to find out what car company an American Megan Malone drives for."

Dismay rounded Saoirse's eyes. "Oh no. That will be on me, then."

Megan wrinkled her face. "I'd say you made it a tiny bit easier for her, but no, I'm pretty sure she'd have figured it out anyway even without my name. Come on," she said gently. "Let's get you back up to the clubhouse and into the warmth, at least. That blouse is very pretty, but it's not at all good for walking around a beach with northerly winds coming in. You're turning blue."

As if made aware of the cold by Megan's comment, Saoirse shivered from the bones out and nodded. They rose, the wind wrapping Saoirse's hair around her face again until Megan took off her own chauffeur's cap, tucked all the loose red curls together, and clamped them down with the cap. Saoirse raised her eyes dubiously at the cap's brim, riding high over her forehead. "You've a small head."

"I'm a small person compared to you. Imagine if it didn't have to fit over *my* hair." Megan touched the French twist she usually wore her hair in while at work. Saoirse smiled wanly.

"I wouldn't be able to wear it at all. Thanks, though."

"In the future I'll carry ponytail holders," Megan promised. They scurried down the beach, propelled by the wind, until Saoirse cut right and started climbing a dune. Megan followed uncertainly, but the young woman knew exactly where she was. The clubhouse lay directly in their path and looked warm and sheltering against a cloud-lashed blue sky. Most of the crowd had moved on with the game, leaving the green littered with only a handful of hangers-on, people whose conversations meant more to them than watching whatever dramatics were taking place on the links. All of them, Megan noticed, were men in flat-soled shoes and windbreaking coats; the women had either moved on or moved inside.

"They're going to descend upon you like locusts if you go in there."

"I don't need to go in." Saoirse, though flushed from windburn, had bad color. "I'll just go around to the parking lot. I need to—to go . . . funeral . . . I have to . . ."

Megan nodded. "Is there anyone to help you? Someone drove you over to Dublin yesterday, didn't they?"

"A friend of mine, but she had to turn around and go back to work. I have some university friends here, it's just—everyone's working. Other people's lives don't stop." Her jaw trembled, but she managed, just barely, to hold her voice steady. "And there's no family. It's only me."

"Would Heather help you?"

"After I slapped her husband? Probably not. Besides, she'll be out there, cheering him on, even if he never goes to her games."

"*Really?*"

"Hardly ever," Saoirse amended. "Just often enough to look supportive where the cameras can see him, for a big game."

"You really don't like him very much, do you?"

"Uncle Martin? I used to. Then I found out how nasty and shallow he really is." Saoirse took a deep breath, squared her shoulders, and gave Megan her cap back. "You won't have to deal with him long enough to find that out. Be glad."

"Look, Saoirse, if you need anything, call me, okay? Here." Megan got one of her cards and handed it to the young woman. "My hours are erratic, so I might be able to come help you out when other people can't."

Saoirse looked at the card a long moment, then at

Megan, with her hair wrapping into her eyes again. "Why are you so nice? You don't even know me."

"It's to make up for the rude American stereotype."

"Most of the Americans I know are pretty nice."

"I think most people are pretty nice," Megan confessed. "Maybe it's naive, but I'll cling to that belief as long as I can. Go ahead and call me later. I'll at least text back, even if I can't answer."

"Thank you." Saoirse put the card in her hip pocket and left Megan standing alone on the edge of the windswept green. She watched as Saoirse entirely avoided the clubhouse, then, hands in her pockets, turned toward the links.

Aibhilín Ní Gallachóir was almost certainly out there, covering the main event, since the juicy human interest story on the side had temporarily run dry. Megan had no doubt the reporter would go after Saoirse for some unfiltered commentary, nor any doubt that she would approach Megan, too. Mouth pursed, Megan took her phone out, texted Paul Bourke with **no emergency, but call when you can,** and hardly had it back in her pocket when it rang, a round B for Bourke dominating the screen. Megan answered with, "Hey. I should get your picture so my phone doesn't think you're just another letter of the alphabet to me."

Bourke's purely astonished silence filled the line for a few seconds. "Sure that can't be what you were texting for so."

"No, I just thought of it when you called. You've missed a whole kerfuffle at the Royal Dublin this morning."

Astonishment slipped from Bourke's voice, replaced by professionalism. "What happened?"

Megan outlined Saoirse MacDonald's dramatic entrance and the ensuing conversation with Aibhilín Ní Gallachóir, ending with, "I'm sure she's going to try to talk to me again. What should I say?"

"Em . . ." Megan could visualize Bourke casting a searching, thoughtful gaze upward. "I wouldn't say you know anything that isn't already common knowledge, so I don't see any harm in you talking to her, as long as you keep it to the events of the day. What's the story with Saoirse and Martin Walsh, do you think?"

"She thinks it's his fault her dad is dead. She's convinced if there's a way, he's the one that killed him."

"Unless there's a way Walsh could hit him with a stray ball across half the green without ever losing a ball himself, I can't see how he did it. Still . . ." Megan heard a page turn; Bourke was clearly taking notes. "Anything else?"

"Am I your assistant now, Detective? Is there a cool name for a detective's assistant over here? Do I get to be Assistant Detective Inspector Adjunct, or something?"

"*You* called *me*, Ms. Malone." Bourke sounded amused, though. "Are you with Mr. Walsh now?"

"No, but I could probably catch up, why?"

"It'd be interesting to see how he's performing under pressure, and whether his relationships are showing any cracks." Bourke trailed off leadingly, and Megan, grinning, started hoofing it across the green toward the distant game.

"And I just *happen* to be employed by your person of interest, and just *happen* to have been invited along on his game, and if I just *happened* to notice anything unusual, I might just *happen* to mention it to you?"

"Something like that," Bourke allowed.

"Is that legal?"

"You're a private citizen doing private citizen things," Bourke said loftily. "Sure it's no business of anyone's if you relate your day to a friend over a pint, later on."

"Okay, but I want that Assistant Detective Inspector Adjunct badge," Megan warned.

"Amateur Inspector Detective Adjunct," Bourke suggested. "Do you like opera, Ms. Malone?"

"I thought we were going for a pint. Look, I've got to book it if I'm going to catch up to them, so I'll call you later." Megan hung up and jogged across the green, smiling with anticipation.

CHAPTER TEN

Her enthusiasm, she decided half an hour later, had been sadly misplaced. Walsh was playing a magnificent game, with Anto at his side murmuring and pointing like an orchestra conductor. Neither of them looked rattled by the emotional display earlier. In the time she'd been watching, Walsh had sunk two shots that clearly impressed people who knew what they were watching, judging from the soft *oooo*s of approval that rose and fell. Once Anto noticed Meg and dropped his head in the most subtle of nods, acknowledging her, but he was clearly every bit as involved in the game as Walsh.

Megan worked her way around to Heather Walsh, who kept just out of Martin's line of sight as the game moved forward. She looked cold: colder than Saoirse had looked, in fact, although unlike Saoirse, Heather was at least nominally dressed for the relentless, changeable wind.

She wore warm, flat shoes and wide-legged slacks beneath a hip-length raincoat that had both a hood and a soft, fluffy collar that could be, and was, turned up to brush the bottoms of Heather's ears. She'd pulled on a dark-blue knit cap as well, her honey-colored hair spilling from under it to tangle in the coat collar. Despite all that, her arms were folded tightly around herself, and her smile looked frozen on her face. Megan hadn't been any too warm on the beach, but now, tucked into the body warmth of the crowd, she felt pretty comfortable, and sorry for Heather. She didn't speak as she settled in at Heather's side, but as the game, and thus the crowd, moved forward, Heather noticed her. Megan flicked a smile at her, keeping her voice down to say, "If I'd realized it would be this cold and windy, I'd have brought a giant thermos of coffee with me."

"I'd kill for a cup of good American coffee," Heather said, then blanched. "I mean, not *kill* . . ."

"No, I know what you mean. I know it won't do any good today, but I'll bring you some tomorrow," Megan offered. "My best friend sends me beans every few months from our local coffee shop."

Heather's face lit up, then dimmed again. "I can't tomorrow. I'm playing, and Martin keeps me away from caffeine on game days."

"I could say it's decaf. I'm a very good liar."

A light laugh escaped from the other woman. "Maybe after the game. In celebration, win or lose."

"I assume win, though," Megan said. "Mr. Walsh's caddie says you're very good."

Dimples appeared on Heather's cheeks and disappeared almost as quickly. "Does he? I like Anthony, but Martin won't share him. It's nice to know he thinks I'm good." Her gaze went to Martin, who stood with the other professionals as the crowd slowed and stopped, waiting for the next round to be played. "I'm not as good as Marty is in these winds, though. Hardly anyone is."

"Maybe they'll have died down tomorrow." Megan watched the first player in the round line up his shot, hesitating as the wind buffeted him, and then struck the ball with what looked, to her, like an entirely respectable hit. Heather, though, winced, and Megan, astonished, murmured, "That wasn't good?"

"It wasn't *bad*. None of these players will hit a *bad* shot. But wait." Two more men played their round before Martin stepped up. He looked a picture compared to the others, whose costumes were more muted and ordinary, but Megan had to admit he drew the eye, and that his style made her want to root for him. He spoke with Anto for a moment, both of them nodding as Anto twirled a hand. Then the caddie stepped back, and Martin turned himself at an angle none of the others had taken as they prepared for their turns. Megan saw him make a minute adjustment to his grip, one that made no visible difference to *her*, but which must have meant something to him. Then he waited what seemed an excruciatingly long time, as if someone had hit pause on his play, before swinging a powerful stroke just as the wind suddenly died.

The ball soared with such speed and grace that even Megan gasped, though the sound was lost beneath the general response from the crowd and, more critically, the wind gusting up again. In the distance, it caught the ball, curving it, and an incredulous shout carried across the green as the ball hit the earth, out of Megan's sight. Eager to see what he'd done, Megan was swept along with the observers until they'd reached the next hole, where it was

clear Martin Walsh had come within two metres of a hole
in one. His opponents' balls were scattered far and wide,
comparatively, and he tipped the ball into the hole in one
easy shot while they each took two more to score.

Megan, astonished, said, "How did he do that?"

"I told you. No one knows the wind like he does. Especially on Bull Island, but he's got a gift for it no matter
where he plays. A day like today favors him in a way no
other conditions do."

"How's, um, how's *he* doing?" Megan looked ahead,
like she could see the sport's number one star somewhere
in the distance, and Heather smiled briefly.

"He's only two strokes ahead of Martin, but he's not
likely to lose the advantage. Martin will probably take
second place. Later, he'll say he did it for Lou." Heather
smiled again, but it wavered and disappeared quickly.

"Would he have done as well if Lou was playing
today?" Megan asked softly.

Heather's shrug barely moved stiff shoulders. "Lou
had a longer drive and knew the wind nearly as well as
Marty does. Lou might have edged him out in the last few
holes. We'll never know now."

"Yeah. I'm sorry for your loss. How are you doing?"

"*Me*? Why me?" Heather gave her a sharp look.

Taken aback, Megan blinked. "Well, he must have
been your friend, too, right? If he and Martin were so
close. And on top of that, you're there to help Martin
through it, too. I know it's not easy."

Mrs. Walsh turned her face away, as if embarrassed.
"Right. Sorry. I just—it's been a hard twenty-four hours.
The story had gotten mixed up on its way to St. Anne's
yesterday, and I thought Martin had died, not that he'd
found a dead man. I dropped my club and ran all the way

here. Golfers walk." She laughed, a small, rough sound. "I like to swim for cardio, so I don't know the last time I ran that far. I almost threw up. And Martin—he tamps it all down. It's hard to know how he's feeling, unless he wants to make sure everyone knows."

"He seemed shaken this morning, when I drove him to the course."

"But look how well he took that awful scene with Saoirse MacDonald." Heather had stopped walking along with the crowd, and now she and Megan stood more or less alone on the green, their conversation as private as possible. "He just smiled and went to play the game."

"Yeah. I don't think I could have done that. What was that about anyway?"

"I don't know, but I know it's breaking Martin's heart. He was Saoirse's 'Uncle Martin' up until a few years ago. He thinks college changed her, and maybe it did."

"Well, that's kind of what college is supposed to do. Was it the game that broke them up? Did he think she was going to go into it, like her family?"

Heather smiled unexpectedly. "Maybe. Oh, she was so good, Megan. She was out on the courses with her parents all the time as a child, and as she grew into her height, she just got better and better. Martin coached her for a while, but she decided on wildlife management instead of sports and things were never really the same after that. He never had children, so I think his hopes were set on her being not just his legacy, but all of theirs. His, Susan's, Lou's, Kimberly's."

Megan screwed up her face, looking for a way to ask an indelicate question. Heather saw the change of expression and sighed. "Yes, I'm certainly young enough to have children, but Martin was so destroyed after his first wife's death that he had a vasectomy, and by the time he met me, it was too late to reverse it. We tried, but . . . he tries to be light-hearted about it sometimes. 'I can shoot a hole in one on the green, but . . .' "

With an effort, Megan rearranged her expression into something understanding and neutral rather than the *that was more information than I needed to know* that she felt. "I'm sorry. That must be very hard."

"It is." Heather's voice quavered and she lifted her chin, turning her gaze away until she trusted her control again. "And it's hard on Martin that his relationship with Saoirse has soured. And it's hard for me, knowing that I probably had something to do with it, although Martin's certainly never blamed me and I don't even know if he thinks that." At Megan's quizzical look, she said, "I'm only a few years older than Saoirse, and I think she finds that kind of creepy."

"Ah. Yeah. Families are complicated."

Heather nodded, then breathed hard a few times, like she was facing a race. "I'd better go catch up. Martin doesn't acknowledge me, but I know he knows I'm there. I don't like to leave him, especially in a game as big as this one."

"Do you mind if I join you?"

"No, of course not. Martin invited you, didn't he? You have the badge and all." Heather nodded at the staff badge Anto had procured for Megan. "Did Collins get in a snit about you being there?"

"Oh," Megan said dryly, "you've met him, have you."

A laugh burst free before Heather clapped a hand over her mouth, eyes sparkling. "Martin says he runs this place like a well-oiled machine, but he's the most condescending man I've ever met, which is saying something in a sport like this one."

Megan, outraged all over again, said, "Did you know this club doesn't allow *women* to be *members*?"

"Why do you think I play at St. Anne's?" They complained quietly to each other about similar offenses as they made their way back to the crowd, arriving in time to watch Martin hit another extraordinary shot. The next holes were merely good, but the congregation were buzzing with excitement as the game wrapped up and the golfers waited for the scores to be tallied.

Martin Walsh's one concession to overwhelming excitement was a fist clenched in joy as Heather's prediction proved right and he placed second, just three strokes behind the handsome leader. Cameras whirred and flashes went off as the two men, and the third-place winner, stood together, shaking hands and smiling broadly while coaches, caddies, and fans pressed in to get a picture with them—or at least to be in the background of those pictures. Megan noticed Oliver Collins slithering his way into an embrace with Martin, photographic evidence of which would no doubt end up somewhere on a clubhouse wall.

Once the worst of the shouting and congratulations had passed, sports reporters broke up the winning trio, asking more focused questions. Aibhilín Ní Gallachóir led the pack of people hoping to speak to Martin Walsh, and Martin, as he'd promised earlier, turned his full attention to her. "Tell me about what this victory means to you in the wake of Lou MacDonald's death, Martin," Aibhilín pressed.

Martin pulled a self-deprecating smile, shaking his head. "Well, I wouldn't call it a victory, Aibhilín. The better man won today, no doubt about that. But it does my heart good to have done well today. I thought of Lou with every stroke, and if I didn't know he'd rise from the grave to give me hell about it, I'd even say his spirit was there with me today, guiding me." A chuckle went around the gathered reporters, and Martin's eyes became earnest. "Today wasn't about me. It was about the love Lou and I both had for this sport. It was about honoring my friend. It was about doing our best in the face of adversity, something that Lou and I both knew a lot about."

"You're speaking of the deaths of your first wife, and of Lou's wife, Kimberly MacDonald, of course," Aibhilín said. "How has that affected your game over the years, Martin?"

"Susan wouldn't take it wrong, I think, to hear me say it made me more focused. And Kim brought Lou into the sport. I don't know that I could have continued playing without his support, and hers, in the years following Susan's death. They didn't just affect my game, Aibhilín. They affected my life. I wouldn't be the man I am without them."

"And what happened this morning with Lou's daughter, Saoirse MacDonald? That was a deeply emotional moment."

"It was so, and I don't want too much read into it, now. We've all suffered a tremendous loss, and that poor girl is an orphan now. I'd say she needs someone to take out her anger on, and Saoirse is my family in all but blood. Sometimes we lash out at those closest to us, because in their way, they're the safest to do so with. Family keeps on loving you, no matter what." Tears stood in Martin's eyes by the time he was done speaking, and Aibhilín kept the camera on him as he discreetly wiped them away before saying, "Thank you for your time, Martin."

"You know my time is yours, Aibhilín." He smiled at

her and said, "If you'll excuse me" to the others. Anto stepped in, making a space for Martin to pass through, and Megan saw astonishment on the faces of the reporters he'd dismissed. Martin wore a pinched smile of satisfaction as he approached Megan and Heather. He embraced his wife, smiled at Megan, and slipped out behind Anto.

Megan, in their wake, heard the reporters he'd left behind begin speaking in awe about Walsh taking time to focus on his family and friends after a tragedy, rather than revel in the staging of a dramatic comeback. "I'll be darned," she said under her breath. "Always leave them wanting more."

Martin, evidently overhearing, turned his head and winked over his shoulder at her, then stepped outside into the dazzling, breezy afternoon.

Megan held the door for the Walshes, letting them get settled as she took her place in the driver's seat. "Celebratory meal, Mr. Walsh?"

"That sounds nice," Heather began, but Martin shook his head.

"No, it's back to the hotel for us. Anything else and they'll be crawling up me arse trying to get quotes or pictures, and I want to leave them wanting more. The game on Friday is soon enough for them to see me again."

Disappointment flickered across Heather's face, and Megan bit down on the impulse to point out she didn't have to do what Martin did. Instead, she briefly met Mr. Walsh's eyes in the rearview mirror. "You won't be at Mrs. Walsh's game tomorrow, sir?"

"Ah, Heather plays better without me there, don't you, pet?" He patted her leg, and an irritated chill zinged up

Megan's neck, lifting the fine hairs there. Anybody who
gave *her* that kind of condescending pat would lose their
hand, but Heather only smiled, and Martin went on. "Lou
would have been the man to show up for the games, no
matter which of us was playing, me or Heather or Kim,
back in the day. He was a rock so, and he held with this
men and women's shared tournament nonsense anyway.
I'd say Heather will miss seeing him more than she ever
noticed me not being there."

"The joint tournament is good publicity for us,"
Heather said very softly. "The Golfing Walshes. And of
course I'll miss him," she went on. "But you could stand
in his place, if you wanted."

"And back-seat coach? I'd send you mental."

Heather lowered her head, as if—to Megan's eyes—
hiding emotion. Megan gritted her teeth behind a polite
smile. Martin Walsh didn't seem to be interested at all in
what Heather wanted, just in his own ritual. Trying to
keep her voice pleasant, or at least neutral, she said, "No
problem. Mrs. Walsh, will you want to go anywhere
yourself?"

An equally polite smile shaped Heather's mouth. "Not
the day before a game, no, but thank you, Megan."

"Leprechaun Limos will be on call if you change your
mind." Megan drove them back to the hotel—a quick
jaunt in midafternoon traffic—and did all the polite
things—holding the door, fetching the umbrella that had
ended up back in the vehicle thanks to Anto—and stood
more or less at attention until the Walshes made their way
through the modern entrance to the centuries-old building. Then she allowed herself an explosive sound, pulled
out her phone, and texted Niamh: **I don't think I like this
guy at all.**

A text with **how about this one?** came back almost immediately, even if it was six a.m. in California. A picture of Niamh and her costar mugging for a selfie followed, and then an obviously professional still shot of the two of them locked in an embrace followed that one. **Told you I'd wear the face off him,** Niamh texted. **That second pic is 100% Not For Sharing, though. The studio'd have my head.**

Holy cats, when I said pics or it didn't happen, I didn't think you'd send me one! Is he a good kisser? A series of heart-eyed and kissy-face emojis came back, and Megan laughed. **Good. I'm glad at least one of us is having fun with our job this week. Why are you up?**

In makeup. Niamh sent another picture, this time with sleepy eyes and her makeup only half done. **This is really me right now. What's up with Walsh? Have you figured out who murdered poor Lou yet?**

Walsh is really controlling. No wonder his second wife left him. And no, no news on Lou. Do you know his daughter Saoirse? She showed up and decked Walsh before the game today.

REALLY!?!?! Daaamn! I wonder if the rumors are true, then!

Megan nearly hopped up and down with impatience as the series of texts suddenly stopped, Niamh no doubt having to do something actually job-related instead of gossiping with a friend on the other side of the planet. When her silence stretched into several minutes, Megan, desperate, texted, **What rumors? You're killin' me, Nee!**

You know, the answer finally came back, as if distracted. **The rumors that Martin Walsh had an affair with Saoirse MacDonald when she was only eighteen years old.**

CHAPTER ELEVEN

Megan opened the Lincoln's door and sat hard in the driver's seat, staring at Niamh's text. A few seconds later another one came in: **GTG, they're calling for me, let me know what happens,** and Megan nodded dumbly at the phone like Niamh could see it. After a while, still feeling mentally numb, she texted Bourke with **are we on for that pint tonight?** and waited a moment to see if he responded. He didn't, but he would: Detective Paul Bourke was the most reliable correspondent Megan had ever had. She got into the car properly, put her phone in the glove compartment so it wouldn't tempt her to stare at Niamh's text while driving, and got the Lincoln back to the garage on autopilot.

Orla waved her into the office, a glint in her eyes. "I've a pick-up job tonight. Would you be up for it?"

"What time?" Vaguely mindful that she'd be better off

getting in Orla's good books now, before she discovered that Megan had gotten the company mentioned in relation to a murder, after all, she added, "I can probably do it, as long as it doesn't run too late. I'm supposed to get Mrs. Walsh at half eight tomorrow." That hadn't actually been arranged, but since it was when she'd gotten Martin that morning, Megan reckoned it was about right.

"It's only a collection at the airport. There and back again. Won't be but a minute." Orla all but sparkled her eyes at Megan, who finally felt a thread of suspicion.

"Who *is* it?"

Orla's blue eyes went shifty. "Carmen de la Fuente."

"Oh, *God,* Orla." Megan threw herself into the couch with the vigor of a teenager asked to do something totally unreasonable, like empty the dishwasher. "Do I have to? I mean, all right, *fine*, I will, but why does that woman keep *hiring* us? How much are you charging her now?"

"Seventeen hundred per hour," Orla said serenely. "She wants a gold chauffeur's uniform this time."

"I don't *have* a gold chauffeur's uniform!"

"I know. I told her I needed a week's notice and three grand an hour to give her that, and she put an order in for the uniform herself, on the condition that you yourself are her driver."

"Oooorlaaaaa! Why me? Why does she like *me* so much?" Orla looked her up and down with a frankly assessing gaze that made Megan's ears heat. "All right, I know *why* she likes me so much, but . . . argh!"

"You'll do it, though?"

"Yes, of course, but I want some of that seventeen hundred quid as my bonus for dealing with her. She's . . . she's . . ." Megan made strangling motions with her hands, and Orla, looking almost apologetic, laughed.

"I know, love, but Jaysus she's rich, and willing to spend it. If you ever wanted a rich girlfriend . . ."

"No one wants a rich girlfriend *that* much," Megan said dismally, although that was manifestly untrue. Carmen de la Fuente usually had two or three women hanging on her arms, dripping with lavish jewelry and, often, not much more. She had a truly piercing laugh that she employed like a weapon and a seventy-foot yacht anchored in the Malahide Marina, where parties too legendary for ordinary people to even hear of them took place twice a year. Megan had never in her life met anyone as unable to understand that they were not the center of the universe, and that included the handful of toddlers she'd known over the years. "Why does she keep *hiring* us?"

"Because I bilk her unrepentantly. She thinks if I charge her that much, there's something special about us, that we're worth it, and it makes her all the more eager to hire us. I raise the prices every time she calls and I'm still not charging enough." Orla pointed a sharp-nailed finger at Megan. "When I reach the right price, she'll start telling her friends we're the only ones in Dublin worth hiring, and then we'll retire rich, my chicken."

"Really, you're going to share the bilking with the whole team? That's great. In that case I'm happy to drive her any time you need." Megan drove de la Fuente any time Orla needed anyway, because Carmen always asked for her, and usually gave Megan a truly eye-popping cash tip. Fortunately for Megan's sanity, Carmen only spent a few days in Dublin a couple of times a year, but the sharp pitch of her laugh gave Megan chills even in memory.

"If you wear that gold uniform for her, I'll give everybody a bonus every time you drive her," Orla promised.

Megan sat bolt upright, pulled out her phone, and hit voice record. "Say that again." The glint in Orla's eyes turned to a glare, but she repeated herself, and Megan saved the note. "You're on. What time am I picking her up?"

"Half seven, from the Weston Airport. Drive the limo."

"As if Carmen would accept anything else." Megan glanced at the time on her phone. "It's already almost four. If I'm getting Carmen, I need to go get my makeup and hair done."

"Charge it to the company."

"As if I would do anything else." Megan would have anyway, but knew perfectly well Orla would pass the cost on to the client. She was out the door and making calls for an emergency makeover before she realized she hadn't mentioned the minor Aibhilín Ní Gallachóir fiasco. A giant sigh overtook her, but she shrugged it off as she ran up the stairs to her apartment. Orla would probably get over it with a Carmen de la Fuente paycheck coming in this evening.

A note on the door told her that her friend Brian, another American who lived nearby, had been over at lunchtime to walk the dogs. She texted him a series of hearts as she went inside, and took three minutes to lie on the floor and be climbed on by licking, wiggling babies and nuzzled by a vaguely interested mama. They all went for a quick walk before Megan deposited them back in the house, saying, "I'll be back in a couple of hours, babies. I've got to go get beautiful."

Detective Bourke texted while one person worked on her hair and another on her nails. Megan, who hated the heaviness of nail polish and the weight of false nails even more, was eager to pull her fingers away and respond to the text, and got smacked on the back of the hand for her efforts. She wailed, "But this is important!" and received a pointed, skeptical look that made her give the woman her hand back, if reluctantly. Eventually, her nails were proclaimed modestly suitable, and she was allowed to retrieve her hand and check the text, which said **Grand so, what time?**

She tried texting back, but her new nails got in the way. Exasperated, she tapped the dictation button and, after several tries, got an ungarbled **I have to work at half seven, so how about nine?** to send to him. He responded with another **grand so**, and Megan closed her eyes to let the stylists work on her.

Forty minutes later someone else entirely looked out at her from the mirror. Contours, highlighting, downlighting, backlighting: she hardly knew what they'd done, but she had to admit she looked amazing. Her hair, which she almost always wore up, framed around her face in waves. Her lips looked fuller and her eyes larger, and she wished she was going out with Jelena, not just picking up a very rich, very self-centered woman at the airport. The lead stylist, smiling, said, "You'll do," once Megan had finished admiring herself, and took Megan's picture for the salon's digital before-and-after wall. Even the picture looked professional, and Megan, pleased, said, "Could you send me that?"

"Sure, love." A minute later Megan's phone buzzed, and she forwarded the photograph on to Niamh, saying, **see, you're not the only one who cleans up well.**

You're driving Carmen tonight, aren't you? Niamh wrote back.

What, it shows?

Niamh sent back laughing emojis and **you look gawges**. Megan scurried home, feeling slightly ridiculous being so made-up in the late afternoon, and fed the dogs before pulling her uniform back on and returning to the garage. Orla met her at the office door with a peculiar expression, and gestured Megan in.

The reception counter was half-filled by a cream-colored box with a genuinely enormous, glittering gold ribbon and bow wrapped around it. An equally gigantic name tag dangled from the bow. Orla lifted her eyebrows in challenge and Megan, cautiously, edged forward to check the tag. Intellectually, she knew it would have her name on it or Orla wouldn't be making such extraordinary faces, but she was still astounded to see *Megan* written on it in elegant calligraphy. "Open it," Orla commanded, and Megan, befuddled, did so.

Nestled in white tissue paper lay a sharp-shouldered, plunge-lapeled golden suit that caught the light even without moving. The thinnest of rich russet lines between golden stripes gave the gold incredible depth. Gaping, Megan lifted it from the box, knowing before she did so that it would be her size, and proven right as the jacket unfolded a little to show that it would fall past her hips to midthigh. Slacks lay beneath the jacket, the russet brown dominant with thin gold highlights. Megan worked her jaw, trying to speak, but couldn't manage anything more than squeaks.

Orla flipped the slacks back and revealed a pair of three-inch gold heels buried in the box beneath them. "Are yis *sure* you don't want a rich girlfriend?"

"How . . . how? How is . . . how? When did you talk to her? Wh . . ." Megan gave up and simply stood there gaping at the coat in her hands.

"Around half eleven, I'd say. She's had somebody on this all day. Jaysus, look at that fabric, that's got to cost more than the company makes in a year. D'you think that's real *gold*?"

"I hope not!" Megan's voice broke on the three words. "I can't—I can't wear this! I can't *accept* this!"

"Well, no one else can either," Orla said pragmatically. "That's been made for you alone, my girl, and Carmen de la Fuente is now paying us four grand an hour for you to wear it."

"But that's *insane*!"

"That's rich people. Go on, go get changed."

"There's no *shirt*!"

"I'd say yer wan sees that as a feature. I'll pop over to Boots and get you some of those stick-on plastic bra things. D'yis suppose she wants cleavage or clavicle?"

"*Orla!*"

"Clavicle it is." Orla left the office, cackling, and Megan was still standing there, the jacket in her hands, when she returned. "Go on with yis! Go on now!"

"Orla, I can't! I can't!"

"Of course yis can. Don't make me strip you down myself, chicken." Orla tossed the sticky bra package at her, and Megan nearly dropped the jacket trying to catch it. They both hissed in alarm, and Megan, somehow defeated by the near miss, went to change clothes.

Wolf whistles might have been easier to deal with than the awed silence that met Megan when she went out to collect the limo. People who hadn't been at work twenty minutes earlier were there, standing in a respectful, jaw-dropped line, and Megan, feeling perfectly balanced on a line between absurd and awesome, started to grin. "What're you all gawking at?"

"*Damn*, Megan," somebody said, and as if it unleashed the floodgates, a buzz of laughing excitement washed over her. Tymon had brought his camera—his real camera, not his phone—parked the limo against the brightest white outdoor wall of the garage, and for about twenty minutes he ran around treating Megan like a supermodel. She laughed helplessly and flirted with the camera, kicking up her heels and doing her best sultry looks, until Cillian, who'd missed all the setup, walked in for a shift and tripped over his own feet. "Holy Methuselah on a bicycle, are we doing a pinup calendar this year or something? Megan, you look deadly!"

Megan, laughing, climbed off the limo's hood and straightened her jacket. "No calendar. Just driving Carmen tonight."

Cillian's eyebrows shot into his hairline. "That's not all she wants you to be doing tonight," he predicted.

"Cillian!"

He spread his hands. "I'm just saying. Look, don't forget us when you're all *Lifestyles of the Rich and Famous,* okay?"

"I don't think there's much chance," Megan said dryly. "Carmen's going to be totally unimpressed when she finds out I can't drive in three-inch heels."

"Naw, mate, that's where the sexy lady driving barefoot shot comes in, in the film."

"Oh, there's a movie now?"

"It's the life you were born to lead. Embrace it."

Forty minutes later, Megan stood beside the limo as a small, private business jet rolled to a stop precisely alongside her. She'd gone past feeling ridiculous—it helped that she knew she looked amazing—but her breastbone was cold, something no one ever mentioned when talking about wearing high fashion. And for someone who disliked having her nails done, she did wish she'd known about the open-toed, high-heeled sandals, because she felt very slightly undressed, as if having toenails to match her fingernails would have completed the look.

The jet door hissed open, and Carmen de la Fuente swanned out, paused at the top of the airstairs, and shrieked so loudly that the whole airfield seemed to pause and look her way. "Megaaan! Megaaan you *wore* it, Megaaan you look *fab*ulous!" She came down the steps in a blur of brightly colored silks and glittering boots to air-kiss Megan's cheeks before gesturing imperiously for her to turn, showing off the ensemble. "The color is perfect for you! I knew it would be! You are perfection!"

"You shouldn't have, Miss de la Fuente, but thank you. It's beautiful."

"You are beautiful! Girls! Girls! Is Megaaan not beautiful?" Even when Carmen wasn't shrieking Megan's name, she stretched the *a* out in a way that—despite the woman's flaws—Megan rather liked. *Megahn,* as if she was flirting with just the use of a very soft *a.*

Three extraordinary women, all with varying levels of petulance on their flawless faces, emerged from the plane and minced down the airstairs to rake Megan with scathing eyes. They all towered over Carmen, who was small and brown and curvy, with pixie-short black hair that made her brown eyes look enormous. She had a type that could easily be summarized as exactly her opposite, which was why Megan didn't really think the wealthy young Spaniard was actually into *her*. Finally, one of the women—an icy-pale Nordic blonde an entire *foot* taller than Megan—relented with the admission of, "Very beautiful. I could never wear that color so well." She gave Megan a knee-weakening smile, and scooted elegantly into the limo when Megan opened the door.

Only as the other women stepped in did Megan realize there was a suspicious theme to their outfits. The Nordic blonde wore light, sparkling blue; a rangy black woman's gown was delicate leaf-green, and an almost-translucent white woman with gobs of curling red hair wore teal green with bits of gold knotwork in the very short hem. Carmen's silk was red and fluttery, and Megan, suddenly suspicious, looked down at herself. "Um, Miss de la Fuente? Am I . . . *Belle*?"

Carmen screamed again, making Megan's ears ring. "I knew it! I knew you would understand, Megahn! You see, girls? I told you she would understand!" She pointed to each of the women in order, imperiously caroling, "Elsa, Tiana, Merida," before pointing at Megan, "and Belle! And now you must come to my party, Megan, for you understand!"

"Oh, gosh, I—couldn't!"

"But you must! I will not have all the princesses if you do not come! You may bring the Beast," Carmen said with a dismissive sniff. "But he must be handsome, Megan, or I cannot bear it." She stepped into the car, leaving Megan to close the door and murmur, ". . . but I had plans . . ." Shaking her head, walking back to the limo's driver door, she took her phone from her pocket— the expensive, gold-threaded slacks had *pockets*, for which all of Carmen's transgressions could be forgiven— and called Detective Bourke. "Um, hi. About that pint . . . do you own a tux?"

CHAPTER TWELVE

Paul Bourke did, in fact, own a tuxedo. Not just a tuxedo either, but the same kind of slim-cut suit he favored, with a flawlessly fitted waistcoat in—of all things—muted gold that happened to match Megan's bold suit beautifully, down to the subtle brown-and-gold striping in the wide tie tucking into it. Patent leather dress shoes were shiny enough to reflect the dockside strip lights, and as he walked up to her, Megan said, "You *own* that?" incredulously.

Bourke, equally astonished, said, "*You* own *that*?" in return, and for a few seconds they simply stood there admiring each other with small, approving gestures and amazed smiles. Then Megan giggled.

"I didn't own this a couple of hours ago. It was a—I don't even know what it was. A gift or a bribe, or maybe just showering some noblesse oblige on the little people,

I don't know. I drive Carmen de la Fuente sometimes, do you know her?"

"No, but I'd say she's the one percent." Bourke rocked back on his heels to look up at Carmen's yacht, towering over them at the dockside.

"I think she might be the one percent of the one percent," Megan admitted. "She's having a princess party and decided I should be—"

"Belle?" Paul smiled at Megan's surprise. "She's the only one who wears gold. Not gold pantsuits, but—wait. Does that mean I'm the Beast?"

"I suppose it would be better if this—" Megan touched the lapel of his tuxedo jacket lightly—"was very, very dark blue, but you've got the gold highlights, so we'll call it good."

"I'm flattered. Why on earth didn't you invite Jelena?" Bourke offered his arm, and Megan tucked her hand into it as they walked up the gangplank.

"You and I already had plans for tonight, so it didn't even cross my mind. I'm apparently bad at dating."

Bourke's pale eyebrows lifted. "I hate to agree, but I think you might be."

Megan made a face, then breathed, "Holy moly" as they stepped onto the yacht's . . . she didn't even know what it was called, besides a deck. Prow, maybe, at the front of the ship. The deck gleamed, polished wood catching the final pinks and blues of sunset and turning fiery under the brilliant tones. The ship's white sides bounced the light around even more, casting flattering glows on people in phenomenally expensive clothes, and even more expensive jewelry, who circulated with drinks in their hands and smiles on their lips.

"Wait," Bourke said, "stop." He dipped his hand inside

his jacket pocket and withdrew his phone, then pointed with it at the ship's railing. Megan tossed her hair and went to lean, with her best sultry supermodel look, against the railing, with the sunset and the ship glamorous all around her. After a minute of taking pictures, Paul put his phone away, but Megan said, "Uh-uh, my turn," and took a bunch of photos of him, and then a ton of selfies of them both grinning like idiots. Fortunately, other people were doing the same, although Megan murmured, "I don't think we're acting as cool and collected as we're supposed to" when she finally put her own phone away.

"I think I can live with that. Can I send one of these to Niamh?"

"Oh, God, send all of them!" Megan cackled and peered up at the next tier of the ship as he did so. A third deck rose above that, too, and she caught glimpses of what she imagined was the most exclusive group on the ship, on the very top deck. The princess theme was in full display, ranging from outfits that would have made cosplayers weep with envy to decidedly interpretive costumes that Megan couldn't identify. Suits ranged from tuxedos all the way to full-blown prince outerwear, and Megan seized Paul's arm, trying not to point too obviously at a ginger man she was pretty certain was an *actual* prince. "Deadly," he said without interest, and turned Megan in the other direction, "but look at *her*."

He indicated an older woman, her hair an elaborate crown of braided buns and a tunic gown of understated blue, with a starburst neckline and a square cutaway front that revealed a lighter-weight undergown. Megan's eyes filled with tears and, like a beauty queen, she flapped her hands at her face. "I can't cry, it'll ruin this makeup. Oh, but she looks *just* like her, that's perfect. Oh my God. What do ordinary people like us do at a party like this, squirm around the edges and gawk?"

"Sounds good to me." Bourke nabbed a couple of champagne flutes from a passing waiter and gestured for Megan to choose a path through the crowd. "I've never been on a yacht. Let's explore. What'd you text me about?"

"Oh, God. I talked to Niamh this afternoon."

"Oh?" Paul brightened. "I haven't talked to her for a few days. How's she doing? How's her shoot going?"

"Really well, I guess. She's having fun." They stepped through polarized glass doors into a living area done in cream leather and walnut wood, all of it polished to a gleam. Huge windows were open to the night air, cooling the room and giving a glimpse of the other boats, and Malahide village, sparkling in the background. The lights were either recessed or chandeliers, which somehow struck Megan as absurdly funny. She choked back a giggle, and Bourke grinned.

"We're a couple of culchies, aren't we?"

"We are so," she agreed, and dropped her voice to say, "Look how *beautiful* everyone is. It's like they're not real." And then, as if it was a natural segue—and it kind of was—she added, "How are things with you and Niamh anyway?"

"Same as you and Jelena, I think. Casual. She's amazing." Bourke sounded momentarily awestruck. "I knew she was savage on stage and a relentless social justice warrior, so I thought she might be fierce all the time like. She's gas, though." He tipped his head like he might add a caveat, and Megan said, "But?"

"But she belongs in a crowd like this one, and I'm a

homebody. It could be that would work out, having a lad to come home to, but I can't see myself dropping a case to fly off and do the red carpet with her, you know? And I don't think she would expect me to, but it's hard to have a relationship if you're not there to celebrate the highs and the lows together."

"Who knows, though. You might go do one of those events and discover you love it."

Bourke grimaced broadly. "And then her private life wouldn't be private at all. It's tricky."

"I hope you'll figure it out." They had, by that time, edged their way down the living room, past women wearing more expensive perfume than Megan had ever smelled, and a group of young men with the best haircuts she'd ever seen. "I feel like I'm the 'normal person' extra on a film set. You know, the one girl at the prom who's dumpy, to give the scene veracity?"

"Are you sure you've seen yourself in that outfit? I know what you mean, though. This is a nice tux, but I think it costs less than some of these lads' shoelaces. There's the stairs. Do you think we need a secret password or a speakeasy knock to get up them?"

"Probably." Megan tapped out a pattern with her fingernails as they mounted stairs that, although constrained by the limitations of the ship, still managed to sweep dramatically in an upward curve. No one challenged them, although a dapper man with grey at his temples did give Bourke an *extremely* appreciative smile as they passed each other. Megan elbowed Paul cheerfully. "Want a sugar daddy?"

"If I were even the smallest wee bit bisexual, I would step up for that, but I've long since come to the conclusion that I am, in fact, depressingly straight."

Megan laughed. "'Depressingly'?"

"Ah, it's always struck me as a bit limiting, you know? Only being attracted to the one gender? I can admire a handsome lad on an aesthetic level, but I have no desire at all to do anything about it."

"I've never had that problem," Megan said cheerfully. "Anyway—oh, gosh." They'd bypassed the yacht's second floor entirely, emerging on the highest, smallest deck, where Carmen and an actual bevy of princesses were backlit by deep blue streaks in the sky and the promise of moonlight on Malahide Bay. "Oh my gosh, this is beautiful. But maybe we'd better get back downstairs before—"

"Megaaan! Megan, there you are, my Beauty and her Beast?" Carmen's shrill voice, and then Carmen herself, burst out of the crowd to embrace Megan and look Paul up and down with a critical eye. "Yes, very handsome, if this is the type you like. You must meet the other princesses, Megan, you have met our ice queen and frog princess already, but here is a fierce warrior and my darling sleepy beauty and—" Princesses, all taller than Megan and most taller than Paul, surrounded them, caroling greetings and admiring Megan's suit. In the midst of it, feeling crowded, Megan turned away to get a breath of air, and collided face-first with a glittering purple seashell bra.

"Oh my God, I am so sorry—" She looked up to meet the mermaid's eyes and found an astonished Saoirse MacDonald blinking back down at her.

"M–*Megan*?" Saoirse sounded as disconcerted as Megan felt. "Megan *Malone*?"

"Yes? I mean, yes! Saoirse? Holy—you look amazing. I'm sorry about—you know—being in your boobs—" At forty-one years and one month of age, Megan thought she should probably be able to get through a surprise encounter without fumbling it like a teenager, but there were simply moments in life when her adult persona shriveled up and left an awkward, easily amused thirteen-year-old in its place. The only saving grace in this painful truth was the knowledge that virtually every other adult she knew suffered the same problem. People didn't really grow up as much as she'd thought they did when she was a kid. Or even when she was Saoirse's age, midtwenties and still knowing it all. "Saoirse, what are you doing here?"

"What are *you* doing here? You look deadly."

Megan made a feeble hand wave in Carmen's direction. "I'm her driver. She dressed me."

"I think she dressed all of us." Saoirse pressed her lips together, the skin around them turning very white. "Da met her years ago and made her laugh, so she invites him to these things. Invited," she said in a strained voice. "She thought I should come along tonight even though . . ." She shook her head rapidly, then looked beyond Megan, saw Paul, and paled further. "Is that the detective on Da's case? What's going on? Is everything okay?"

"It is, but we're—I was supposed to go out for a pint with him tonight, but Ms. de la Fuente invited me to this, so I invited Paul. It's nothing to do with the case."

Bourke stepped up to offer his hand. "Ms. MacDonald. Paul Bourke. Not Detective tonight."

"Wouldn't you always be, though?" Saoirse shook his hand and glanced around. "Not that you'd want to be with this crowd. Da played a gentleman's game, so he could be seen with the likes of these, but only as a poor relation like. A curiosity. A trained monkey like."

"Not much use for the proletariat," Bourke said with a nod. "I won't tell if you don't. How are you holding up, Ms. MacDonald?"

"Please call me Saoirse. And I don't know. Very badly, but as well as I can be. Have you—do you know anything?"

Bourke cast a sideways glance at Megan, who twitched an eyebrow in return, suddenly aware that they'd gotten sidetracked on the topic of their respective love lives and she hadn't told him the rumor Niamh had shared with her. Bourke, apologetically, said, "Nothing yet" to Saoirse, who shuddered almost imperceptibly, but nodded.

"I didn't think so. I've been wracking my brains, trying to think who would want to hurt Da, but I just don't know. Not if Martin's out of the picture."

"Can I—I talked to Heather Walsh this morning, after you escaped Aibhilín," Megan said, almost apologetically. "She said she didn't know why you and Martin had grown apart, but she was afraid it had something to do with her. I don't mean to be rude, but—"

"Of course it did," Saoirse snapped. "She turned up like a gold digger and wrecked what Martin and I had. Nothing was ever the same after he started seeing her." A few absurdly well-dressed people—princesses—glanced her way as her tone carried, and Paul invited her to the stairs with a small gesture. Megan, her heart racing with the thrill of uncovering information, kept the conversation going as they moved, saying, "She said Martin had been your coach. It must have been very difficult to have someone else come into that dynamic."

Saoirse's cheeks flushed. "You have no idea. All of a

sudden he wanted her to come with us, wanted *her* to show me a swing, because *she* was a woman, *she* could teach me better—" They tucked just inside the top steps, Megan, the smallest by a considerable margin, still on deck and Paul a couple of steps down, so Saoirse wouldn't feel crowded. She didn't seem to notice, fire still building in her cheeks. "I'd no need for another coach. Martin was everything I wanted. But what he wanted mattered more, so there were three of us in it when all I wanted was himself and me. I thought she'd go away, but instead they got married! Him! And *her*! And herself four years older than myself, like some old hag, but sure he was a laughing-stock for marrying her, half his age and all. Now if *she'd* been killed—" The color left her face in a heartbeat, leaving her the color of skim milk. "I never said that."

Paul Bourke's pale-blue gaze met Megan's for a moment before returning to Saoirse's, reassuringly. "Even gardaí say they'd kill someone like, in a moment of heat, and Mrs. Walsh is safe and sound. Don't worry your head over it."

Instead of worrying, the young woman slid down the staircase wall into a heap of stifled sobs. Bourke met Megan's eyes again, a question in his arched eyebrows. She lifted her chin a bit, indicating she'd take Saoirse duty while he did whatever he had in mind. A brief smile of gratitude crossed his face, and he stepped past them both, returning to the upper deck and the princess party. Megan giggled unkindly at the thought, making Saoirse lift a dripping gaze to her, and Megan sat on the step below her, sliding an arm around the young woman's lower back. "Nothing, I was just thinking, how like a guy to run away from the crying girl to go hang out with a bunch of rich princesses."

Saoirse's laugh emerged as the worst combination of crying and snorting possible and left her coughing and wiping her eyes. "Men are fecking awful, aren't they?"

"Oh, well, I don't know. They have their moments, and I've noticed women aren't always sunshine and light either. So tell me, do you want to get off this boat or to raid Carmen's extensive liquor cabinet?"

"I could stand a drink," Saoirse admitted through sniffles. Megan nodded and helped her to her feet, then paused, astonished, to examine Saoirse's face.

"Whoever did your makeup must have thought you were a real mermaid. I've never seen mascara that actually stayed put when someone cried."

"You've never spent enough money on mascara, then."

"That," Megan agreed, "is almost certainly true. Okay, is the best booze up there, or down there?"

"Probably up there, but I don't think I can face Carmen right now. If she thinks I've been crying, she'll be so *extra* about it."

"In Ms. de la Fuente's defense," Megan said as they made their way down the stairs, "I think *extra* is her only method of engaging with the world." They threaded through the crowd in the second-deck living area, making their way to a bar appointed with a more expensive array of whiskeys than Megan had seen in any tony hotel in Dublin. The bartender, a young man with long black hair, sharp features, and a black suit highlighted by a green vest scarf with gold pointing, poured them each a generous couple fingers of a whiskey literally as old as Megan was. She turned away, drink in hand, with his costume itching at the back of her mind, then spun back with an objection on her lips as it finally struck her. He, clearly prepared for this, said, "Disney owns Marvel. He's a Disney prince."

Megan, gleefully, said, "He's the shapeshifting mother of Sleipnir, too, so I think that makes him a Disney princ*ess*."

The kid grinned broadly. "I was hoping somebody would catch that."

Megan laughed, raised a toast to him, sipped the whiskey, and said, "Wow," aloud, reverently. "Holy cow. This is amazing. Saoirse, did you—"

Saoirse slammed her whiskey and tapped the bar for another. Megan murmured, "Wow" again in a totally different tone, and offered Saoirse her own tumbler. "I can't drink it all anyway. I have to drive the company car back to the garage tonight. I can drop you at home on the way, if you want to get obliterated."

The green-and-black-clad bartender intervened, plucking Megan's crystal glass from her hand and pouring it deftly into a silver flask that he topped off before screwing it shut and handing it back to Megan with a wink. At virtually the same time, another tumbler appeared at Saoirse's fingertips, this one containing amber liquid that Megan suspected cost a great deal less than the drink Saoirse had just totally failed to appreciate. It was no doubt still more expensive than any apartment Megan had ever rented, but she supposed to the obscenely wealthy, these things were relative.

"No, it's fine, I can get home on my own," Saoirse muttered. "You should go find your detective boyfriend before he hooks up with a princess." She threw back the second drink as quickly as the first and looked suddenly cross-eyed.

"Give me your phone," ordered Megan. Saoirse did, and Megan programmed her own phone number into it. "You call me if you need *anything*, all right, Saoirse? Do you hear me?"

"All right already." Saoirse had a third drink in her before she got her phone back in her aquamarine fishtail skirt's cleverly hidden pocket: the scales disguised it perfectly, without destroying the skirt's line. Megan backed off, giving her the room she needed to get very, very drunk. She had no intention of leaving the girl to fend for herself once the alcohol had rendered her numb, but neither would she get in the way. It wouldn't help. Megan knew that, and maybe Saoirse did, too. It wouldn't help, but she might need it in the moment anyway, and sometimes people just needed to be given the space to do something stupid, safely.

She bumped into Paul Bourke as she backed away, and he murmured, "Oh good, I was looking for you. I don't know what you wanted to talk about over pints tonight, but I wonder if it had anything to do with the ladies upstairs being quite sure Martin Walsh broke that young woman's heart."

CHAPTER THIRTEEN

A minute later, having rousted a pair of lovebirds out of an extremely comfortable chair meant for people of intimate acquaintance, Megan muttered, "In my misbegotten youth we would have called Walsh 'skeevy,'" as she and Bourke tried to take over the seat without wrapping up in each other.

"Was your youth misbegotten?"

"Not really, but leave a girl her illusions." The lovebirds, both more than a little intoxicated, blinked at Megan with the air of young people who didn't know what to do next. She suggested, "Find a room?" and they, clearly stunned and delighted by the idea, clasped hands and disappeared from sight. Megan tried again to sit with, or beside, Paul, but it was clear that entangled was really the only way for two people to share the seat. After a moment she managed to mostly balance on the arm. She could keep an eye on Saoirse from there, but had to lean, with an arm on the chair's back, to talk with the detective. It put her carefully taped cleavage indiscreetly near his nose, and there was no real way to keep her leg from brushing, or crossing, his. Their attempts at conversation kept dissolving into self-conscious laughter, until Megan finally said, "Honestly, we're adults, we can do this without giggling."

"Apparently we can't." Paul Bourke offered one of his brilliant grins, and Megan felt heat crawl down her breastbone to warm her unexpectedly.

"We *can*. Anyway, their story corroborates Niamh's rumor—"

"How does she know the goss on everyone in Dublin?" he interrupted, mystified. "If the guards had half her contacts . . . !"

"Focus, Paul. If it's true . . ." Megan looked toward Saoirse, who had stopped drinking and now slumped at the bar, her red hair pooling across its gleaming walnut surface. "Honestly, I think it is true. She said earlier today that her last boyfriend had married what *she* thought was the bit on the side. And she was furious when we asked her about Heather."

"Do you think Heather knows?"

"I don't. I think she'd think it was skeevy, too. But what I can't see is how it gets us any closer to figuring out who killed Lou."

"'Us'?" Bourke sounded amused, and Megan looked down her nose at him.

"Don't tell me there's not an 'us' in this, copper. Assistant Intern Associate Detective, remember?"

"Accidental Investigative Detective Adviser, but you're not." Bourke grew serious a moment. "Never mind the hell I'd catch for letting a civilian help with an investigation, Megan. Things got dangerous with the Darr case. You could have been killed, and that would have been on me."

"It certainly would not have been. I make my own decisions."

"That may be true in cold hard fact, but it would do nothing to alleviate the guilt I would feel if something happened to you. You're not my assistant."

Megan tilted her chin toward the ceiling—the recessed lights glowed through refracting lenses she was certain were lead crystal—and sighed. "All right, fine. We're a couple of mates out for a pint to discuss a bit of gossip about the death of a man whose daughter we both know. And I still don't see how knowing about this affair helps. If *Martin* had ended up dead and Lou was the murderer, I'd get *that*, but it's not what happened."

Bourke shifted, making her balance change, and she caught herself before falling into his lap. "Or if Martin was dead and herself over there the killer, it'd be an open-and-shut case, but that's not it either. There's something we're—*I'm*—missing yet."

"Had Lou any enemies you've learned about?"

"I could never tell you."

"I hate that I can't tell if that means no, yes, or maybe. Separated by a common language." Megan craned her neck to look at Saoirse again. She'd been approached by a tallish man in a suit that somehow seemed more like Bourke's than the tuxedos worn by other men that evening: expensive, but not incomprehensibly so. Saoirse shrugged the man off and he turned away, not looking particularly miffed, and Megan frowned. "I've seen him before. I think he was at the game this morning."

Bourke followed her gaze. "Ah, he's a . . . banker, or something. I remember his face from the news when the banking crisis hit in the Aughts, though I wouldn't know his name. He wasn't a big man in the scandal. I'd say he came out of it well enough, if he's here. People must still trust him with their money."

"Do people go to golf tourna . . ." Megan stopped herself and laughed. "To rub elbows with money. As if there's not a whole culture of business deals done over golf games. Do you think he knew Lou?"

"Or her own self." Paul nodded toward Saoirse, which brought his nose into Megan's cleavage again. "Sorry so."

Megan waved it off. "There's nothing to be done unless I actually sit on your lap. Which might be less awkward, except I've never really liked sitting on laps. I feel like I'll squish them."

"You? You're only a wee small thing."

"But in my mind I'm an Amazon."

"I don't see why the one has to be exclusive to the other." Paul, however, didn't try to convince her to sit on his lap, for which Megan was grateful. She *was* comparatively small, and men often thought that meant she should be happy to take an available lap. Some people were. Megan wasn't one of them.

"Tell you what." Megan twisted to look at Saoirse again. "I'll drive her home—wait, do you have a car, or can I give you a ride?"

Bourke snorted suppressed laughter so hard it sounded painful. Megan looked back at him, eyebrows furled in confusion, and found his blue eyes watering with censored amusement as his face slowly turned hot pink from his collar up. She stared at him, bewildered, then suddenly realized her error and half-shouted, "*Lift*! Can I give you a *lift*!"

A number of people looked around at her as Bourke gave up all hope of containing himself and threw his head back in breathless, body-shaking laughter. After a minute he wiped his eyes, peeked at Megan, found her waiting it out with hot-cheeked resignation, and burst into laughter again, this time shifting to put his head down on the arm of the chair as he guffawed into it. Megan fixed her gaze on an opposite wall and, with the long-suffering patience of an American pretending she failed to find the humor in using a locally insinuation-laden phrase, said, "Right after I moved here I took a yoga class, but I'd forgotten part of my workout gear. One of the teachers had extra things with her, and I said to her, 'Can I borrow your pants?'"

Bourke's shriek of laughter nearly drowned out the end of Megan's story, although she continued, stoically, to tell it. "The poor woman gaped, turned the hottest shade of red I'd ever seen on a human face, and gasped, 'Do you mean me *trousers*?' back at me." Paul's long legs kicked straight out and he kicked his feet against the deck floor like a little kid before collapsing in a boneless, laughing heap in the chair. All of Carmen's very wealthy friends were staring openly at them by now, and even Saoirse had lifted her head from the bar to look blearily in their direction. Megan, in sepulchral tones, said, "I've never gone anywhere without yoga *trousers* since," and Paul, weeping with laughter, wiped his eyes again and tried to gather his dignity.

"What did you say before, separated by a common language? Oh, God, that was funny."

Megan, maintaining the morose tone, said, "I'm glad

somebody thought so," and finally broke, giggling, too. "Honestly, on some level I knew about the pants thing, but 'give you a ride' is totally Irish. We don't put any weight on that in the States. It must be our car culture or something."

"I need neither a lift *nor* a ride," Bourke assured her, his grin still bright and broad. "Go on with you, give Saoirse *a lift*, and keep your nose out of police business."

"I will if police business keeps its nose out of mine." Megan, smiling, disentangled herself from the laughing detective and made her way to Saoirse's side. The young woman had lost interest in their hysterics and drooped at the bar again, tracing patterns in the circle left by condensing water on the whiskey tumbler. The black-and-green-clad bartender stood a few feet away, clutching a bar towel and twitching toward Saoirse's little mess every time it looked as though she might be done mucking with it. "Come on," Megan said to her. "Let's get you home, and let that poor man wipe the bar down. He's going to have a heart attack there."

"There's nothing for me at home," Saoirse mumbled dismally, but she let Megan lever her off the bar-stool. The bartender swept in and wiped down the counter, his shoulders relaxing visibly as the reflective smear of water disappeared. Megan chortled and waved at him with her fingertips as she maneuvered Saoirse toward the spiraling staircase at the other end of the room, and thought their escape nearly complete when Carmen appeared in a flurry of flowing silk and long, loose hair.

"Megan! You are not leaving already? And with my mermaid instead of your prince? I heard you were very laughing, the two of you. A lover who makes you laugh is important."

Megan opened her mouth and shut it again on a correction about the nature of her relationship with Bourke. "I wish I could stay, but I have to be up early to drive another client, Ms. de la Fuente. Thank you for the invitation, and I'll have this"—she gestured at her outrageous suit—"dry-cleaned and returned to you."

A mixture of insult and amusement creased Carmen's face, and she indicated her body shape relative to Megan's. "It would never fit me. It's a gift for you to wear when you drive me. You're very handsome in your black uniform," she promised Megan, "but it lacks a certain . . ."

A flighty motion of her hand indicated the only phrase that could finish that sentence, and Megan, a little wryly, said, "Je ne sais quoi?"

"But of course," Carmen said with a smile. "All right, very well. And you may bring my mermaid home, too, as she looks a little seasick, poor dear." For all her theatrical capriciousness, a trace of concern showed in Carmen's brown eyes. "She has had very hard days. If she needs anything, Megahn, call me." The deliberate drawing-out of the second vowel in Megan's name returned, as if Carmen had realized she was showing a bit of soft underbelly and decided she'd better return to her usual outrageous personality.

Megan, surprised, thought maybe she had never really seen anything beyond Carmen's shrill voice and sharp laugh. There was, perhaps, more kindness in her than she had imagined. She said, "I will," and Carmen nodded, satisfied, as she ascended the stairs again.

Saoirse, who seemed to have gotten a great deal more drunk in the minute Megan had spent talking to Carmen, shouted, "Thank you, Ms. de la Fuente!" after her, then clapped a guilty hand over her mouth and stage-whispered, "That was too loud, wasn't it?"

"It's okay. Come on, let's get you home." On the way off the boat, they passed the older woman in blue with the crown of braids, and Megan blurted, "Excuse me, I'm sorry, but I just wanted to say your costume is amazing and perfect" to her. The patrician lines of the woman's face turned upward in a blossoming smile, and she waved as Megan and Saoirse staggered down the gangplank.

"People like you," Saoirse muttered. "They liked me da, too. They don't like me as much. Martin didn't like me as much as he liked Heather. Heather doesn't like me at all. The lads in school fancy me until they find out I won't shag them, and then they think I'm a cold fish and won't help with my own projects even if I've lent a hand with theirs. Everybody in Donnybrook likes me because I kept that bastard Sean from turning their green into a housing development, but that's not *me* they like, it's what I did for them."

"If it were me, I'd like the person who did all that work for us, too. Which bastard is that?"

"Sean Ahern. He was here tonight, but he fecked off after I told him I'd vomit on him if he spoke to me again."

"Oh, the tallish guy? I saw him talking to you." Megan walked Saoirse down the dock, taking a few seconds to catch glimpses of the rows of white boats and ships making ghostly, shifting, bright spots against the black water. Overhead lights cast pools of yellow and blue into the rippling bay and made well-maintained dock slats safe and easy to walk, even at night. The water's constant, gentle slosh against ship hulls drowned out most of the sound from the town beyond—and the party behind them drowned out the rest—leaving the moving lights in town a silent dance and nothing more. Megan took a deep breath, inhaling the sea scent, and wished she had more time to appreciate it, rather than thinking about murders and unwelcome visitors. "Paul thought he was a banker."

"Might as well be," Saoirse spat. "They're all after screwing the country, and instead of being in jail, he's trying to turn the bay into a sewerage dump and murder my island and my birds." She climbed into the limo's front seat when Megan opened the door for her, and slid most of the way into the footwell. Megan, lips twisted with concentration, got her far enough up again to buckle her in, and went around to the driver's side, asking, "Where are you staying?" once she got in.

"At me da's house down in Dalkey."

"Oh, gosh. That's . . . on the other side of Dublin from here. Would you be okay with staying at my apartment in Rathmines tonight? I've got to go walk my puppies before their bladders explode."

Saoirse's eyes lit up. "Puppies? Can I sleep with them?"

"I think *not* sleeping with them would be the challenge."

"Yay!" Saoirse clapped her hands together like a child, then slithered as far down in the seat as the seatbelt would let her. "I feel awful."

Megan, gently, said, "I know. It's been a hard couple of days for you, and I'm afraid it's not going to get any easier for a while." She pulled out of the parking lot, leaving the marina behind as they drove down the coast, back toward Dublin city centre. There were glimpses of the northern train line along the way, caught between centuries-old residences that lay beside modern buildings. "Can I ask you something that's none of my business?"

"Pfffshh. Sure."

"Was Martin Walsh the boyfriend who dumped you for his bit on the side?"

Saoirse bolted upright in the seat, a flood of tears pouring from incredulous eyes. "How'd you know that? No one knows that!"

"I was thinking about what you said this morning, and how angry you were when I asked you about Heather this evening, and I made a guess," Megan said, more judiciously than truthfully. "Saoirse, do you—"

"Do I know how awful everyone would make that? Do I know they'd all say he *groomed* me? Do I know they'd think it was gross that he fell in love with his 'niece'? Of course I do! It's why we had to keep it a secret, and the secret is why he started dating somebody *else*. For *show*, he said. To help us stay *hidden*, he said. Only then he chose her over me. I could kill her," Saoirse snarled. "I could kill *him*. He *betrayed* me. He said he loved me, but he dumped me for *her* like he didn't even *care*—"

"Do you think your dad knew?" Megan interrupted, driving Saoirse into shocked silence.

"No. No? No! He—he wouldn't have understood. Nobody understood." Saoirse put her face in her hands, her shoulders shaking, although Megan heard no sobs. "He hated that Uncle Martin and I had fallen out, but I couldn't tell him why, because he wouldn't understand."

She kept on in that vein, the words occasionally broken with audible tears, while Megan turned over in her mind what she could, or should, say. Being judgy obviously wouldn't help, and moreover, Saoirse clearly understood, whether she could admit it consciously or not, the deeply problematic aspect of her relationship with Walsh. Carefully, not wanting to engage the young woman's defenses, she asked, "What do you think he would have done if he had known?"

"Oh, God, he'd have killed Martin like!"

"You don't think he would have—no," Megan said to herself, and to the road in front of her, more than to Saoirse. "No, he wouldn't have told the press. He wouldn't have tried ruining Martin's career, would he? Because he wouldn't have wanted to drag *you* through that whole mess."

Saoirse dropped her hands, staring at Megan in wet-faced horror. Her makeup hadn't survived the second bout of tears quite as well; thin streaks of black straggled down her cheeks, and her lips were their natural shade again, not the shimmering pink of before. "He'd never have done that," she whispered hoarsely. "Never!"

"No, I don't think he would have." Megan took a deep breath. "Would he have threatened Martin with it, though? To get him to stop playing, maybe?"

"No!" Saoirse wrenched her gaze to the street ahead of them. "Maybe . . . maybe."

"And what would Martin have done to keep that secret from coming out, or to counter that threat?"

Saoirse shook her head, her eyes glazed. "Anything. He'd do anything, but everyone says—*you* said—you were *with* him when Da died. He couldn't have done it."

Megan bared her teeth and thumped the heel of her hand against the steering wheel. "Yeah. Yeah. Dammit, that was looking so tidy, too." She turned onto Rathmines Road, the drive having gone very quickly in the lack of midnight traffic, and flushed guiltily as Saoirse asked, "Is that what you want my da's death to be? Tidy?"

"I'd like the solution to be tidy. I'd like there to be answers that make sense. On paper, at least. They're not likely to ever make sense in your heart." Megan pulled into the garage, waving at Tymon, who was mostly sacked out on a couch tucked against one wall. He got to his feet, yawning enormously, and ambled after the vehicle as Megan drove it into the back parking lot. He also shot Megan a look of disconcerted worry as Saoirse clambered out of the car, all tearstains and mermaid skirts. Megan shook her head minutely, and Tymon developed a set of magical blinders that sent him around the car the long way, collecting what he needed to clean it, as Megan escorted the tall redhead out of the garage. As the door closed behind them, her phone buzzed with a text from Tymon: **you're going to *have* to explain that!**

Later, Megan promised. It was only a few minutes' walk from the garage to her apartment, and Saoirse's eyelids were drooping by the time they got up the stairs and into the flat. Even the puppies couldn't keep her awake, and by the time Megan returned from a quick potty trip with them, Saoirse had curled up on the couch and fallen asleep. True to her promise, Megan tucked Dip and Thong into the blankets with her and tiptoed off to bed herself.

Noise in the kitchen woke her a few hours later, making Megan sit up in alarm before remembering she had a house guest for the night. She blearily made her way out to find Saoirse nursing a huge cup of coffee at the little kitchen table, two puppies sitting on her feet and Mama Dog lying beside the chair with an air of brown-eyed expectation.

Saoirse said—pleaded—"Don't even talk to me," and Megan raised her hands in agreeable silence as she went to fill a mug of her own. The puppies scampered over, winding around her ankles like they were determined to fell her and break her neck. Megan snorted and sat on the floor with them, smiling as they wiggled their way into her lap.

"Good babies. You make even early mornings less awful, don't you? Yeah. Yeah." She wrinkled her face as Dip stood on his hind legs, front feet on her shoulder so he could lick her face. His tongue went up her nose as she inhaled, and a series of shouts, spilled coffee, and coughing fits later, peace was restored to the sound of Saoirse's pained, hung-over giggles. Not at all to Megan's surprise, the young woman's laughter slid toward tears, and Megan, briskly, said, "Why don't you get into the shower real quick, and get ready for the day? I'll find you some slightly less inappropriate daywear."

Saoirse fled to the bathroom, where she could cry— and shower—in peace, and Megan took the dogs out, promising them an excess of quality time once the golfing weekend and its attendant murder was past. "Because normal people promise their dogs quality time," she said, mostly to herself, as they trotted back up to her flat. She did find a hip-length-on-her T-shirt that would reach Saoirse's waist, and a pair of ankle-length, flared yoga *trousers* that would probably be a flattering calf-length on Saoirse's long legs. She couldn't do anything about replacing the aquamarine high heels the young woman had worn the night before, as Saoirse's feet were at least four sizes larger than her own, but at least she wouldn't have to go home dressed as a mermaid.

"I can give you a lift as far as Clontarf Castle Hotel," she called to Saoirse after handing the clothes through a cracked-open bathroom door, but the other woman came out a minute later, toweling her hair and shaking her head.

"I don't want to see the Walshes. I'll take a taxi."

"All right." Megan had already pulled her chauffeur's uniform on, reckoning she could make it a day without a shower, especially with her hair still in remarkably good shape after the previous day's makeover. "I've got to get to the garage. Let yourself out when you're ready, but be careful of Dip. He likes to make a break for it."

"Okay. Thanks. Megan?" Saoirse's voice stopped her as she headed out the door. "Thanks very much."

Megan smiled. "No worries. Call if you need anything, and I'll see you later." She took the stairs down two at a time and got to the garage just after seven, comfortably in time to make it to the Clontarf without rushing it.

Tymon, still awake, pointed at the office as she strode into the garage. "You owe me last night's story, but Orla wants a piece of you right now."

"Oh no, a piece of me?" Megan made a face of mock alarm and hurried into the office, calling, "What can I do for you, Miz Keegan?" ahead of herself.

Orla's voice, as cold as ice water, splashed over her. "You can tell me why this woman came to visit us at half six on a Thursday morning."

Megan, the garage door banging closed behind her, looked up to meet the smug and sparkling gaze of sports journalist Aibhilín Ní Gallachóir.

CHAPTER FOURTEEN

"Megan Malone." Aibhilín looked genuinely de-lighted to see her. "Ms. Malone, it's a pleasure to meet you again. I had the most *interesting* afternoon yesterday, looking into you. It's not my usual beat, but surely somebody had to remark on the fact that you've been caught up in two murder investigations in as many months?"

Megan, faintly, and fully aware that Orla's murderous gaze lay on her, said, "It's two in four months, to be fair," and flinched with the conviction that a stapler or possibly a computer screen was about to come flying at her head.

"And *both* of them tied to Leprechaun Limousine clients," Aibhilín proclaimed, as if she had never heard anything as interesting in her life. Maybe she hadn't. Megan had to admit it *was* interesting, in the may-you-live-in-interesting-times sense of the word. "How did all of this come about, Ms. Malone?"

"Through outrageous coincidence," Megan replied as steadily as she could. "If that's all, I have a job to do, Ms. Ní Gallachóir—"

"Oh, but it's not. I'm altogether desperate to hear how you found Lou MacDonald's body." Ní Gallachóir's eyes danced with challenge. "Give me that interview and I'll forget what I've learned about the *two* recent murders connected with this company."

Aware of Orla's enraged attention, and thinking of Detective Bourke's request that she not talk to the media, Megan smiled until her teeth ached. "Can it wait until after I've done my pick-up this morning?"

"As it happens, I'll be covering the tournament at St. Anne's today," Aibhilín said. "I'd be delighted to meet you there. Say half nine?"

"Let's make it ten," Megan said through her teeth. "Just to make sure Mrs. Walsh doesn't require my services."

"Perfect." Aibhilín drawled the word into the very Irish "pair-fect" pronunciation, which normally Megan loved but which, right then, raised hairs on her nape. "I'll see you then, Ms. Malone." She left with the air of a victor, and Megan braced herself on the counter, both wrists turned out, before daring to look Orla's way.

"A fine job you've done of keeping us out of the media," Orla said shortly, and with that stalked away. Megan watched her go, then turned her gaze to the ceiling, as if there might be answers there. There weren't, of course, so with a sigh she went back to the garage, collected her keys, and said, "I'm sorry, I can't even right now" to Tymon's hopeful gaze.

"There's a pint in this for me when this is all over!" he called after her, and Megan, feeling that was probably reasonable, lifted a hand in agreement as she got into her car and drove away.

As if the city itself felt Megan needed an apology for siccing Ní Gallachóir on her, the drive through Dublin was spectacularly beautiful, with soft morning light turning condensation-wet streets blue and pink with the sky's reflections. Traffic wasn't even that bad—Megan wanted, someday, to see an analysis that explained why Thursday mornings generally seemed to be lighter in traffic in the capital city—and she had time to enjoy the Clontarf seafront on her indirect route to the castle hotel.

She arrived early enough that Heather Walsh hadn't yet put in her appearance. Tempted to wander the grounds, Megan instead exited the car, leaned on the hood—*bonnet*, she reminded herself—and texted Paul Bourke with **1. How late were you out with the princesses? & 2. Aibhilin Ni Gallachoir (how do you even do accents on phones) accosted me at work this morning and is going to drag my company into the media's eye if I don't give her a play-by-play of finding Lou's body. How should I proceed?**

Sunlight, split by bare branches, stretched in golden slats across the parking lot, coloring even the asphalt warmly and picking tiny prisms out of the dew clinging to blades of grass. Megan watched the light change, lazily, with half an eye on the castle doors so she wouldn't miss Heather's arrival. Her phone buzzed before the golf star came out, and she glanced at it to see Paul's return text.

1. none of your business so. 2. hold down the letter, it'll come up with accent options. 2a. bore her, and then, a moment later, **3. u know regular ppl use abbreviations in texts, not complete sentences?**

I know it, Megan texted back. **I just don't hold with it. Roger wilco.** She pressed a few letters on the phone's keyboard, delighted to see he was right about the accents, and sent a nonsensical text of tildes, umlauts, and cedillas to him as a follow-up. She was still smiling at herself when Heather Walsh appeared, somehow looking visibly thinner and frailer than she had the afternoon before. Megan stepped forward, worried, but Heather offered a smile that suggested nothing was wrong. Skeptical, but aware the woman had an important game ahead of her, Megan only said, "Good morning, Mrs. Walsh," and held the car door for her. Once they were both inside again, Megan, testing the conversational waters, said, "Lovely morning. Not much wind."

"Not here," Heather agreed. "Maybe on the island, though."

"Are you like Mr. Walsh? Do you like playing in the wind?"

"No one likes playing in the wind as much as Martin does."

"Did Lou?"

To Megan's surprise, Heather stiffened, jaw tightening as she looked out the window. "I'd rather not talk about Lou, if you don't mind."

"Of course not. I'm sorry." Megan hesitated, then released a breath that made Heather look back at her. "Nothing," Megan said apologetically. "I was about to ask you for advice, but you'd just asked me not to talk about—I'm sorry. I shouldn't have said anything."

"You haven't said anything." Heather sounded irritated. "What did you want advice about?"

Megan sighed. "It's just that Aibhilín Ní Gallachóir learned I was there to find Mr. MacDonald's body, and she wants to interview me. I barely knew him, and I just— I wondered what someone who knew him well might want someone to say about him, if they had the chance."

Heather Walsh softened again, though her gaze remained on the approaching shoreline. "Lou MacDonald loved more deeply than anyone I'd ever met. He kept playing golf out of love for his first wife, and he'd want that to be his legacy. That and Saoirse. He was so proud of her."

"His first wife?" Megan asked, surprised again. "I thought he'd only been married once."

Heather shook herself a little. "Yes, of course."

Curious, smiling, Megan glanced in the rearview mirror, hoping to catch Heather's eye. "Was he seeing someone? Oh," she said, as dismayed as she'd been hopeful a moment earlier. "Oh no. Seeing someone Saoirse didn't know about, maybe? Someone who can't even come forward to mourn?"

Heather gave her a brittle smile in the mirror. "I can't imagine anyone in Lou's life being unable to publicly mourn him. But really, that's all I can talk about him right now. His death is a huge blow to us and . . ." Her smile fractured. "And I have a game to play, one that he wanted me to do well in. He was going to caddie for me this week, between his own games. Can you believe that? He used to do it all the time when he wasn't competing himself, but can you imagine taking the time when he had a competition of his own?"

Megan smiled. "He must have thought very highly of your skills. Who will caddie for you today instead?"

"Anthony volunteered." Heather shook her head. "He knows Martin's game inside and out, but I don't know if he's as conversant with mine. Martin doesn't like to share, you know."

"Yes," Megan said softly. "You mentioned." She had taken the longer way around, adding almost a whole kilometre to their journey, in order to drive along the coast. As they approached the wooden bridge, she glanced at Heather in the rearview mirror. "I'll drive up the causeway instead of the wooden bridge, if that's all right, Mrs. Walsh? It's closer to St. Anne's."

"Yes, of course." The road ran straight along the sea-walled coast, as unnatural a front as Bull Island's, until Megan turned onto the double-lane causeway, crossing mud flats and marshy wetlands before reaching the sandy body of the island. The gated entrance to St. Anne's was nestled in the very middle of the island, an unobtrusive little turn that led to the quiet green.

Megan liked Bull Island's second golf course better than its first, although she'd been given to understand that the Royal Dublin was the superior course. Not being a golfer, that didn't matter much to her, but the clubhouse design at St. Anne's had struck her with its low, rounded roof, shaped much as if the wind itself had swept down and formed it along with the sand dunes. Enormous windows and balconies lined most of its upper floor, making it look open and more part of its environment than the older, more formal buildings at the other club.

Besides, St. Anne's encouraged women to be members, so even if the clubhouse had been nothing more than a firepit with some marshmallow sticks stuck in the sand beside it, Megan would have liked it better for that reason alone. She pulled into the parking lot on the eastern side of the clubhouse and got out to open the door for Heather Walsh, who gave her a tired smile of thanks.

There were more personal cars and fewer media vans at St. Anne's than had been at the Royal Dublin the day before. Megan, counting the media vehicles, made a face, and Anto, approaching from the clubhouse to escort Mrs. Walsh inside, said, "Isn't it always the way," as if he understood Megan's unspoken complaint.

Megan, mimicking a pundit or sports announcer's voice, intoned, "As you know, Bob, there's never the audience for women's sports that there is for men's, which couldn't possibly have anything to do with the media focusing over ninety percent of its sports coverage on male-dominated sports, and don't get me started on the shocking pay gap between male and female athletes!"

Anto laughed, a big sound that bounced off the sand dunes, and even Heather smiled. "It helps to have people like Aibhilín in the sports room, though. I'm glad she's covering today's game."

"Is it different?" Megan asked. "Having a woman sportscaster? Do they ask different questions?"

"They ask questions at all," Heather said dryly. "I've been in postgame interviews where every question was either directed at my husband, or about him. But that's not useful to think about right now." She turned her attention to Anto. "Has anyone dropped out, Anthony?"

The big man met Megan's eyes briefly, then shook his head, addressing Heather. "No, ma'am. The course is as hard and dry as it gets this morning, and the wind has fallen off, so there's not much danger in the parallel holes." He caught Megan's quizzical look and pointed down the course. "St. Anne's is narrow, for a green. A load of the holes are more or less next to each other, separated by some low dunes. On a windy day a ball can fly over and crack somebody in the teeth."

"Well, that's horrible."

"Bystanders get injured, sometimes badly," Heather said matter-of-factly. "Not often, but often enough."

"Yeah, Anto mentioned that. Wonderful. I think I'll go for a walk on the beach, or stay safely in the car while you all hit tiny, deadly weapons around a field." Megan pressed her lips together, belatedly aware that although she meant to be funny, her client had reason to find such commentary upsetting. Fortunately, Heather smiled faintly and shook her head.

"You can, of course. I don't need you on the green with me, and I'm afraid there's no one as exciting in today's game as the men's tournament featured yesterday. But the odds of injury really are very low."

"And yet . . ." Megan said.

Heather chuckled. "And yet. Well, I certainly won't need you back before one, and the island isn't very big. You can probably explore most of it before I need you again."

"I'm looking forward to it. And you have my number if you need to leave early, Mrs. Walsh. I won't be far out of reach." Megan was ready to set off as Anto and Heather went into the clubhouse, only remembering at the last moment, and with dismay, that she had to wait on Aibhilín Ní Gallachóir.

The RTÉ News van pulled up just as she got comfortable in the Lincoln. Megan scowled at the cameramen getting out, checked the time, and set her phone for a wake-up in forty-five minutes.

About two minutes later Aibhilín knocked on the car

window, shouting, "You don't seem busy, Ms. Malone!" through the glass.

Megan, both annoyed and incredulous, sat up and unrolled the window. "I was resting, which is a kind of activity. Our appointment isn't until ten, Ms. Ní Gallachóir."

"You made it for ten on the chance Mrs. Walsh would need something from you. She doesn't seem to, and I've a game to cover. It'd help me along to do our interview now."

"Brilliant." Megan muttered the word and pulled her coat and tie off, leaving them beside the driver's seat of the car, and unbuttoned the collar of her shirt as she got out. Aibhilín watched with visible amusement and a trace of inquiry. "The only reason I'm doing this is to keep my boss happy," Megan said. "Wearing the company logo during the interview wouldn't exactly keep it on the down-low."

"Ah, sure, grand so. Here, up here on the hill. Most people won't know we're not at the Royal Dublin, with the coastline in the background." Aibhilín drove Megan up the hill like she was a sheep and scampered up after her like a goat. Megan supposed that made the cameraman, coming lumbering up behind them, something like a bison. "Look at me, not the camera," Aibhilín instructed. "Try not to blink too much."

"*Blink* too much?" The request became clear when the cameraman turned on a filming light that shone brilliantly white in Megan's eyes. "Jeez, is that necessary in full daylight?"

"It never hurts to have extra lighting. Besides, the light wash will make you look younger."

Megan, offended, said, "I don't *need* to look younger!" and received a dubious click in response. For a furious moment while Aibhilín continued setting up, Megan considered stomping off and letting Leprechaun Limos fend for themselves, but before she had, Aibhilín brought a microphone up and spoke into it brightly.

"This is Aibhilín Ní Gallachóir here on Bull Island with American immigrant Megan Malone. RTÉ Sports have learned that Ms. Malone was with legendary pro golfer Martin Walsh when he found the body of his best friend, golfer Lou MacDonald. Ms. Malone, can you take us through the discovery?" Aibhilín put the microphone under Megan's chin. Megan, disconcerted, tucked her chin and looked down at it, eliciting a huge sigh and "Cut" from Aibhilín. "Don't look at it, Ms. Malone. Look at me."

"Don't shove it into my collarbone!"

Aibhilín rolled her eyes, turned back to the camera, and gave exactly the same speech she'd done before, her inflections and enthusiasm identical. Megan blinked at her in astonishment and forgot to answer when the sportscaster put the question to her, and, exasperated, Aibhilín had to start all over again.

A wicked impulse to keep messing it up crept over Megan, and she broke into giggles twice at the idea, ruining the takes again. "I'm sorry!" she caroled, not very sincerely. "I've never done this before."

By the seventh try, Aibhilín had given up on doing the opening spiel, which Megan assumed would be edited in properly later. Megan finally stopped flinching at the microphone and, prompted by Aibhilín's impatiently elevated eyebrows, said, "We came over the hill. We saw a body in the water. Martin and I pulled it out. It was Lou," in a not *deliberately* mechanical voice, but even she could tell she sounded stiff as a robot.

Aibhilín lowered the microphone incredulously. "What was that?"

"I don't know! I'm not a TV personality! This isn't my kind of thing!"

The sportscaster took a deep breath. "Let's try again." She coaxed answers out of Megan with leading questions—"What did you *feel* in the moment of discovery?"—and grew increasingly tense-jawed as Megan's absolutely honest answers—"Cold"—failed to give her the revealing human-interest story she was going for. Aibhilín finally put the microphone away and folded her arms, frowning at Megan. "I know you're smoother than this, Ms. Malone. You bamboozled me yesterday with that nonsense about my name. Are you stonewalling me on purpose?"

"I didn't have a camera in my face yesterday." Megan shrugged stiffly. "Maybe I'm only quick-witted when it's not being recorded for posterity."

A glimmer of frustrated recognition came into Aibhilín's eyes; apparently Megan had hit on a thing that really happened, although she knew perfectly well she wasn't *trying* to charm and delight just then, either. "All right," Aibhilín said with a sigh. "One last time. Jerry, can you back off a bit? It might help Ms. Malone relax."

The cameraman moseyed back several steps, adjusting his camera lens so, Megan assumed, the fact that he was farther away wouldn't make any noticeable difference to the quality of the recording. She kept stealing glances at him as Aibhilín asked questions, until the sportscaster burst out with, "For God's sake, woman!"

"I'm sorry!" Megan half-shouted back. "It's just that I know he's still there!"

Aibhilín all but threw her hands in the air as she faced Jerry. "We'll have to cobble something together from what we've got. It's not going to get any better." She took a couple of audible breaths through her teeth, then turned a professional smile on Megan. "Thank you for your time, Ms. Malone. I appreciate your effort."

Megan, sounding much more sincere than she felt, said, "No problem, Ms. Ní Gallachóir. I'm sorry I'm terrible on camera."

Ní Gallachóir, tightly, said, "I suppose if we were all good at it, everyone would be TV personalities or actors. Good morning, Ms. Malone. I'd better get onto the green now."

Megan, trying hard to look apologetic, nodded and scooted down the grassy knoll. A cheek-splitting grin worked its way across her face by the time she reached the dunes and the beach beyond the golf course. Windswept and cheerful, she pulled out her phone to text Detective Bourke, and tripped over a body.

CHAPTER FIFTEEN

Megan's hands splayed as she stumbled. Her phone went flying, but she caught herself before falling, instead lurching a few ungainly steps past the black-clad legs sticking out of the sand dune. She stood there a few seconds, staring blankly at the distant Poolbeg chimneys across the water, waiting for her heartbeat to slow a little. Waiting to see if her mind decided it had gone on an over-active rampage and that she'd really tripped over an unfortunately shaped piece of driftwood.

She was pretty sure she hadn't.

Carefully—*very* carefully, as if great caution would unwind the last half minute and return some degree of normalcy to her world—she bent and collected her phone, brushing sand off it and making sure it was undamaged. Her last session of texts with Detective Bourke were on the screen, and the three lines of accented characters seemed very frivolous just then. She moved her thumb to the little receiver icon, pretty certain she would have to call the detective as soon as she turned around, and then, as prepared as she could be, she turned.

A man's slacks-wearing lower half lay a few feet behind her. There was not, to her relief, a huge, brownish-red stain in the earth around his buried waistline, suggesting that the rest of him was also there, just hidden from sight by drifting sand. He wasn't wearing shoes, and his feet, grey-white with death, had no visible chunks missing, which meant no wildlife had really had a go at him yet. He probably hadn't been dead long. Beyond him, the beach swept toward the distant wall, its rough blocks of stone and concrete a dark shadow making up the island's southern end; light blue skies riddled with high, quick-moving clouds met earth and sea all around them, with the century-old chimneys jutting up from the mainland at the decommissioned Poolbeg Stacks. An admiring murmur of voices rose and fell on the wind as the golf game went on just over the ridge, and the deep, rich scent of salt water and marine life washed over everything. Megan saw and heard it all unnaturally vividly, as if nature, presented with death, felt she should capture the surrounding life in an indelible image. Wind rifled seagrasses, still green in September because Ireland's greens never faded, and seagulls, annoyed that she stood between them and a meal, shrieked at her from above.

Megan, mechanically, pressed the call button on her phone and brought it to her ear, the electronic tones of the call going through a surreal contrast to the endless break of surf against the changeable shoreline. Bourke picked up with a friendly, "What's the story?" and, after Megan's silence drew out longer than normal, said, "Megan? What's wrong?"

"Well, the good news is I gave Aibhilín the worst interview imaginable." Megan sounded wrong even to herself.

Bourke's voice became very serious. "What's the bad news?"

"I just tripped over a dead man."

"*What?* Where? Are you all right? Are you sure he's dead? Who is it?"

"I'm fine, I'm grand so." Megan doubted the truth of that—she was rattled, at the very least—but in the grand scheme of things, she was well enough. Not, for instance, dead and buried in a sand dune. "I'm on the beach at Bull Island, on the northern end. I don't know who it is—he's half-buried—but I'm sure he's dead. This is not normal, Paul. People don't just keep stumbling on dead bodies."

"No kidding," he said grimly. "Stay where you are. If anyone comes along, shoo them off. I'll get a team together and we'll be there in twenty minutes."

"There's a golf tournament going on," Megan warned. "You're going to have rubberneckers all over the place."

"Grand. Deadly. Brilliant. All right so. See you soon." Bourke hung up, muttering, and Megan folded her arms around herself, wishing she'd put her jacket back on. Of course, she'd expected to be walking briskly, not standing in the sea breeze making sure no one disturbed a dead body. A couple of brightly colored kites rose into the air farther down the beach, and Megan watched them swoop while hoping their owners stayed put. They did, but dog walkers, too many of whom didn't follow the leash law, appeared, too. She was trying to figure out how to head them off when police vehicles drove down a stretch of beach clearly marked *vehicle free zone,* and made a barricade around her as they parked.

People from farther down the beach immediately headed their way, but at that point it wasn't Megan's problem. Detective Bourke got out of one of the cars and strode over to her, his long coat flapping in the wind and orange galoshes kicking sand up as he came. "Are you well?"

"I'm fine. *He's* not so great." Megan nodded at the body, shivered, and accepted Bourke's coat when he handed it to her. It came to his knees and her ankles. Remembering he'd lent her a coat after the Darr murder, she said, "This is getting to be a habit."

"I wish it wasn't." Bourke, having taken her at her word, left her alone to go crouch beside the body as a forensics team began photographing and recording details that Megan didn't have the expertise to recognize at all. After a minute of discussions, he rose and returned to her side, this time with a notepad—this one dun brown—in hand. "All right, what's the story?"

"I told you literally everything I know on the phone. I came down the hill after talking to Aibhilín. I got my phone out to text you, wasn't looking where I was going, and tripped over his legs."

"'His'?"

"I assume so. Those look like man feet to me. Then I called you."

Bourke sighed. "You were a soldier before you moved to Ireland, right?"

"Yeah, twenty years in the army. Combat medic and driver."

"Tell me. How many bodies a month did you person-

ally average in the military? More or less than you're av-
eraging here?"

Megan ducked her head. "Heh. More, while I was on
tour, Detective. And a lot more wounded. On the positive
side, at least with me finding them, you can be sure you
won't hear about it through social media before it comes
in through official channels."

"Yeah," Bourke said sourly. "Because you're very
concerned with hierarchical escalation and not at all interested in finding things out for yourself."

Megan's gaze, and eyebrows, rose in mild offense. "I
was a good soldier, Detective. I followed the rules and I
went through the proper channels. But I'm not a soldier
anymore, and of course I'm interested in finding things
out for myself, especially when people keep dropping
dead at my feet. Obviously you're interested in finding
things out, too, and furthermore, I *am* going through the
official, hierarchical channels, so I'd appreciate it if
you'd back off on insulting me."

Bourke wet his lips and thinned them until they disappeared before nodding. "Sorry. This isn't . . ."

"Normal?" Megan said. "Yeah. Pretty sure I told you
that myself." She shrugged his coat off, handed it back,
and stalked several feet away, watching the forensics
team while, in the background, uniformed garda fended
off onlookers drawn by their presence. Bourke didn't approach her again, which suited her just fine. She wanted
to stomp down the beach and release some of her irritation in exercise, but she knew if she left the police
perimeter she'd never get back in. In fact, she counted
herself lucky she hadn't been thrown out, and figured that
under the circumstances, if she left now, she wouldn't
hear anything unofficial about the body until the sanitized

version of the story hit the news. So she stayed, arms folded, jaw bunched, and anger keeping her warm.

The forensics team finished taking pictures and began, with great delicacy, to move sand away from the body's upper half. The man was slim and well-dressed, even with beach stains on his clothes, and it took some time to dig him out, with the team taking pictures and making notes while they worked. Eventually he was uncovered, and, as they rolled him over, Megan saw them exchange glances and shrugs. Her own view was blocked, but Bourke gestured to her, inviting her down to have a look. "Do you know him?"

She slid a few feet down the dune and made her way to Bourke's side, convincing herself as she went that she wouldn't know the dead man, and would only feel a clinical sense of loss at seeing his face. He was balding, with thin, light-brown hair, and cadaverous cheekbones above a disapproving mouth, and Megan, shocked, blurted, "Oh, thank God!"

"*Excuse* me?" Bourke gaped at her, and heads everywhere turned, from the forensics team to the uniformed guards to the dog-walking and kite-flying people who were trying to see what was going on.

Megan, horrified, clapped her hands to her cheeks. "That's Oliver Collins. He's the general manager at the Royal Dublin Golf Club. Or he was."

"'Oh, thank God'?" Bourke asked disbelievingly.

"I'm sorry. That was really inappropriate. I was afraid it would be someone I knew and liked." Dismay crashed through Megan. "That sounded even worse. He was awful.

A real snob. I only met him yesterday morning for a minute."

Bourke, under his breath, said, "I'm beginning to think you shouldn't make casual acquaintances," before saying, "Are you sure?" aloud.

"Yeah, pretty sure. Positive. He left an impression. Not a good one, but an impression." Megan stared toward the Royal Dublin, on the far end of the island from where they stood. "I can see why somebody would want to murder him, but what's it got to do with Lou MacDonald?"

"That's my job to find out. Thank you for your help, Ms. Malone." Bourke nodded toward one of the uniformed guards, who stepped up to escort Megan off the scene. She went along politely, restraining the urge to kick Bourke's shin as she went by, and headed down the beach for her much-delayed walk. A number of the onlookers rushed after her, and for a few minutes she led a little crowd away from the investigation, although they dropped off as it became clear she had nothing interesting to tell them. Most of them, she noticed, didn't bother to go back, for which she felt Paul should, and wouldn't be, grateful.

Once she'd lost her troop of spectators, she took her phone out again and texted Saoirse with a **make it home okay?** that she didn't really expect an answer to. Still, if the young woman *did* answer, she might be able to figure out how to ask about Lou's relationship with Collins without raising suspicion and, more importantly, without annoying Paul Bourke.

Her phone rang a few seconds later, Jelena's picture coming up. Megan, smiling, answered, "Hey there," and Jelena's pretty accent replied, "Hey. I missed you at the gym this morning."

"Well, I missed you yesterday. How are you?"

"Good. My shift doesn't start until two. Can you have coffee?"

Megan groaned. "I would like nothing better, but I'm out on Bull Island with a client and won't be done until at least half one, probably later."

Jelena tsked. "Our schedules are not in sync. Tomorrow evening, then?"

"It's a date," Megan promised. "How about Lebanese? Can I take you out to the Cedar Tree?"

"Ah! Yes. I just won't eat anything between now and then."

"Yeah, me either. We have to get that walnut stuff no matter what mezze we order, okay?"

"Muhummara," Jelena said with confidence.

Megan groaned happily. "Yeah, that. Oh, man, I'm hungry already."

"Good thing they feed you all the food, then. All right, pa, Megan, *do jutra*."

"*Do jutra*," Megan echoed, and although technically they'd said goodbye, Jelena stayed on the phone a moment to say, "Very good, your accent is improving," and laughed when Megan said, "Sure, as long as I only say two words."

"A little at a time is how babies learn, too. *Do jutra*." Jelena hung up, and Megan wiggled her shoulders happily as she started to put her phone back in her pocket.

Then she said, "Ooh!" out loud and texted Jelena with **oh, dress up tomorrow night? I got a crazy new outfit to show off to you,** before putting the phone away and striking out along the beach, finally feeling pretty good about the world.

The city council was talking about banning dogs from

the island, and, watching one lope down the beach chasing geese, Megan thought maybe they should. On the other hand, unless somebody enforced the law, making it wouldn't do any good, and she did want to be able to bring Dip there someday. If they instead enforced the leash laws that were already in place, probably they wouldn't *need* to ban animals—or people—from the beach. Megan made a face at the free-running dog. It always came down to funding: the law could be enforced if they had more feet on the ground, and they could have more feet on the ground if they had money to pay them. It was easy to get outraged about that in Ireland, where the population was small enough that everybody knew everyone's business, up to and including the glad-handing going on between politicians and corporations, but the problem was hardly limited to Ireland.

Her phone buzzed repeatedly in her pocket and she took it out, seeing an **okay!** from Jelena and **home safe** from Saoirse, which didn't invite much in the way of further conversation. But it rang almost immediately with Saoirse's number, and Megan very proudly remembered to say, "What's the story?" as she answered.

"I need help," Saoirse said in a shaking voice. "I've got all of this funeral arrangement stuff to deal with, and I'm just after hearing from the lads in Raheny that the St. Anne's Park development deal is underway again. I don't know what to do, Megan. I can't do all of this. I can't do any of it!"

"Okay, wait, what?" Megan stopped on the beach, looking across the narrow stretch of water at Raheny itself. St. Anne's Park dominated an enormous stretch of land in city terms: a couple hundred metres of waterfront greenery, stretching back into over two hundred acres of land. She'd walked through it a couple of times, which hardly constituted exploring the space, but knew it had sports fields, gardens, and cafes within its borders. And, as if the square mile containing it, Bull Island, and the Howth Head peninsula needed somewhere else to golf, a pitch-and-putt course. "Start again, Saoirse. Remind me about the development. How can I help?"

"They want to develop the old playing fields by the park." Saoirse's voice still shook, but knowing what she was talking about helped steady her. "I told you I was involved in the environmental assessment that stopped them moving forward? That they failed because they went through fast-track planning?"

"You told me some of that, at least, yeah. Okay. What's happened now?"

"We knew they would probably submit a new application like, but they've paid someone off or something and they've a hearing set for tomorrow to argue their case. I've got to be there. I'm the residential side's expert. But I can't, not tomorrow." Her voice rose, fluttering with panic again.

"Okay. Okay. Listen. Listen, they have to put up notice of development at least twelve weeks before they can break ground or anything, right? That's how it works here? They didn't sidestep that, did they?"

"There's a new scheme in place that *does* sidestep that," Saoirse said urgently. "If they get this permission a second time, if they've got an assessment that says they won't have the environmental impact the local community claims it will—which it *will,* they'll have only found someone to reinterpret the data, or choose the numbers they want so they say what they want them to—they may be able to start breaking ground this month. But Da's *funeral* is tomorrow, Megan. I can't change that."

"That soon? God. Okay." Megan bit her upper lip, staring across the water at the threatened park. "First, I know it might not do any good, but do you have the—who's doing the hearing? A judge? A lawyer?"

"An Bord Pleanála, the planning board."

"Okay. Look, call them first, or better yet, if you can, go over to them today, right now, in whatever state you're in. Explain your situation. They might be sympathetic." At Saoirse's sound of disbelief, she sighed. "Yeah, I know, it's not likely. Bureaucracies aren't usually. But it's worth a shot. I'd go for you, but it'll be harder for them to say no to the bereaved. Tell me what I can do for you right now, so you can do that."

"The wake is tonight," Saoirse replied in a small voice. "I haven't the drink for it yet. I'm meant to be at the off-licence now."

"Tell me what you need and where to bring it, and I'll sort it out for you," Megan promised.

"Da's house is out in Dalkey. I'll text you the address." Saoirse took a shaking breath. "Thanks a million, Megan. You don't have to be doing this."

"Sometimes people just need a little help. Text me that address, and the list of the booze you want." Megan hung up and rang her friend Fionnuala, making a face as the phone went straight to voice mail. "Hey, Fionn, this is Meg. Look, a girl I know, her dad's just died and her job has just gone into crisis mode, and she's trying to do it all, including the wake tonight. Can I fling myself on your mercy on her behalf and pick up some food platters from the restaurant around . . ." Megan moved the phone to check the time and made a face. "Around five? I think I'll be free from driving by then. I'll text you, too." She hung up, put the phone on voice recognition, and dictated the same message, except full of errors, to Fionnuala, then climbed up the ridge of long-grassed sand to see if she could cut back across the island to the car without getting brained by a stray golf ball.

A small horde of people spread across the low, flat greens, all trailing along behind the golfers. Some had moved off to the northwest, looking toward the roofs of police vehicles that Megan could just barely see over the tops of the dunes. Most, though, hadn't been distracted from the game, which appeared to be approaching the final holes. Megan judged the ground quality in front of her and decided it was worth risking a jog across, since the parking lot was only six hundred metres away as the crow flew. To her relief, Anto's estimation of the hard earth proved right, and she didn't sink in any sandpits. The prospect did make her smile, though, remembering the innumerable quicksand traps of her childhood media. She, like many people her age, had grown up imagining that they would be much more of a problem in their adult lives than they actually were.

A few long strides took her down a dip and up its other side. Cresting it, she saw Martin Walsh in the parking lot, arguing vociferously with Anthony Doyle, whose round face was florid with rage. Walsh, with his back to her, stepped forward threateningly, as though he'd throw a punch at Anto, but the caddie caught sight of Megan and snapped a warning that had Walsh turning, all smiles and charm, as she came down the hill toward them.

CHAPTER SIXTEEN

"Megan!"

"Mr. Walsh." Megan smiled, deciding it behooved her to pretend she had neither seen nor heard their altercation. "I didn't expect to see you here this"—she made a show of checking the time—"afternoon. Or you, Anto. Aren't you supposed to be out on the green with Mrs. Walsh?"

"She switched caddies for the back nine." Color crept up Anto's jaw again, outlining stubble that Megan hadn't noticed that morning. "Happens sometimes."

"I didn't even know that was allowed. Is she all right out there? I know it must be hard to play so soon after a friend's death." Megan turned her oblivious smile on Walsh. "By the way, Saoirse told me Mr. MacDonald's wake is tonight. Will I be driving you?"

A flicker of disguised emotion danced through Martin Walsh's eyes as he nodded. "That would be grand."

"Great. Oh! I hope you don't mind. I've asked a friend for some snack platters, and I might have them in the car with me. Probably in the boot, along with some alcohol."

"Not at all. We can stop for any errands you need to run. I won't tell Orla." Walsh dropped a wink, then clapped his hand against Anto's shoulder. "You'll find me in the clubhouse when Heather's off the green." He walked away as if nothing out of the ordinary had occurred. Megan, eyebrows elevated, watched him a moment before looking at Anto.

"Everything okay?"

"Mr. Walsh really wanted me by Mrs. Walsh's side today." Anto looked uncomfortable. "He doesn't like disappointment."

Megan, dryly, said, "It must be very hard on him indeed when he loses, then."

Anto's eyebrows twitched agreement, though his larger body language was a noncommittal shrug. Megan went to get her coat from the car and replace her tie, saying, "Can I ask what happened that Mrs. Walsh sent you off the green today?" over her shoulder.

The big man sighed. "I'd say Mr. MacDonald let her call her own shots when he caddied for her, and she didn't like me having an opinion."

"That surprises me. She said it was nice to hear you thought she played well."

"Ah, sure, but it's one thing for me to think she plays well and another altogether for me to tell her what shot I thought she should take."

"Isn't that a caddie's job?" Megan sat on the car bonnet, heels on the fender, and considered that Orla would have her hide if she saw her doing that.

"It is, but that's why we work with an athlete for a long time. You get into a way of doing things, a way of talking to each other, that builds trust. I've got Mr. Walsh's trust, not her own self's. She thought I was steering her wrong."

Megan bit back the obvious *were you?* and nodded instead. Anto, given an audience to air his grievances at, carried on with increasing heat. "But Mr. Walsh didn't want her out there alone today, never mind that he could have caddied for her himself and she'd never have sent *him* away. Not that he knows this green as well as I do, either, but he's got no cause to lash out at me when it's his own life that's falling apart through no fault of mine!"

"Is it?"

"Isn't it?" Anto demanded. "His best mate dead, his wife in bits over it, and him only caring if he got the right numbers to go into the tournament this weekend? I'll tell you something, Ms. Malone, that one never knew about Lou's wake tonight, so he didn't. It was news to him, and I don't think Saoirse MacDonald will thank you for telling him, either."

"Oh, no." Megan slumped. "Oh, no, I didn't even think of that. Oh, no! You're right, she's going to kill me. *Crap.*"

"Well, it's no use crying over spilt milk," Anto said, suddenly phlegmatic. "You'd better warn her, though. It's bad enough having your da's wake without unexpected guests showing up."

"Yeah. Yeah, I will." Megan took her phone out to text Saoirse and found a message from her detailing how much alcohol to buy and where to bring it. The phone buzzed again, reporting **I've got in to see the board,** and

Megan, deciding this was not the time to bring further turmoil into the young woman's life, only responded **good** and put the phone away again. "Are you going?"

"To the wake? I suppose I am. Mr. Walsh might not think it's right, but Lou was my friend, too. It'll make for a long day tomorrow, though. Mr. Walsh has a game in the morning and the funeral at three, and—have you ever been to a wake, Ms. Malone?"

"I haven't, why?"

"They're grand old parties," Anto said with a brief smile. "Everyone drinks and sings and sees who can make the others laugh the most with remembrances of the dead, and they run late. Very late. You may be driving himself from the wake to the green, and then on to the funeral, with no sleep in between."

Megan, weakly, said, "But I have a date tomorrow night that I need to be awake for."

Anto cracked a wider smile, advising, "Coffee and not a drop of the old devil liquor in it."

"Not that I could have the drink when I'm on the job anyway." Megan sighed. "I'd better see how my boss wants to handle this. I don't usually stay on call past early evening. Maybe one of the others can collect them if they're out carousing until all hours of the night."

"Maybe," Anto said, "but Mr. Walsh doesn't like to be disappointed."

A cheer came from the course as he spoke. Heather Walsh appeared at the head of a crowd, flushed with pleasure and shaking hands as they were thrust at her. A young woman walked in her wake, carrying her golf clubs and fixed with an adoring gaze. Behind them came the rest of the field of golfers, most looking pleased, though a few wore the surly expressions of athletes who hadn't lived up to their own expectations. "I'd say Mrs. Walsh has done well," Megan said, smiling. "Good for her. Will Martin come out to celebrate with her?"

Aibhilín Ní Gallachóir swooped in, her cameraman trailing behind her, to meet the golfers just before they left the green. Megan, remembering what Heather had said about interviewers asking about her husband, thought maybe it was best if Martin Walsh didn't come out. But, as if she'd summoned him with her question, he exited the clubhouse, arms spread wide and a proud smile stretching his face. "Congratulations, my dear!"

The RTÉ cameraman swung around to catch Martin approaching Heather for an embrace. She smiled as they kissed before Martin turned them both to face Aibhilín. "I get so nervous watching her," he confessed directly to the sportscaster. "I can't even watch on television. I have to immerse myself in something else until the news reaches me, and I'm always delighted to hear it. Isn't she magnificent?"

"You are, Mrs. Walsh," Aibhilín said to Heather. "If I've kept track correctly, this is your eleventh win in a row. Does that steady your nerves, on a day like today?"

Heather took a breath to speak, and her husband laughed. "Heather doesn't have nerves. She lets it all flow through her and uses it to channel her game. The truth is, I wouldn't want to be up against her in a tournament."

"Fortunately," Aibhilín said, so acidly Megan was surprised her voice didn't etch scars in the microphone, "you don't have to be, Martin. Heather, please tell me about the game today. How did you feel out there, in the wake of Lou MacDonald's death?"

Martin opened his mouth again, and Aibhilín, still sharply, said, "*Mrs*. Walsh, please, Martin."

"It was a difficult game today," Heather said into the startled silence left by Aibhilín's interruption. "Lou has been at my side for so many games, and I felt his absence tremendously."

"Is that what led to changing your caddie on the back nine? You'd been with Martin Walsh's caddie for the first nine holes, had you not? But a young woman finished the course with you this afternoon." Aibhilín gave a short nod toward the girl, who stood behind Heather with a smile so bright Megan thought Jerry probably didn't need the extra light he shone down on Heather.

"Anthony and I have a long-standing relationship," Heather with a quiet smile. "I knew he'd understand if I gave a young woman a chance out there on the green. I'm proud of the game we played today. I think Lou would have been, too. Right now, I think that's all we can ask for."

"What will tomorrow bring? It's the third day of Ireland's first all-inclusive golfing tournament, and we'll be leaving Bull Island for the Howth Head golf courses. How are you and Mr. Walsh feeling, headed into the fierce competition lying ahead of you?"

"Confident," Heather said before Martin could speak. "We both have a lot to prove this weekend, not to ourselves, not to the golfing world, not to the fans, but to Lou's memory, and to the future of a sport that I hope will grow increasingly inclusive over the next years and decades."

Aibhilín smiled like she'd gotten the sound bite she wanted. "Thank you for your time, Heather, and good luck on the green tomorrow." She turned to Jerry, signaling to the Walshes, and the crowd behind them, that they were no longer on air. "That was rising star Heather

Walsh, playing through the adversity of a close friend's death just forty-eight hours ago. Golfer Lou MacDonald, an advocate of this week's global debut tournament featuring alternating days of men and women's golf, died under suspicious circumstances on Wednesday, just south of here on Bull Island. We'll be back later with more exclusive details on that tragic event, and will be following this week's tournament closely from on the course at Howth Head. This is Aibhilín Ní Gallachóir for RTÉ Sports." She kept smiling at the camera until Jerry made a cut sign, then lowered her microphone to give Megan, just within her line of sight, a flat look.

"Sorry," Megan muttered, knowing the sportscaster couldn't hear her. "I'll work on being more charismatic for your interview the next time I'm on the periphery of a sports murder."

As if she *had* heard, Aibhilín squinted suspiciously at Megan, who waved and went to situate herself at the car so she'd be available to find out what the Walshes wanted to do next. She waited over an hour, long enough to call her friend Brian and ask him to walk the puppies—he already had—and to send Niamh a text asking how filming was going. Fionnuala called back with a promise of snack platters, and when Megan asked how much it would cost, huffed indignantly. "Anything for a friend, love."

Megan thought that was preposterous, but said, "You're a star," and made a note to check with the restaurant's manager about how much she should pay for the food. Despite all the busy work, she still had time to nearly fall asleep in the driver's seat before the Walshes emerged from the clubhouse. They were all smiles and waves at what remained of the crowds, even stopping to sign autographs, but the moment Megan closed them into the car, bickering erupted.

"We weren't invited, Martin—"

"And what does that matter? He was my oldest friend—"

"—and you're the man who's always been set on a quiet night before a big game. Tomorrow is going to be a more challenging field and you know it. The weaker players have been weeded out, and if you want to make the final cut, and the Ryder Cup team—"

"I'll never miss Lou's wake," Martin snapped. "I'd think you didn't want to be there at all, the way you're carrying on."

"Of *course* I want to go! He was my friend, too! But I know Saoirse doesn't like me, and your relationship with her has soured, and it's her father, Marty."

"I don't give a damn what she wants!"

They had reached the causeway connecting the island to the mainland by then, and Megan, in as unobtrusive a voice as she could manage, murmured, "Will we be returning to the hotel, sir? Madam?"

In a limo with a privacy divider, they would have lifted it at that moment. In the Continental, without that option, Megan always found it interesting to see what clients would do when reminded of a third party privy to their conversations and arguments. Some people still didn't seem to realize an actual person was there, listening. Others fell into a furious, wary silence, angry not only at each other but also at Megan, for having heard them breaking social norms by fighting in front of someone else. Martin snarled, "Yes," while Heather, calmer, replied, "No, thank you. I'll need to go to town after you've dropped Martin off."

"Where the hell do you think you're going?" Martin barked.

"I'll need something appropriate to wear to the wake, if we're going," Heather said very steadily. "I didn't bring mourning clothes with me."

"*Mourning* clothes? Jesus, what is this, Victorian England? Will I paint the railings black and—"

"That's a myth," Heather said coolly. "Victoria had her staff wear black armbands for years, and wore it the rest of her life, but they didn't start painting the railings black until decades after her death, when fast-drying paint started coming on the market."

"Ah, you have to be so fecking smart, don't you, ferreting out all the little truths and lies about people. You think it's a way to keep your own secrets safe," Martin snarled. "Don't count on that, my dear. You're not half as clever as you think you are. It's a good thing you're pretty or you'd never have amounted to anything at all."

"Except being a brilliant golf player and a good friend."

"Watch and see how good a golfer you are with a broken ankle."

Megan's hands tightened on the steering wheel, but Heather gave a light, sharp laugh. "You wouldn't dare. Don't think I don't know how much money you owe Anthony, or how many of my winnings you've used to pay him back with. You might be free of him if we both win this weekend and you get the Cup wild card position, but you won't be without my money, so don't think you scare me, Martin Walsh."

"'Martin Walsh,'" he mimicked in a high, nasty voice. "You were happy enough to take on that name when we got married."

"Live and learn," Heather said. "Live and learn."

Martin could not, evidently, find a satisfactory come-back to that, and they fell into an enraged silence that lasted the rest of the drive to the hotel. Martin got out of the car, slamming the door behind him, before Megan had a chance to kill the engine, much less get out and hold the door for him. She waited a few seconds to see if he would turn back for any reason, then, as neutrally as she could, said, "Where to, Mrs. Walsh?"

"Brown Thomas, I think, thank you, or the Power-scourt Centre."

"I'll take you to the Brown Thomas car park? It's the most reliable parking for that end of Grafton Street, and it's only a minute or two to walk to Powerscourt."

Heather nodded quietly and fixed her attention out the window as they passed through the broad, wealthy streets of Clontarf, heading south past Connolly Train Station and finally across the River Liffey into the warren of small streets of Dublin's city centre. They were waiting to pull into the parking garage at Brown Thomas, one of Grafton Street's upscale retailers, when Heather said, "I'm sorry for subjecting you to that," out of the blue.

Megan met her eyes in the rearview mirror, saying, "To what?" lightly enough that she hoped the blond woman would understand she was pretending nothing had happened.

A relieved smile flashed over Heather's face, and Megan nodded, then took a quick, preparatory breath. "I do have to ask, though, Mrs. Walsh. Do you believe you're in any danger? That did sound like a . . . a credible threat, and I'm required to report things like that, even if I, uh, didn't hear anything."

For a moment Heather Walsh looked very tired. "No, I don't think I'm in any danger. I meant it when I said he wouldn't dare. He certainly never has dared in the past, anyway, and he can't afford to alienate me right now."

"Yes, ma'am." Megan had every intention of letting Paul Bourke know about the volatile relationship between the Walshes, but trusted Heather's assessment of her personal safety for the near future, at least. She glanced in the mirror again as they pulled into the dark parking garage and began winding through its cavernous aisles. "Will you want me to come along and carry bags?"

To her surprise, Heather laughed, a bright, genuine sound of pleasure. "Is that part of your job? You're a better husband than the one I've got." She sighed, her smile fading. "Lou used to come shopping with me. Martin complained that we always spent too much, but he hated coming with me himself. It's more fun to go with someone, though."

Megan smiled at her in the mirror. "Well, I'm at your disposal."

"No, that's all right. Martin said you were picking up food for the wake tonight, and I'll probably get maudlin. Dealing with that is definitely *not* part of your job."

"You'd be surprised." Megan nodded, though, parked the car, and held the door for Heather, who glanced at the time and said, "Meet you back here at four? And I have your number in case I run late."

"See you then," Megan promised, and scurried away to call Detective Bourke with all her latest gossip.

CHAPTER SEVENTEEN

"That is *not* a happy marriage," Megan told Bourke a few minutes later as she headed up Grafton Street toward a nearby Luas stop, in hopes that the tram would be the fastest way back to Rathmines and the puppies. "Emotionally abusive at best, and Heather's obviously used to being self-effacing in his presence. You should have seen her postgame interview, with Martin trying to horn in. Oh, well, I guess you can, on the news tonight. What's the story with Collins?"

"Somebody strangled him," Bourke said in the tone of a man who knew better than to share that information. Megan rolled her eyes at the phone, then squinted at the Luas sign, which was still too far away to read. There were no trams in sight, though, so at least she hadn't just missed one.

"No kidding. I mean, it looked like it, right? But was

there any skin under his fingernails or anything incrimi-
nating like that?"

"You've been watching too many television shows.
No. They used some nylon boundary rope and dumped
him."

"Why not dump him in the water?" Megan wondered.
"Weight him down and drop him into the surf? Or at least
bury him?"

A long pause came over the line before Bourke hung
up and called back on a video application, his blue eyes
gone grey with dismay. "Do me a favor," he said bleakly.
"Never become a criminal. I'm afraid you'd be good at
it." He sighed, gaze losing some of its storminess. "I'd
say the killer probably panicked. Most of them do. And
you've no idea how hard it is to bury a body, Megan. Do
you know the best way to keep from being caught, if
you've killed someone?"

"No," Megan said, fascinated. "What?"

"Bury the body six feet deep. We'll never find it."

Megan blinked at him. "That sounds easy."

Bourke shook his head. "No. It's *simple*. It's not *easy*
at all, which is why hardly anybody does it."

"Ah. Yeah, okay, fair enough. But weighting a body and
dumping it off the Bull Wall can't be that hard, can it?"

There was a tram in two minutes. Megan touched her
Leap Card against the terminal to pay for the ticket and
leaned against a wire-and-steel railing to watch passers-
by as Bourke conceded, "It's a lot less hard than digging
a six-foot deep hole, but it's still not easy. You've moved
unconscious bodies."

Megan, with a shudder, remembered hauling Lou out
of the pond just two days earlier. "Yeah. Okay, it's not
easy. They weigh a lot."

"So combine inconvenience with panic and you end up with the odds being good that Oliver Collins died within a few metres of where you found his body."

"On a beach where the water washes away all signs of struggle." Megan made a face. A tram pulled up, doors dinging pleasantly as they opened, and she fell into line with other people waiting to board. "Was he in the habit of early morning beach walks?"

Bourke's pale eyebrows shot up. "How did you know he died early this morning?"

"Nothing had eaten him yet."

She was treated to another silent stare as she got on the Luas, except this time he didn't have to hang up and make a video call to deliver it. "Have you ever considered law enforcement as a career, Ms. Malone? I'd say you have the stomach for it."

"I've done enough enforcing, thanks. I'd rather drive people around and listen to their gossip."

Bourke inhaled and exhaled it so deeply Megan's chest started to hurt in sympathy before he finally said, "As it happens, Oliver Collins *was* in the habit of taking an early morning walk around the island before going to work. Apparently, he was out there rain or shine, unless the conditions were so adverse as to constitute weather warnings."

"And I suppose anybody who worked at the Royal Dublin, or who regularly went to Bull Island early, or who knew Collins, knew that. And I also suppose a lot of people made this kind of face"—Megan flared her nostrils and twitched her upper lip—"when asked if Collins had any enemies."

Obviously despite his better judgement, Bourke laughed.

"As a matter of fact, yes. He was not, as it turns out, well-liked. Widely lauded at being very good at his job, but not well-liked by anyone but the wealthy or influential."

"Yeah, I saw him in action. He was really good at kissing up to people he thought could do something for him. Martin Walsh liked him, but his caddie, Anto, didn't." Megan's stomach roared suddenly, and she clapped her hand over it. "I need to eat something. I haven't had anything but coffee today, I don't think. Do you want to meet for lunch?"

"I have several dozen more people to interview," Bourke said dryly. "Maybe another day."

"Right. Anything I can do to help out in the meantime?"

"*Megan*," Bourke said in despair. "You are not a garda. This is not your job."

"Right, yeah, no, I know." Megan waited a beat. "So is there anything I can do?"

Bourke groaned and hung up. Megan, still snickering at herself, got off the Luas a few minutes later and stopped for Indian at Tadka House before knocking on Brian Showers's door.

He opened the door with an air of amusement and a sparkle in his brown eyes. Puppies rolled out the open door, wriggling excitedly around Megan's ankles. She laughed, handed over the bag of food, collected both the little dogs, and stood up. "Cutting to the chase, are we? I didn't think you'd bring them here. I'm sorry I stuck you with them today. I didn't expect to be working all night."

"It's fine, except my cat thinks they, and therefore you, are the devil incarnate. But it was easier to bring them here than run back and forth to your place all day. Come on in." Brian—taller than Megan, black-haired, bespectacled, and wearing professorial tweed—stepped out of the door, opened the takeaway bag, and sniffed appreciatively. "You're bribing me, aren't you?"

"Is it working?"

"Magnificently."

"Then yes, I definitely am." Megan kicked the door closed behind her and put Dip and Thong back on the floor, where they began climbing over each other in an attempt to get back into her arms. "Thank you for taking them."

"I'm consoling myself with the knowledge that in another few weeks their bladders will be more reliable and you'll start sneaking them around with you in the limos."

"Orla would straight-up murder me." Megan followed Brian down a wood-floored hallway into a small, bright kitchen overlooking a tiny, concrete garden dominated by a shed where the oil tank resided. He laid lunch out on a small, blue-topped table while she got silverware out, and they sat down to eat with two exceedingly hopeful puppies and one equally hopeful but more dignified mama dog watching them. "How's the book business?"

"Oh, you know what they say." At Megan's querying eyebrows, Brian smiled. "If you want to make a small fortune in publishing, start with a large one."

Megan laughed. "Oh dear. You, er . . . you didn't start with a large fortune, did you?"

"I'm afraid not, but I'm nearly twenty years in the business now anyway." Brian tilted his head toward the spare bedroom where he ran his small press, focused mostly on Irish Gothic and horror literature, from. "It's not a bad oeuvre."

"Well, you've reprinted all kinds of things *I'd* never read before anyway."

Brian sniffed. "Uncultured American, not knowing who Le Fanu is."

She snorted back. "Unlike you, who is cheese-cultured?"

"Ooh, a low blow!" Brian had moved from Wisconsin to Ireland long before Megan had even started considering retiring to her grandfather's native country. "So why is it I'm dog sitting overnight, and why is it that Fionnuala, who is supposed to soon be the adopted mother of one of these little beasties, is not?"

"I have a wake to go to, or at least to drive people to and from, and Fionn's working tonight."

"Fionn works every night. Are you sure she's going to be able to have a dog?"

"Well, her partner doesn't work nights."

"But does *he* want a dog?"

"You know what, I assume that's a conversation they've had and I don't need to." Megan bent to rub Dip's chocolate-colored nose. "But I know you don't want one, and I promise to either get a regular pet sitter or somehow flatter Orla into letting me take Dip with me when I'm working a long day."

"My *cat* doesn't want one," Brian corrected. "I don't mind dog sitting, particularly when there's free lunch involved."

"Because you didn't start with a large fortune," Megan said with a smile.

"Exactly."

They finished lunch before Megan, guiltily, looked at the time. "I have to go buy an entire off-licence's worth of booze, pick up snack platters from Canan's, *and* be waiting at the car for Mrs. Walsh when she gets done shopping at half four."

"In other words, you have to run. Fear not. I'll fend for the puppies."

"You're my hero." Megan kissed Brian's scruffy cheek and hurried back to the Luas, feeling a little as though she'd been on the run all day after her comparatively luxurious, slow morning. It seemed barely possible that she'd tripped over Oliver Collins's body only a few hours, rather than a few days, ago. "No," she muttered to herself, "a few days ago you found somebody *else's* body. Great!"

There were three whiskey stores within a five-minute walk of the St Stephen's Green Luas stop, and Megan, preferring the Celtic Whiskey Shop's selection, went to it, even though it was farther away from the car. She had about ninety seconds of lugging bags of bottles down the street and deeply regretting her choice before one of the bicycle rickshaws wobbled up beside her and a plucky young man said, "Would you be looking for a lift?"

"Oh my God, yes." Megan loaded the bags behind the driver and crawled in after them, her arms already feeling wobbly from having carried the alcohol a scant hundred metres. "Can you cycle me all the way into the BT car park? I'll pay for your time in there if they try to charge you, leaving."

"Sure so."

"Thank God." Megan flopped dramatically across the seat, an arm flung out, and watched the tops of Georgian buildings go by through the little plastic window in the rickshaw's canvas. Her driver made an effort *not* to run people down as he turned up Anne Street South, which couldn't be said for all rickshaw cabbies, and after a few breezy minutes, pedaled into the Brown Thomas car park. Megan paid and gave him an outrageous tip after he helped her load booze into the Lincoln's boot, then, checking the time again, Megan ran around the corner behind Brown Thomas to Canan's in the old St Andrew's Church.

The statue of Molly Malone, which had been moved from Grafton Street to in front of the church during the extension of the Luas tram line, still stood there, an unfortunate reminder, to Megan, of a food critic's death. She said, "My life has gotten pretty weird" to the statue, which, unsurprisingly, had nothing to say in return, neither then nor several minutes later when Megan exited the restaurant with Fionnuala, both of them burdened with platters of finger foods.

"This is way more than you should have done," Megan said for at least the third time. "I just wanted to bring her a little something for the wake, not enough to feed the whole army of them."

Fionnuala, her heart-shaped face already pink from working in the kitchen, and turning pinker from dodging passers-by, shook her head. "Know what's worse than a load of drunks at a wake?"

"No?"

"A load of drunks who get smashed in the first hour because there's no food to pace themselves with." Fionn puffed a breath of air upward, knocking back an errant lock of reddish hair. It fell into her eye again almost immediately. "I should have left me hat on."

"Well, you're a star," Megan said. "Floppy hair or no. Thank you for this."

"You saved my restaurant, Megan. There's no favor too big to ask me." Even with stacks of food, the walk

back to the car park only took a few minutes, and Fionnuala stood patiently holding platters while Megan tried to
arrange them in the boot so nothing would be crushed or
fall over. Heather Walsh appeared while she was still
working on it, said, "Oh, man," and put down her shopping bags to help.

After a minute they had it sorted, and Megan turned a
grateful smile on her friend. "My hero."

"Mmm-hmm." To Megan's astonishment, Fionnuala's
hands were clutched in front of her stomach, wringing
around each other as she looked, wide-eyed, at Heather.
"Mrs. Walsh, hi, I'm a friend of Megan's, I'm Fionnuala
Canan, a restaurateur, and I know it's ridiculous, and
you're not—you're not working, but I love watching you
play, and I wondered—I wondered if—well, I wondered
if you might come to Canan's, I'd love to have you, but
also—I wondered—a picture—?"

Heather's cautious smile grew broader as Fionn fum-
bled her way through the request. "Yes, of course. I'd be
delighted. And where's your restaurant?"

"It's—tourist church—St Andrew's—Megan knows—"

Megan, grinning hugely, said, "I'd be delighted to bring
you there tomorrow or Saturday night, Mrs. Walsh. It's
just around the corner."

"Of course. I know where the tourist church is. Megan,
would you mind taking our picture?" Heather handed
Megan her own phone, causing Fionnuala to squeak in
thrilled dismay.

"Mine! Mine! I wouldn't—bold!" Fionn thrust her
own phone at Megan, who took them both and snapped
several shots on each, silently despairing about the unat-
tractive car park backdrop. Fionnuala, however, looked
chuffed as Megan handed back her phone, and Heather,

still smiling, shook the chef's hand, said, "It's lovely to meet you, Fionnuala," and got in the car herself, without Megan opening the door for her.

"*Fionn*!" Megan hissed gleefully. "What was that? Starstruck? You know Niamh O'Sullivan, for heaven's sake!"

Fionnuala, pink-cheeked, flustered, and clearly over-whelmed with excitement, whispered, "But Nee is just Nee!" back at her. "That was *Heather Walsh*!"

Megan, still beaming, hugged her friend. "I absolutely adore you and I'll bring her to dinner Saturday night. Make something special."

"I *will*!"

Fionn capered off and Megan, trying not to giggle out loud, got into the car to meet Heather's eyes in the rearview mirror. "That was really nice of you. I didn't even know Fionn liked golf."

"People usually get excited over Martin," Heather replied with a smile. "It's nice to not be overshadowed, sometimes. Is her restaurant good?"

"So good," Megan said with a happy groan. "New Irish cuisine. It's all local, with some seafood specials, and Fionn's always in there pouring her whole heart into every dish. I think you'll love it."

"I can't wait," Heather said sincerely, and Megan got her all the way back to the hotel to change clothes and collect her husband before remembering she hadn't warned Saoirse that the Walshes would be at the wake that night.

CHAPTER EIGHTEEN

She rang Saoirse while Heather went in to the hotel to get changed. Saoirse answered with, "It didn't work," and for a few seconds Megan had no idea what she was talking about.

"What didn—oh! Oh no, the appeal to put the hearing off until Monday? Oh no, Saoirse, I'm so sorry." Megan crushed a hand against her face. "I've got news that will probably make your day worse, too. I mentioned the wake in front of the Walshes, and they're planning to come."

"Of course they are." Saoirse didn't sound surprised. "I wasn't in any hurry to invite them along, but someone would have mentioned it. Don't stress."

"Still, I'm sorry. Look, I've got booze and snacks for the wake. Is there anything else you'd like me to pick up on the way?"

The way Saoirse said "No" meant there were a whole host of things she wished for, none of which were practical or, in all likelihood, possible. "Can you stay for the wake? I know you didn't really know Da, but . . ."

"But I know you now," Megan said gently. "I'll stay as long as I can. Sometimes it helps to have someone who's mostly on the outside of things there to keep a level head. Okay, so I know I need to get there kind of early to help set up the drinks and the food, but I'm also going to have the Walshes with me. Maybe I can drop them off at a nearby pub for a little bit before it's supposed to start?"

"Oh, Martin would love that," Saoirse said in a tone that meant he wouldn't, at all. "Just bring them in. I'll be busy enough that I wouldn't have to talk to them if I don't want to, and a few of our friends from the West have already come over, so I'm not all alone in the house. It'll be fine."

"Fine" could mean "completely terrible"; the general Irish verb for things being genuinely okay, in American terms, was "grand," and things were definitely not grand. Megan sighed, said, "Okay, see you in a bit," and hung up before the Walshes came out.

When they did, Heather looked shaken to her bones, and Martin, baffled and angry. They got in the car carefully and quietly, moving skirts and long black coats out of the door's way, and after Megan got in again herself, Heather said, "Martin's just heard that Oliver Collins is dead."

"It's impossible," Martin said. "I only saw him yesterday. They say it's foul play."

Megan, feeling as though it wouldn't go over well if she casually mentioned that yes, she knew that, she'd found the body, said, "Oh, no," in a voice that sounded affected and stagy to her. "How terrible. Were you close?"

"I knew him going years back, long before he started managing at the Royal Dublin. He golfed himself, back in the day. He was good, very good, but not good enough. He was after quitting playing when he realized he'd never be a pro, but the love of the game stayed with him, I'd say. We'd play a round or two together sometimes, and I'd introduce him around. It's how he met the right people to get that job. He got to be friends with all the businessmen, the bankers and the developers and the like, and the club thought he'd bring them in as members. They were right, too. I can't believe he's dead. Thank God it's today and not yesterday, or the club might have shut down the tournament."

"The PGA may yet," Heather said. "This is two tragedies in a row, and it's going to gain a lot of negative coverage. There'll be people who'll call it a curse."

Martin chuckled suddenly. "And that it's the result of having a combination tournament. See, love, I told you it was a bad idea. We lads should do our thing and you lasses your own."

Heather turned her face toward the window, voice quiet but venomous. "I didn't hear you complaining about the idea of taking home a double purse on your way to the Cup."

"But it's a stunt, and you know it. Women can't play on par with me." Martin laughed, catching Megan's eye in the mirror. "On par!"

She gave him a flat, polite smile in return, and he settled back in his seat, pleased with himself, though he returned to the topic of Collins's death, mostly in a monologue, for the drive to Lou's house. Heather caught her breath as they turned up the drive, and Megan saw her bite her lip in the mirror as she tried to compose herself. "We'll help you get the food and drinks, Megan," she said as they got out of the car. "It's the least we can do."

"Don't worry about it, Mrs. Walsh." Megan concealed a surge of irritation as Heather, unsurprisingly, went ahead and helped while Martin walked ahead to knock perfunctorily on the MacDonald front door before letting himself in.

The house—down in Dalkey, a posh section of town—had the samey-samey look as its neighbors, which had turned Megan off when she'd first come to Dublin. Now she could recognize the quality of the pale bricks and the care put into maintaining the old house. It sported bay windows on both sides of the front door, and from the matching sizes of those windows, Megan suspected the MacDonald home had never been as simple as the standard Irish "two up, two down" house, with two living space rooms downstairs and two bedrooms up. At the least it had begun its life, 150 years before, as a detached home with at least four rooms on each floor and, like nearly all old Irish houses, had no doubt been expanded since. Whatever expansion had taken place, though, had gone back, not out or forward. The house still had a generous front garden and, given its location, Megan guessed that the back garden expanded far beyond what most Dublin homes offered. She hoped to see it; peeking around at old houses and seeing how they'd been changed—and stayed the same—through the generations was one of her favorite things about living in a country where a hundred miles was a long way, but a hundred years was no time at all.

Martin left the door open behind him. Megan followed Heather inside, feeling like they were the load-bearing cars of a train with an engine that thought it was too good for the job at hand. An image of the Little Engine That Could popped into her mind, and she bit the inside of her cheek, suspecting that bursting into giggles when just through the door to a wake would not be appreciated.

The house did, in fact, go back for what seemed like miles. She'd been right: there were four rooms with visibly older framing and picture rails above them, two on each side of a wood-floored hallway lined with rugs she knew didn't come from IKEA. A switchback stairway with runner carpeting and original features rose beyond the doorway to the second room on the left, and past that lay a doorway to the first extension, which, at a glimpse, looked like a handsome, modern kitchen.

Martin had already gone into the first room on the right, probably once a parlor, now kitted out as a library, and was pouring himself a drink. Saoirse, pale and drawn, appeared from the kitchen and pointed toward the second door on the left, just in front of the stairs. "That's the dining room, so the food should go there, I guess. Thanks, Megan. Heather." The second name was spoken more stiffly, but Heather smiled and nodded pleasantly. "Is there anything else?"

"We got all the food," Megan said, counting the platters as she set hers down on a table a bit too large and considerably too ornate for the room. A lot of the houses she'd been in in Ireland were decorated that way. Lingering ideas of wealth, left over from Georgian and Victorian landlords, still seemed to dictate fashion in houses too small to carry off furniture meant for enormous rooms. A sash window threw late-afternoon light on the table, brightening the space, which was friendly enough, if slightly overcrowded. At least the oversized table held the restaurant platters neatly. Megan arranged a couple more tidily, saying, "There are a lot of bottles in the boot."

"Not anymore." A strapping young man entered with an armful of boxes. Another like him, and a young woman, followed behind him, the latter saying, "I couldn't get the boot closed, sorry."

"No, it's grand so," Megan assured her. "I'll lock it up. Thanks very much."

The girl nodded, leaned in to hug Saoirse and exchange a whisper with her, then, steely-eyed, jerked her head at the young men, who exchanged a look of anticipation and followed her out of the room. A tense little smile of satisfaction played over Saoirse's mouth, and Megan wished Heather wasn't in the room so she could ask if Lou MacDonald's daughter had just set a couple of towering youths on Martin Walsh. Instead, she said, "I am, with the Walshes' permission"—Heather nodded permission—"at your disposal, Saoirse. Tell me what I can do to be useful. Can I go get paper napkins and plastic wineglasses?"

"I think we've got everything." Saoirse sagged against the back of a chair. "I don't know . . . I don't know where I should be. I don't know how to do this." She paled as she spoke but didn't begin to cry, an effort that Megan regarded as Herculean.

"Come to the front room," Heather said, surprising Megan. Saoirse gave her a bleak, startled look, and Heather smiled tightly. "My dad died when I was nineteen. I remember . . . we didn't have a wake, but there was a reception after the funeral, and I remember feeling just like you just said. Like I didn't know how to do it, or where I should be. I didn't want to be *anywhere*, but I couldn't just go hide. But I found out nobody expected me, or my mom for that matter, to really do very much. We were supposed to stay in one place and let people come to us. So come to the front room, and if you'll let me, I'll stay with you and send people back here for food and drinks when you need them to move on."

To Megan's complete astonishment, Saoirse whispered, "That would be great."

Heather smiled more openly than she'd ever done when talking about Saoirse and escorted the slightly younger woman out of the dining room. Megan followed them but went all the way out of the house to close the Lincoln's boot and move the car down to the street, where she wouldn't get boxed in later. Car safely parked, she went back to the house, glancing into the library, where Martin Walsh was boxed in a corner by Saoirse's boyfriends. She wondered how much they knew about her relationship with Walsh and guessed, from their swollen postures, that the answer was "quite a lot." "'Loads'," she breathed, correcting even her thoughts to local parlance, and hurried past before Martin could catch her eye and inveigle a rescue.

She looked into the living room, too, to find Heather, Saoirse, and the girl whose name Megan hadn't caught all huddled together on the couch before guests started arriving. "You're going to be standing up all evening," Heather was saying. "Sit while you can. And maybe put on flats."

"No." Saoirse shook her head. "The heels make it hard for anybody to try to intimidate me. I'm tall enough without them, but . . ."

"No, I get it. It helps, doesn't it? Being able to look down on them? Especially men. It makes so many of them uncomfortable." Heather straightened up even on the couch, like she was proving what she meant. "Even Martin stands up straighter when I wear heels."

"You're as tall as he is anyway," Saoirse said. "It must make him mental when you're taller. Come on in, Megan."

Megan shook her head. "Can I get all of you a drink, maybe? And if you don't mind me asking, where's the toilet?" She could still barely ask the question without embarrassment: the Irish did not, as a rule, ask for the "bathroom" or the "ladies," or even "the loo." Just *where's the toilet?* which, to Megan's American mind, was mortifyingly direct.

"Through the kitchen." Saoirse started to rise. "I can show you."

"I can find my own way," Megan promised. "Drinks when I come back?"

"Not yet. I've got to—maybe not at all. I've got to be sober if there's any chance of making the hearing and the funeral both tomorrow."

The unknown girl said, "Wait, *what*?" and tears flooded Saoirse's eyes, though they didn't quite fall. Megan left her explaining the situation with the St. Anne's Park development project and meandered through the kitchen—galley style, as extended Irish kitchens often were—but surprisingly wide, with a breakfast nook that looked as though it got a lot more use than the more formal dining room space. It had the semiprofessional chrome-and-black design that had been popular for years now, complete with a bar set under a long window that overlooked a row of short, leafless trees outside. There would be plenty of room for people to spill out into the kitchen and garden, if the wake became busy. Megan used the toilet, washed her hands, and returned to find several people had arrived in her absence. Most of them were adults, by which she meant people her own age or older, as opposed to Saoirse and her friends, all in their twenties. Heather looked at home among them, and Martin Walsh, by contrast, seemed much older when he came in, having escaped the young men.

He sucked the attention from Saoirse, drawing mutual friends to his side to express their sympathy. Megan watched cords stand out in Saoirse's neck, although she cast her gaze downward and schooled her expression as quickly as possible. Heather squeezed her arm sympathetically, and despite Saoirse's earlier enmity toward Martin's wife, she now looked grateful. The other girl, whose name Megan still hadn't gotten, leaned in to speak quietly and urgently with Saoirse, who shook her head. Megan took the perimeter of the room, brushing between the overstuffed couch and its coffee table and past a feature fireplace probably as old as the house until she'd circled behind the three women as unobtrusively as possible, and could listen in on their conversation.

"Soar, you've got to call Ellen Million. If you don't, I swear to God *I'm* going to."

"She doesn't know the material as well as I do, Trina."

"No one's going to know it as well as you do, Saoirse," Heather said gently. "But you can't be in two places at once."

Trina, quietly but explosively, said, "*Thank* you!" to Heather, and made a short, hard gesture that encapsulated both agreement and pleading to Saoirse. "Ellen's a solid environmentalist, Soar. Call her tonight and she can at least get her feet under her by tomorrow, and make your case for you."

"It's too much to ask somebody overnight—"

"And under normal circumstances you totally wouldn't, but this is not normal, love. Look, no, listen, I know. It's too much for *you* to ask of somebody, yeah?"

"*Yes!*" Saoirse's outburst drew attention away from Martin, and the intense little conversation broke up as people not only returned to her, but as more came in. Trina met Heather's eyes with a meaningful gaze and, upon receiving a nod of approval, left Saoirse's side and went, Megan assumed, to call Ellen and explain the situation. A knot of worry that she hadn't even known she was carrying came unwound beneath Megan's breastbone. She didn't want the young redhead to lose the opportunity to continue her environmental work with the St. Anne's group but couldn't imagine Saoirse missing her own father's funeral either. It was all rotten timing, as if death could ever be timed well.

Martin was saying, "Thank you, yes, *av carse* I miss him terribly," with an accent laid on thicker than Megan had ever heard, which seemed especially absurd given that everyone around him was Irish, too. It was true that her own grandfather, who'd left Ireland at only twenty years of age, and returned to visit sixty years later, had gotten increasingly Irish-sounding upon landing on his native soil, but Martin was in and out of Ireland all the time. He didn't need the affectation, and had even complained about actors doing the same thing just the day before.

It played well, though, with people clapping his shoulder and pulling him into rough embraces while they were gentler and more delicate with Saoirse. More people flooded in, some going directly to the dining room for drink while others worked their way through the growing crowd. The library filled, people flowing naturally from room to room. Megan stayed behind Saoirse and Heather, watching them well up and accept offers of sympathy, then pull themselves back together for the next wave.

Anthony Doyle came in, went straight to Saoirse, and exchanged a sad look with Heather Walsh before retreating to allow them their space. He nodded when Megan caught his eye and came over to her, dropping his voice. "How are they holding up?"

"As well as can be expected. You?"

"Looking forward to the pub later," Anto admitted. "Will you come around? It's Fagan's in Drumcondra, I don't know if you know it."

"I know where it is. Maybe. I'll have to see how long the Walshes stay before I make any decisions for after the wake."

"Sure so." Anto moved away, talking to someone else, as a familiar-looking, swarthy man entered. Megan couldn't place him until Martin said, "Victor" in surprise, and the man replied, "Martin. I'm sorry for your loss," in a light French accent. They shook hands before the head of the European Ryder Cup team made his way to Saoirse and took both of her hands in his. "*Je suis désolé pour votre perte.* I very much looked forward to having your father play with us in the Cup."

Saoirse, faint with surprise, said, "What?" and Fabron smiled sadly.

"Yes, had he not told you? I had already selected M'sieur MacDonald as my wild card. Martin was never in the running."

CHAPTER NINETEEN

"Da was . . ." Saoirse's voice broke, and her profile, as she looked toward Heather, was disbelieving. "Did you know?" Her gaze shot to Martin. "Did *he*?"

"He can't have," Heather whispered. "He's no good at hiding that kind of thing. He'd be furious if he'd known. He would have—" She paled.

"I had not told M'sieur Walsh," Fabron agreed before she could go on.

Saoirse's voice dropped to a hiss. "That doesn't mean he didn't know. I *knew* it. I *knew* Martin had something to do with Da's dea—" People were beginning to look, and she cut herself off, face flushed with fury.

"He would have been angry enough to," Heather said helplessly, if very, very quietly. "If he'd known Lou had already been picked for the Cup, and that he never stood a chance, no matter how well he did in this tournament?

Martin would have gone into a jealous rage. He would be angry enough to kill Lou over it." Her gaze went to Victor Fabron. "If Lou wasn't able to play, who would be your next choice?"

Fabron's long face went ruddy along the lines of his sharp cheekbones. "The highest-placing European competitor of this tournament, of course. The best golfer, even if he was not such a pleasant person as Monsieur MacDonald. It would almost certainly be M'seiur Walsh," he finished quietly.

Heather gave a tremulous nod. "I thought so. But I don't see how Martin could have done it. He was golfing when Lou died and I don't think . . . his anger runs hot," she whispered. "He's never been the calculating type when he's angry. He wouldn't . . . think ahead. . . ."

She sounded far less certain than she might have, and Megan couldn't help remembering the caddie, Anthony Doyle, saying that Walsh played his best when the world around him was in upheaval. That he had ice for blood, in those cases. Megan wondered if Heather Walsh was thinking of that, and whether Heather had already considered the possibility that Martin was somehow responsible for Lou MacDonald's death. The motivations seemed increasingly obvious. The only difficulty was the time frame. Megan took a deep breath to put voice to her uncomfortable thoughts. "This probably isn't a good place to talk about it, Mrs. Walsh, but you and Anto both told me earlier there were some terrible injuries on the course. Could he have hit him with a golf ball?"

Fabron went white. "But this is terrible. *Non*, surely it cannot be. I would hate to think I am in some way responsible—"

"No." Saoirse spoke quietly but firmly. "No, whoever killed Da, M'sieur Fabron, it's on them, not you. And—" Her cheeks stained red with emotion as her eyes went tear-blurred. "Thank you for telling me. I'm glad to—I would have loved to see him play on the team."

"You once golfed, no? If only I could invite you in his place." Fabron offered another sympathetic smile, then left to, Megan suspected, avail himself of some of the cognac in the next room. She would need it herself, if she thought she'd somehow contributed to someone's death.

Saoirse's glassy stare fixed itself across the room. Megan followed it and found a photograph of the Mac-Donald family on the wall: Saoirse, no more than eight or ten, standing between Lou and a pretty woman who must have been Kimberly MacDonald. All of them had golf clubs and tremendous smiles as they stood on a course that, judging from the sea-swept background, had to be one of the two on Bull Island. "If I hadn't given up golfing . . ."

Megan began to say it wouldn't have mattered, that it wouldn't have changed anything, but Heather spoke first. "You could always take it up again. In his name, if you wanted."

Rage contorted Saoirse's face, a smash cut from grief to wrath. "And you'll be my coach, I suppose? Wouldn't Martin fecking love that, his two bits snuggled up together on the course so's he could imagine them shagging like that in bed? I don't fecking think so, you man-stealing *cow*—"

"*What?*" Heather's voice cracked two octaves out of her usual range, color slamming out of her face, then back again in a curdling blush. "*What?*"

"Oh, don't pretend you don't know, you stupid cow!

Don't pretend you didn't waltz in and steal him from me, don't pretend you don't know about his stupid nasty fantasies, don't pretend—" Saoirse's shrill tones rolled through a room—a house—gone utterly silent with shock and avidly interested horror. "We were *happy* until you came along—"

"*Martin?*" Heather spoke, hardly a whisper beneath Saoirse's shouting. Even Saoirse fell silent at that tiny word, as Heather looked for her husband in the room, moving as though she'd been flash-frozen and could barely command her muscles to respond.

He stood surprisingly alone for a man in a crowded room. Everyone he'd been speaking with had backed off, leaving him at the center of a small, empty space. His color, too, had drained, leaving him pallid and even trembling as he searched for something to say. He looked utterly caught out, a king with a castle of cards falling down around him, and when Heather whispered, "*Martin?*" again, he flinched.

"I–I—Heather—I can—explain—"

Heather fell back one clumsy step and lifted shaking hands as if making a barrier between herself and Martin Walsh. "Oh my *God*." Then she fled, pushing through a crowd reluctant to make way for her. Martin reached for her arm as she passed, and she threw off his hand with violence. *"Don't touch me!"*

A moment later she was gone, leaving everyone— leaving *Saoirse*—staring after her, aghast. Saoirse whispered, "She didn't . . . she didn't know, did she."

Martin blurted, "Heather!" and ran after her. The gathering parted for him, as they hadn't for her, and Megan lurched a few steps after them before pulling up and turning back to Saoirse, unsure who she should support.

"Go on," Saoirse said hoarsely. "If he did kill Da, God knows what he might do to her."

An uproar met her words, mourners closing in with questions as Megan pressed through them to chase after the Walshes. Heather, twenty years younger, taller, and highly motivated, had cast off her heels and bolted down the street, leaving her husband standing hopelessly at the end of the MacDonald driveway. Megan skidded to a halt several steps behind him and, after a judicious pause, said, "Shall I drive you back to the hotel, Mr. Walsh?"

Martin spun around, staring at her, then shouted, "No! Get in that car and follow her!" He ran to the Lincoln, yanking on the locked door handle, and gave a bellow of inarticulate rage. "Let me in!"

"With pleasure, Mr. Walsh, but I won't chase Mrs. Walsh." Megan unlocked the doors while Martin bared his teeth, snarling with anger.

"You'll do what I tell you! I'm paying you!"

"So you are," Megan said, opening the door for him, "but not to stalk someone who clearly doesn't want to be with you right now. You can take it up with Ms. Keegan, if you like."

"I sure as hell will!" Fumbling with anger, Martin took out his phone, searching for the Leprechaun Limos phone number, while Megan took a judicious step back from the car and rang Orla herself.

"Ms. Keegan? This is Megan Malone. We've had an altercation and I believe Mr. Walsh would like to speak with you." She handed her phone over to Martin, who spat with fury as he said, "Tell this dumb bitch driver of yours to *follow my wife* when I tell her to!"

From his changing expression, Megan thought it safe to say that Orla was telling him no such thing. She did her best to keep her face professionally unreadable as his grew even angrier. Then, with a roar, he threw her phone to the ground.

Glass and plastic shattered everywhere, despite its protective covering. Megan jerked back a step, less afraid than genuinely appalled. Then anger rolled in. Very carefully, with deliberate control, Megan moved forward again, closing and locking the car door. Sheer hatred flew across Martin's face, and Megan, exquisitely aware that she was within his reach, crouched to pick up the broken pieces of her phone before rising and walking to the driver's side door, saying, "Your contract is canceled, Mr. Walsh. Good evening."

"You can't do that! You can't do this, you *bitch*!" Martin's howls followed her down the street.

Megan worked at not looking at him in the rearview mirror, focusing instead on driving, and watching the sidewalks until she saw Heather Walsh, carrying her high heels, walking in the distance. After a moment she pulled up beside the golfer and rolled down the window. "He's not with me. Would you like me to take you somewhere?"

Heather looked down the street behind her, at Megan, at the street in front of her, and back at Megan, then got into the front seat beside her. She didn't say anything as Megan drove her back to the hotel, said, "I'll wait," and did, as Heather went inside, packed, and came back out within a mere five or six minutes. She threw the suitcase in the back seat and got in the front again, and finally spoke.

"I have nowhere to go."

Megan took a breath, but before she spoke, Heather went on in exceptionally calm tones. "The credit cards are all in his name. I can withdraw money—I'd better, before he thinks to freeze the accounts—but his name is on them, too. What did it matter, when we were going to be together forever? I thought it was funny. A throwback to the seventies, before women could have credit cards in their own names. That's what changing my name was, too. A lark. And we thought it would look good on the marquees, being the Walshes. And the whole time he was really playing the *Mad Men* game, wasn't he? Screwing around with his—" Her voice cracked in horror. "With his *niece*. Lou didn't know. *I* didn't know." She regained control over her voice again and looked out the window. "I have nowhere to go."

"We'll stop at the first bank so you can withdraw as much as possible on whatever cards you have on you," Megan said. "And you can stay with me tonight."

Heather Walsh turned an astonished face toward Megan. "What?"

"I have a couch. It's not exactly the Ritz, but it won't spend the money you have, and there are puppies to keep you company."

A smile, almost a laugh, cracked Heather's calm façade, and nearly shattered it entirely. Megan watched her slide toward hysterics and drag herself back with a massive effort. "Puppies sound wonderful. Why would you do this?"

"Because you look like you need a friend." Megan paused judiciously. "That, and I don't think it would occur to Martin that you might end up staying with me, and frankly, I think he might be dangerous."

"No, he's not, he's—"

"He shattered my phone when I wouldn't drive him after you."

Heather blanched and turned her attention out the window again, jaw tense. "Maybe," she finally said, quietly. "Maybe you're right."

Megan, reminding herself she was the help, bit back everything she wanted to say about what she'd seen of their relationship. Instead, she pulled over at the first bank, as promised. Heather put her heels back on, exited the car, and spent several long minutes withdrawing money from more credit cards than Megan had owned in her life, never mind at once. She returned tucking what Megan believed was technically referred to as *a wad of cash* into her purse, and once more turned a glazed look out the window.

Traffic hadn't thinned out much by the time they hit city centre, and what was really only a short drive took a long time, especially in Heather's silence. As they finally approached Rathmines, Megan cast a cautious glance at her passenger. "I need to bring the car back to the garage. Would you like me to drop you off at my apartment first?"

"Yes, please." Heather kept her gaze on the buildings—some old and beautifully cared for, some old and less well cared for, and all with modern ones interspersed—slowly gliding by. "I should probably meet Ms. Keegan to explain what's happened, but honestly, I just don't think I'm brave enough. I feel like a total chickenshit right now."

"It's fine. You're going through a lot. I'll introduce you to the puppies and deal with Orla myself, which I'd end up having to do anyway." Megan pulled into a barely legal parking place up the street from her flat and paid the parking fee on the meter machine, figuring it was better to pay a couple extra quid than a parking ticket. She got Heather's suitcase out of the Lincoln's back seat and hauled it up the stairs to her apartment with the argument "I'm not in heels," which silenced Heather's perfunctory objections. Once inside, she pointed out the amenities: kitchen, bathroom, and, to her own surprise and confusion, no puppies. "Oh, dang it. They're at Brian's. Look, I'll get them after I bring back the car, okay? I thought I was going to be out all night, so a friend is dog sitting them. There are leftovers in the fridge, or there's a ton of takeaway places right nearby, although Brian's got my spare keys, so you'll have to wait unless you want to order in. I'll be back in . . ." Megan considered the conversation she was about to have with Orla and hedged, "An hour, probably."

"Okay." Heather sat on the living room couch, looking around for—as it turned out—a router. "Is there a wifi password?"

"Oh. Yeah, it's on the router behind the TV. The network is 'nofastsuchfurious.'"

A little smile twisted the corner of Heather's mouth. "Internet service is the same everywhere, huh?"

"Ain't it though. Look, I'd better get the car back and face Orla's wrath. I'll be back in a while." Megan left Heather behind and drove the final two minutes to the garage, pulling in where she was directed to park and getting out of the car with a sigh.

To her complete surprise, Orla flew from the office with a mixture of fury and concern creasing her features. "Jaysus, Megan, are you well?" She embraced Megan and stepped back, anger taking precedence once she saw Megan was unhurt. "What the hell happened? One moment I had that sorry gobshite roaring in me ear about paying for a service and you being a bitch, and then the line went dead and I couldn't ring you up again! Neither would himself answer his own damn phone, so I've been out of my mind with worry!"

"Mr. Walsh threw my phone on the ground and destroyed it."

Orla's snapping blue eyes went dead with rage. "Are you well?"

"I'm fine. I'm fine, Orla. Honestly. There was a minute there when I was picking up the pieces of my phone— I wanted to make sure I kept my old SIM—where I thought he might try kicking me or something, but he didn't, and then I drove off without him."

"*Good.*" Orla's teeth bared in a brief snarl. "He'll pay for every minute of the service we're contracted for, and a new phone for you besides. What happened to the wife? Why did she walk away from him?"

Megan, with feeling, said, "Oh my *God*," and flung her hands in the air.

Orla laughed sharply. "That bad, was it?"

"You have no idea. Look so, it started this morning with tripping over another body . . ."

Orla shrieked, and Megan threw her hands up again, this time preventing the inevitable tongue-lashing. "I promise nobody but the police know I found him. Look, just listen, okay?" By the time she'd recounted even half the day, the entire garage crew had given up on even pretending they were working and had gathered around her in a semicircle, with Orla standing over them all on the step up to the office. When she reached the climactic revelation about Saoirse and Martin, Cillian, who had come in late, recoiled.

"Forget I ever called that bastard my cousin," he said in disgust. "What a gobshite. She can't be even half his age."

"She's not," Megan agreed. "Look, this is all—don't gossip about it, okay? Saoirse's going to have a hard enough time of it with all her friends hearing the whole sordid story. She doesn't need us spreading the gossip, too."

"Sure, but one will get you ten that it'll be all over the sporting news by tomorrow even if we don't say a word," Cillian predicted.

"Maybe so, but don't let it come from us." The chill warning in Orla's tone was enough to make Megan's spine straighten, and Cillian looked abashed. Megan finished up with Martin's street-side temper tantrum and the destruction of her phone, which drew any remaining humor from Cillian's square-jawed face. Orla finally released Megan from her audience—without, a little to Megan's surprise, any kind of lecture—and returned to the office, presumably to charge the rest of the Walshes' bill to Martin and excoriate him if he dared object.

As soon as she was gone and everyone began drifting back to work, Cillian stepped in closer to Megan, dropping his voice to ask, "Are ye well, Megan? Do you need someone to come around and check up on you tonight? I can stop by around half ten, before my late job."

Amused, Megan shook her head. "No, I'm fine, Cill, I'm grand so." Worry wrinkled his dark eyebrows together, and a thump of charmed affection ran through Megan. "It's nice of you to check."

"It's not that I don't know you can take care of your own self," he said hastily, color rising in his cheeks. "It's just a thing like that can creep up on you and leave you needing someone there without knowing it's happening. Not that ye need me, although it'd be grand if ye did. I mean, having someone you could count on beside ye.

You could count on me." By the time he finished speaking, he'd turned scarlet, and a penny slowly dropped in Megan's mind, leaving her fighting off a flattered smile.

Cillian Walsh had to be at least a dozen years her junior, but that apparently hadn't stopped him from developing a crush. She lowered her own voice, leaning in to murmur, "I didn't want to tell Orla for fear she'd come wring the payment out of her, but I've got Heather Walsh staying at my flat tonight, and maybe for a few nights. I think we'll be fine, but thank you, Cillian. It's very good of you," and realized that didn't sound one single bit like she was shooting him down.

And maybe she wasn't. A little unrequited lust made most jobs less boring, and Cillian, with his dark hair and light eyes, the classic black Irish look, was as handsome as they came. And, at the moment, flushed with pleasure, too, which wasn't a bad look at all. Megan winked at him and, despite the chaos of the day, slipped out of the garage feeling absurdly good about the world.

CHAPTER TWENTY

She went by Brian's house first to collect the puppies, much to his surprise. All three dogs rolled indolently out the door with the fat bellies of animals who had successfully deployed puppy dog eyes at a defenseless human. They stopped for takeaway as they headed home, Megan picking up a heap of burgers and chips, figuring that although Irish burgers weren't quite like American ones, the familiarity might give Heather some comfort.

Heather didn't seem to have moved in the hour or so Megan had been gone, although when the puppies came swarming in, she slid off the couch and let them introduce themselves all over her new, expensive black dress. Tiny white hairs went everywhere, and she buried her face in their kisses. Muffled, she said, "They're adorable," and Megan chuckled.

"Yeah. I didn't mean to keep them. I'm *not* keeping all of them. Thong is going to go live with—"

"*Thong?*"

"The chocolate-nosed one is Dip, his sister is Thong, together the—"

Heather lifted her gaze to give Megan a positively severe look. "Diphthong. Shame on you."

Megan cackled. "See, at this point I can't change their names because I love making people give me that look. But Thong is going to go live with Fionnuala, the chef you met earlier today? Oh, crap." She looked vaguely north, in the general direction of the MacDonald house. "I've got to go get her platters. Well, not tonight. Anyway, they were born in her restaurant—"

"They were *what*? Didn't she get penalized for that?"

"It kind of paled in comparison to the murders, so, uh, no." Megan, listening to herself, had a moment of wondering what she'd done in a past life to end up casually mentioning multiple murders in this one.

Heather stared at her over the wiggling puppies, then said, "Nope," and put her head back down, clearly not ready to hear whatever story went along with that sentence. It seemed like a not only valid, but fundamentally wise choice to Megan, who didn't try to press the details on her.

"Anyway, she's adopting Thong and swears she'll change her name. I should—" Megan made an aborted move toward her ruined phone, then drooped. "Never mind."

"No, you're right, you should. Use mine." Heather took her phone from her purse, thumbprinted it on, and opened the camera so Megan could take a picture of her, glammed up but sitting on the floor covered in dog hair, with Thong snuggled beside her cheek. When Megan handed the phone to her so she could see the picture, Heather sighed and held it against her chest, eyes closed. "When I look back on this absolute shit day in my life, I'm going to use this picture to remind me that at least there was puppy love in it. If I send it to you, will you get it?"

"I've still got my SIM card. I'll get a new phone in the morning."

"And expense it to my"—Heather visibly edited a word from the sentence—"husband?"

"That's the plan, yeah."

"Good." She went quiet a minute while Megan finally put the takeaway bags on the kitchen counter and started unloading them on to plates. "It wasn't bad at the start," she said over the sound of Megan unpacking. "It was great, at the start. He was so charming."

"People keep saying that. I haven't seen a lot of it myself."

"Honestly, it didn't last very long. I don't think I realized it had gone bad for a long time, though. Not until we came to Ireland for a six-month holiday and I actually—" She gave a broken laugh. "I started having fun again. Lou was a riot, and we got on like a house on fire. Martin had stopped golfing with me when Saoirse quit the game. Oh, *God*." A hard, hiccuping cry, almost like a laugh, broke from her chest and made Thong stand up in her lap to lick her jaw with concern. "God, I'm so *stupid*. I didn't realize until just now when I *said* it. Martin stopped golfing with me when Saoirse quit. I just thought—I didn't think anything! Not about *that*."

"You had no reason to," Megan said quietly, more to the chips than Heather herself. Heather went on as if she hadn't heard Megan, and maybe she hadn't. "So I'd been out on the course alone, or with caddies, which was fine for the serious stuff, but not for a casual game. Lou played with me, though, and we would laugh until we couldn't hit the ball. We actually got thrown off a green once. It was wonderful." She lifted her chin, gaze empty on the far wall. "But by that time the Golfing Walshes were a thing, you know? A brand. And there were people—Lou was one of them—who were trying to use that to break down some of the barriers in the game. Men and women competing together, old golf clubs with bylaws like the Royal Dublin's got. And I was getting better while Martin was . . ."

"Petering out?"

"Not quite." Heather turned her profile toward Megan, as if remembering she was there. "But he wasn't improving, which meant I was coming up fast on him, and in terms of being poster children for a fair, equal playing field between men and women, that . . . worked." She put the puppies down and got up, making a futile attempt to brush dog hair away as she came around the couch to the kitchen area. Dip and Thong followed her hopefully, while Mama, who had gone straight to her bed, rolled on her back and stuck her tongue out. "Then a PT finally got Martin's shoulder straightened out, and he thought he had one last shot at the PGA Tour. He's been doing well, but there's been all this focus on *us*, and he needs the money from the double win, if we can pull it off, and I thought . . ."

Her gaze went blank again, and she started eating fries mechanically, one after the other. Megan, not wanting her to feel alone but also not wanting to spill ketchup on her own uniform, ran into her bedroom, changed into a dark red T-shirt and jeans, and returned to eat her burger at the counter, like Heather did with the fries. By the time Megan came back, Heather had worked her way through a considerable portion of the equally considerable pile that Megan had set aside for her. Then she paused long enough to say, quietly, "I thought I could leave after that. If we won. So I pretended I didn't notice, or care, that he was getting more and more controlling, because if only he got this money he'd be satisfied, and I could get out." A shiver went through her, and she began eating again, methodically, one fry at a time. "Lou knew I was going to leave."

The pile of chips diminished until it was gone. Heather licked salt from her fingers, then wiped her hand neatly on the takeaway's paper napkins. "Lou knew I was going to leave Martin for him."

Megan choked on the Coke—actually a Sprite, but she was Texan—she'd just picked up to sip from and put it down again, wiping her eyes. "You and Lou were . . . oh my God," she finished more softly as she put it together. "Oh, no, honey. You knew it was Lou, didn't you? When you ran into the clubhouse and collapsed on Wednesday? You knew it was Lou, not Martin, who was dead. Pretending you didn't know, pretending you thought it was Martin, was the only way you could mourn as much as you needed to right then, wasn't it? Oh, Heather. I'm sorry."

She suddenly had an armful of sobbing golfer, Heather Walsh wrapping strong arms around her back and holding on as she cried like her world had ended. Megan sighed quietly and hugged her back, stroking her hair with burger-greasy fingers and figuring Heather wouldn't much care. "I'm so sorry. What a terrible, terrible mess. I'm sorry, Heather."

Heather pulled away, wiping her entire forearm across her face to ineffectually remove snot and tears. "You shouldn't be, I did an awful thing, I cheated on my—" Her sobs suddenly turned to rage, and this time she didn't edit herself, bellowing, "my *asshole husband*!" loudly enough to startle Megan and frighten the puppies.

Their whines and sharp little barks brought Heather back to herself, and she dropped to her knees, extending her hands toward them in apology. Being puppies, they forgave her instantly and rushed forward to lick her fingers while Megan sighed. "I'm not going to cast any stones, Heather. You did what you could to be happy while trying to stay safe."

"But if I'd just left him, Lou would still be alive."

"Not if he's dead because he got the spot on the PGA team that Martin wanted," Megan pointed out, maybe a little too callously. "That didn't have anything to do with you."

Heather stared at her for a moment, then bowed her head over the puppies, shoulders slumped. "I guess you're right about that. But whether it was me or the tour, I don't know *how* he did it, but I'm sure Martin killed him. I'm sure he . . ." She shook her head.

Megan slid down the cupboards to sit beside her, tipping her head back so her chin pointed toward the ceiling. "Everybody thinks he did it, but I don't see how he could have. He was with fifteen people when Lou died. I was one of them. Granted, I didn't know yesterday that rogue golf balls could kill people, but he never lost a ball while we were out there. He was being all man-of-the-people about it, finding his own balls in the rough—" Her inner twelve-year-old surfaced, and she choked back a laugh.

Heather met her gaze with wet eyes and a lopsided smile. "You wouldn't believe how careful we get sometimes, trying not to say things like that. Some days we can all get through it like it's not some sort of stupid, juvenile double entendre, and other days we're snorting and smirking like teenagers."

"I'd believe it," Megan assured her. "Anyway, Martin never had a chance to kill Lou out there on the green, as far as I can tell."

"Then he paid someone to do it," Heather said, bleakness returning.

A chill sluiced down Megan's spine, and she straightened. "Oliver Collins, maybe?"

Heather's jaw fell open, but if she had a protest, it never made it farther than the workings of her throat. Megan got to her feet, suddenly full of nervous energy. "Was Collins a decent golfer? Yes, Martin said he was. Could he have? Would Martin have killed *him*, to keep him quiet?"

"Or to keep from paying him," Heather said with a curled lip, then shook herself violently. Dip, looking delighted, did the same, and fell over on Thong, who put her paw in his eye as retaliation. Dip nipped at her, and an instant later they were both running around the apartment, yipping wildly at each other. Megan and Heather both stared after them, faintly dumbfounded by the normality of their behavior. Heather, after a moment, smiled weakly. "And there's life, going on regardless of what we have to deal with."

"At least it's cute life." Megan bent and picked Thong

up as she ran headlong toward Megan's ankles, kissed the squirming puppy on top of the head, and put her back down to chase her brother. "Do you think Collins would have killed someone? That he would have killed Lou?"

"I'd think he'd have rather killed me and kept girl cooties out of his clubhouse, but . . . yeah, he might have. He was a weasel. Good at his job," Heather said grudgingly, "but a weasel. And I'm dead sure"—she winced at the phrase—"that Martin would kill somebody to shut him up, or to avoid paying him, if he thought he could get away with it. God, why did I marry him?"

"All right. Okay, I have to call P—" Megan turned a dismayed gaze toward the fragments of her phone and sighed. "Paul. Um, crap. Do I still have . . ." She went to look through a junk drawer, hoping she would find the card Paul Bourke had given her months ago, with his phone number on it. "Maybe it's on my dresser. Are you okay here for a minute, Heather?"

As she asked, the puppies, having exhausted themselves, staggered back to collapse on Heather's lap, dropping more short, white fur on her black skirt. She nodded, and Megan collected the bits of her phone, trying to work a piece that impact had welded in place off, so she could get to the SIM card. It snapped open just as she went into her bedroom, sending pieces flying again. Her next step centered itself on a wedge of plastic and she fell onto the bed, hissing and growling with pain, but she got the card out and snarled at it triumphantly. Not that it did her any good, she realized a heartbeat later: the phone was the first she'd bought in Ireland, so she had no old spares lying around.

Neither, after a couple of minutes' search, did she have Paul's business card. "Heather? I'm going to go out—"

She limped back to the living room as she spoke, although the pain of jabbing her foot was fading. "I'm going to go out to the office to borrow somebody's old phone until I can get a new one. Can I get you anything? I have spare keys now anyway, I got them from Brian." As if, she thought, Heather Walsh knew who Brian was, and clarified, "My dog sitter. Will you be okay?"

"Go ahead." Heather, still laden with puppies, hadn't moved from the kitchen floor. Megan waggled the spare keys and dropped them on the table so Heather would know where they were, and trotted downstairs, heading for the garage.

CHAPTER TWENTY-ONE

There were no fewer than five spare phones in one of the office drawers and, Megan knew, at least that many more again in one of the garage toolboxes. One of the office phones had a few percentage points of battery left, so she put her SIM into that one and sat on the floor behind the counter next to an outlet, where she could plug in the phone but not be in the public eye. Although, it being after nine p.m., she probably didn't have to worry all that much about being interrupted by clients needing to suddenly hire a car.

It took a minute to convince the phone to see her network, but once it did, she called Paul, her eyes closed as she listened to his phone ring. Voice mail picked up and she said, "Hi, this is Megan. Heather and Lou were having an affair and Heather thinks Martin could have paid Oliver Collins to kill Lou, then killed Collins to tidy up loose ends. Call me back." She hung up, thought about how she'd just said all that as if it was perfectly normal, and indulged in a slightly manic giggle.

The phone rang, startling her. More surprising was that it was Saoirse calling, not Paul. She thumbed it on and brought it to her ear. "Hey, Saoirse. Is everything . . ." Her face screwed up as she finished, ". . . okay? I mean . . ."

"Oh, it's *grand*." Saoirse sounded so dry it bordered on drunkenness. "Martin had the balls to come back in after you left him—you left him! I don't know whether to kill you or kiss you."

"He smashed my phone," Megan said, almost mildly. "I don't have to drive someone I consider a physical threat to my well-being."

"Nah, I don't blame you so. Wait. We're talking on the phone."

"I got the SIM and put it in a burner. Are you okay?"

"I've no idea. The wake was banjanxed. Nobody wanted to talk about Da anymore, except to ask what he would have thought. Or tell me. Or tell one another. And then Martin came back in in a fury and got madder still when the whole crowd gave him the cold shoulder, so he was shouting how he'd done nothing wrong, and the lads told him he should leave, and he threw a punch at somebody, and so anyway someone called the guards to come and take him away."

"What? He's in custody?"

Megan straightened, then slumped again at Saoirse's, "Nah. He went off and called a taxi when he saw they meant it. I'd say things went back to normal after that, but they didn't. Everyone who came in heard about it all before they got past the threshold, so there I was being stared at more than sympathized with, until my girlfriends decided I'd had enough and threw everybody out a little while ago. A wake's meant to go all night." Her voice cracked.

"I am so sorry." Megan sighed. "Is it any use saying you should get a good night's sleep so you can face tomorrow on its own terms?"

"None at all." Saoirse sounded almost cheerful in that moment, though it faded mercurially. "I'll try, though. My friend Ellen, she's come over and is going to stand in for me tomorrow at the planning board hearing. I might—it's at half one and the funeral is at three. I might try . . ."

"That's mental." Megan got up, forgetting her phone was plugged in, and nearly jerked it out of her hand when the cord reached its maximum length. "Look, let me . . . can you hang on for a second?"

"Sure so."

"Thanks. Be right back." She put the phone on the counter and stuck her head into the garage. "Hey, is Orla here?"

Somebody shouted, "Orla *lives* here," and somebody else said, "She does so, but she's not, why? Everything all right, Megan?"

"It's grand." Megan closed the office door and collected the phone again. "My boss has canceled the Walshes' contract, so I'm theoretically not driving anybody tomorrow. I might be able to borrow a car and drive you so you can put in an appearance at the hearing and get to the funeral on time."

"I couldn't ask you to do that."

"You didn't. I'll call you in the morning to let you know if I can manage it, all right?"

"Why are you so fecking nice?"

Megan laughed. "You can think of me as being a terrible busybody, if that helps. I love to know what's going
on. And I like people," she said a little more seriously. "I
mean, what are we here for, if not to try to help one another?"

"You're a sound one, Megan Malone." Saoirse sighed
hugely. "I'm a ruin. Maybe I will try to sleep."

"Good girl. I'll talk to you tomorrow." Megan hung
up, saw she had three missed calls from Detective Bourke,
and waited thirty seconds. The phone rang again and she
answered, smiling wryly as she said, "And I hardly even
told you the good stuff."

"There's *more*?" Bourke sounded like a man trying to
rearrange his priorities.

Megan, trying to decide where to start, ended up say-
ing, "There is too much. Let me sum up," in her best
Inigo Montoya accent. Bourke snorted, amused, and Megan
said, "Saoirse admitted to the affair with Martin, which
Heather had no idea about. Heather has, I think, left
Martin for good—she's at my apartment right now—and
Martin smashed my phone in a temper tantrum."

She could imagine, almost see, the detective's body
language change to something cold and still as he asked,
"Are you all right?"

"I'm fine," Megan promised. "Seriously, I'm fine. I
thought he might have a go at me when I was picking up
my phone, so I was pretty adrenaline spiky, but he was either not that dumb or isn't that violent, and you know I
can take care of myself."

"I do." Bourke's voice retained the steadiness of re-
strained anger and concern. "You got another phone?"

"A burner from the office. I had to call you and didn't
have your card anymore."

"Okay. Tell me what you know."

Megan related what Heather had told her—affairs, finances, and all—ending with, "She maxed out the cash withdrawals from their credit cards, so I don't think she's going back, but if you look into their finances to see if there's a connection between Walsh and Collins, you'll see that."

"You said she's at your apartment? I'd really like to talk to her."

"Yeah. I mean, I don't mind if you come over. Should I warn her?"

Paul said, "No," judiciously. "I never like to give people time to think about their story, if I can help it."

"That's a horrible, paranoid way to live."

"See, you don't really want to be an assistant detective." She could hear his smile. "You just want to be the neighborhood gossip."

"I'd be okay with being the neighborhood gossip with fewer murders to gossip about. Did you figure out anything about Collins yet?" Megan tilted the phone to check its battery. At 24 percent, it would probably get her home while they talked. She unplugged it, got off the floor, and locked the office door behind her as she left.

"He was a parsimonious little shite," Bourke replied rather grandly.

Megan laughed. "A *what*? Pars—I don't think I've ever heard anybody say that out loud before. It's like . . . stingy, right? But he dressed really well." The September evening air felt fresh and cleansing, though the office was hardly stifling. It was the day, Megan thought; all of its events carried a lot of emotional weight, and the cool evening lifted some of that away.

"He did, but to hear everyone talk, clothes would be

all he spent his money on. Someone else always paid when he went out or he wouldn't go. It served him well enough, I'd say. He wasn't well-liked, but he was conceded to do his job well. Very well, apparently. Membership in the club rose by forty percent in the three years he managed it, and it's not an inexpensive prospect to join that club. We're talking over ten thousand in fees."

"To play *golf*?" Megan's voice skirled high in offense, drawing the attention of a group of teens passing her. They laughed, the too-loud raucous, judging laughter that could sometimes cut through even the most confident adult's defenses. Megan rolled her eyes once they were past, though their laughter rattled the air a while longer.

"That's just to join the club. There are greens fees on top of that."

"I'm in the wrong line of work. I should have been born rich."

"Sure and it's a moral failing that you weren't. You could always marry her own self."

"Her own—oh, Carmen?" Megan laughed. "I don't know if I want to be rich that badly."

"There's your problem," Bourke said philosophically. "Your priorities are skewed."

"Maybe. On the other hand, I'm not the one who ended up dead in a sandbank this morning, so maybe I'm doing all right." Megan reached her apartment's street-level door and did the necessary rituals, punching in the key code, digging her keys from her pocket, stabbing herself beneath the fingernail all the way into the nailbed with a key as she tried to fish them out. The last didn't often happen, but her nails were still Done, thanks to—or because of, at least—Carmen de la Fuente. It was the little things like that which kept her from having long nails all the time. "How long will it take you to get here?"

"I'm on my way now. Twenty minutes, maybe."

"Okay. You didn't tell me if you got anything on Collins, though." Megan banged the outside door shut with her butt. Her bum, in Irish parlance. Once she'd injured her knee, told someone she had a "bum knee," and gotten such a peculiar look she giggled now as she thought of it, even as Bourke answered her.

"Not that I should be telling you a thing, but this link with Walsh and Collins might be the most solid lead we've got. I've already got someone checking on whether there are any unexplained payments to his account, or unusual spending recently. I—"

"Paul?"

"What?"

Megan nudged puppies back into her apartment with her feet and edged forward far enough to close the door, searching the open-plan space with her gaze. Mama Dog heaved a dramatic sigh and rolled onto her back, pleading, lazily, for a belly scritch, and the puppies, thwarted in their escape attempt, attacked Megan's ankles with nips and head butts and wagging tails. Megan's spare keys were still on the kitchen table, and the takeaway food had been cleaned up. Even the dishes were done. The bathroom door stood open a few inches, the light inside off. Megan took a few more steps into the room, looking around as if she could be missing something, although she knew she wasn't. "Paul, Heather is gone."

CHAPTER TWENTY-TWO

"Where were they staying?" Bourke's voice went flat on the phone. "I'll go there, in case she's going to confront Martin."

"Clontarf Castle Hotel." Megan searched the room, hoping for a note, for anything suggesting where Heather might have gone. The phone beeped in her ear, informing her the battery was almost dead again. "Dang it! I'm almost out of battery, look, I'll meet you there?"

"Don't even *think* about it." Bourke hung up, and Megan indulged in an inarticulate *naaargh!* before scurrying to her bedroom, where she dumped the bedside table's drawer contents onto her duvet. A spare battery pack fell out among the other detritus. She pounced on it, checked its charge, then plugged the phone in to it, trusting its 47 percent charge would see her through the evening. A spark of hope flew through her as she thought maybe Heather had given Megan her number when Megan had dropped her at Brown Thomas, but a quick check through her contacts said she only had Martin's number. She muttered, "Dang it, dang it, *dang* it, I thought modern tech . . ." The rest of the complaint didn't make it as far as her lips, though the petering-out thought ran along the lines of *modern tech was supposed to take the legwork out of solving mysteries.* Maybe, if she was a cop who had Heather's number and could magically trace her phone's location through triangulation, or whatever it was they used on TV, but she wasn't, and she didn't, and besides, she wasn't confident it actually worked that way anyway.

She stopped in the middle of the living room, phone clutched in one hand and the battery pack in her back pocket as she tried to think. Bourke was heading for the hotel, so he'd cut Heather off before she got there, if that was her destination. Megan didn't know the other woman well enough to imagine where she might go otherwise. She checked the time: ten p.m., or close enough, which made it around two in the afternoon in California. She called Niamh, hoping the actor's inexhaustible gossip resources might have an answer, but Niamh's phone was off. Despite herself, Megan smiled as she left a quick message: "Nothing important, but how dare you be, like, working when I want to get gossip. Talk to you later, babe." She hung up, then, struck with a thought, made another call.

A somewhat worried man's voice answered a few seconds later. "Megan? Is everything all right?"

"Hey, Uncle Rabbie. It is, yes. I just have a weird question."

"Grand! What is it?"

Megan smiled at the phone. Robert Lynch, "Uncle" Rabbie, was more accurately her second cousin, but he was a generation older than she, and Megan found it easier to go by generations rather than the vagaries of genealogical technicalities. "You know everybody in Ireland, right?"

"Well," said he modestly, "not *everybody*," and Megan laughed.

"But close enough. Look, do you know Martin Walsh?"

"The golfer?" Rabbie asked in surprise. "I've met the man. I knew his friend Lou better, there was a grand auld soul, may he rest in peace."

Megan clenched a fist in triumph and went to sit on the floor beside a power outlet so she could plug in the phone while still at home instead of draining the battery pack. Dip trotted over and flopped in her lap so she could rub his ears. "It's Lou I'm asking about, really. Kind of. Did you know he was having an affair with Martin's wife?"

A judicious silence came over the line, followed by, "I wouldn't say I *knew* it, no, but now that you've said it, I can't say I'm surprised. There was a fair bit of—what do the young people say today? 'It's complicated.' There was a fair bit of *complicated* about Martin and Lou and their wives all along."

"Don't make me beg for the details."

Her uncle cackled. "They married young, both of them, the first time, and to American women both. Susan Walsh and Kimberly MacDonald were both sound ones like, but Susan died young of the cancer, and I'd say Martin was jealous as the devil himself of Kimberly after that. Kim was a star," Rabbie allowed. "She made Lou into the man he was, gave him direction. He became a great golfer because she loved the game. Susan, now, she shaped Martin, but he had the ambition all on his own. When Kim died . . . that child of theirs and Lou were destroyed, but I'd call it a happy day in Martin's life."

"How'd she die?"

"An accident. Some drunk arsehole plowed into her while she was out for a run. They never caught them as did it."

"Jesus."

"I'd say it probably wasn't him." Rabbie gave a self-satisfied chortle at Megan's startled burst of laughter. "Walsh's second wife divorced him not long after that and took all his money with her. No surprise, though, as he was at Lou's side all the time. Helping him through Kimberly's death and all. Being there for the little girl."

Megan bit her tongue on that, figuring she could catch him up on the gossip later, if someone else hadn't already. "Was he in love with Lou?"

"Hnh." Rabbie sounded like he was considering it. "I wouldn't have thought so. I think he's just a jealous bastard. What's his is his and what's yours is his. He wouldn't even share that caddie of his."

"Yeah, I've heard about there maybe being big money involved th—" Megan broke off, a thrill splashing down her spine. "Oh, shoot! Oh, gosh! I wonder—I wonder—!"

"Do ye now," Rabbie said drolly. "What is it you're wondering, my girl?"

"Nothing—I just—do you know anything about the caddie? Anthony Doyle?"

"I don't. Sorry to be of no help, love."

"Yes, the fact that you don't know the intimate details of *every* life on this island is scandalous. I don't even know how you know as much as you do."

"Ah, well, people like to talk, don't they? And I listen.

And there's all sorts come through the port, Megan, you know that." Rabbie, although he was, to hear him say it, dangerously near retirement age now, still made it his duty to meet the ships at Sligo Port, where he'd been harbour master for decades. Megan thought it wasn't so much the goods as the gossip that got him there every day, and his ear to the ground made him an absolute nexus of information. *Everyone* knew Rabbie Lynch.

"Do you remember the first time I came to Ireland?" she asked, off topic but smiling.

"When you came in to Rosslare like a silly fool and couldn't get a bus to the West?"

"The ferry was late! It wasn't my fault I missed the buses!" A truck driver had taken pity on her, offering to drive her up to Dublin from the port city a hundred miles south of it, and—being Irish—had gotten her name and asked why she, a teenage American, was visiting Ireland on her own. She'd said she was on her way to visit her cousin in Sligo, and the man, in the wink of an eye, put the names together, said, "Wait, you're never Rabbie Lynch's cousin, are ye?" and drove her all the way across the country, delivering her safely to the Lynch family home.

"And I was a Malone," she said now, still mystified.

Rabbie laughed now as he'd done then. "He knew my mother was a Malone before she married, is all."

"Yes, but there are four million people on the island! How could he know *you*?" Except everyone did, or close enough that from Megan's perspective it didn't make much difference. "Tell you what, I'll call you at the weekend with the whys and wherefores of all this, but I've got to go right now, all right?"

"Sure so, bye bye bye bye, bye bye bye." Rabbie was still saying "bye" as Megan hung up and lifted Dip from her lap. He gave her a mournful, brown-eyed look, but sagged back into sleep when she put him on the dog bed with his mother and sister. She didn't know if the unending stream of "bye" so common to Irish partings was something linked to the structure of the Irish language— most probably—or born from a bone-deep determination to get in the last word, but she still had a hard time hanging up on it. Fortunately, she'd gradually learned no one took offense if she did, and that in fact, she was supposed to.

A minute later she was out the door again, feeling a little like a jack-in-the-box, unable to decide whether she wanted to be in or out. Or maybe she was a cat, although presumably the dogs would object to that. She jogged back down to the garage, zipping her windbreaker against the chill, and banged on the big metal door as she went in through the human-sized one beside it. "Hey, anybody here? Is there a car I can hire tonight?"

In theory, borrowing a company car occasionally, when needed, was one of the perks of the job. In practice, Megan had discovered that she was the only one who ever dared to. Furthermore, Orla always charged her for the vehicle's use, as if Megan was a client. She occasionally envied Cillian's personal car and Tymon's motorcycle, but not enough to own either herself, so she just had to accept that Orla Keegan had never met a day she couldn't wring a few extra cents from.

Achojah, a lanky Nigerian driver who had started recently and was tutoring Megan in Yoruba about once a week, came from the back parking lot with a set of keys he tossed to her in an underhand arc. She caught them in both hands as he said, "Tymon still has the Volvo to detail. You can take it."

"I'll detail it myself when I get back," Megan promised.

"I know, and so does Tymon. E se, thank you."

Megan called, "*Ko*, um, ko to ọpẹ?" in hopeful response as she ran into the office to fill out paperwork.

Achojah shouted, "Not bad, not bad," after her, and waited by the garage door until she came hurrying back out. His, "Do you have a date, Megan?" followed her as she got the car from its parking spot, and she rolled the window down on her way out to say, "I wish," with a bit of heartfelt melodrama. "Tomorrow, though!"

"Good woman." Achojah waved as the garage door closed. Megan waved back, rolled the window up, and smiled at the streetlamp-lit street ahead of her. Orla could be a snake, and she'd take you for every penny she could, but Megan liked her coworkers and her job. Although, she thought as she pulled away from Rathmines toward Dublin city centre, she could maybe do with a little less excitement and considerably fewer murders.

With that thought in mind, she plugged her burner phone into the car's audio system and tried calling Paul Bourke again. He didn't pick up, which didn't particularly surprise her. "I just remembered Saoirse told me Martin's in to his caddie, Anthony Doyle, for a lot of money. I thought I'd go see if Heather went to him instead of Martin." As she said it, she realized that Bourke would consider it a phenomenally stupid and dangerous thing for her to do, so she added, "I'll be careful, promise," as if that would actually reassure him. As another afterthought, she said, "He told me he'd be at Fagan's in Drumcondra after the wake. It's his local, so that's where

I'm looking for him first." Then she hung up, feeling she'd covered her own butt enough to satisfy a jury of her peers, if not Detective Paul Bourke.

A "local" was the neighborhood pub, the place where everyone hung out, and the kind of place Megan didn't drink enough to establish herself at. She always felt tremendously self-conscious going in to locals, as if somehow wearing a hat or a sign that said "I Don't Belong Here." Even one like Fagan's, which was large and friendly enough to welcome tourists, made her feel out of place. She sidled up to the bar, though, and asked after Anthony Doyle, which got a laugh from the bartender, a thick-shouldered man in his thirties. "Jesus, what's his cologne, with all the ladies asking after him tonight? He was in earlier for a drink, but he said he was taking himself out to the island. A mate of his died, you know?" At Megan's nod, the bartender nodded, too. "He's taking it hard. Went out to Bull Island to say goodbye, like. That's what I told yer ather wan, too."

"American, like me?" Megan asked. "Honey blonde, about yay tall?" She gestured well above her own head, remembering Heather had been wearing heels when she left Megan's apartment.

"That's the one," the bartender said cheerfully. "You know her?"

"We all knew Lou," Megan said, stretching the truth far enough to break it. The bartender's face grew more solemn, though, and he tried to push a drink across the counter to Megan.

"On the house," he said, disappointment clear when she shook her head.

"I'm driving, sorry. I'll come back and take you up on it another time, all right?"

"All right, but you'd best tell me your name so I have something to pin my hopes on."

Megan laughed. "Oh my God, the nerve on you. It's Megan."

The man looked delighted. "I'm Hugh. Don't disappoint me, Megan."

"I probably will," she told him, and a woman just down the bar gave a shout of laughter.

"That'll learn ya, ya chancer."

"No one ever swipes right," he said to her. "I've got to be bold in real life." The woman laughed again, and Megan was smiling as she left the pub. She checked her messages before getting in the car, but Bourke hadn't called back. That was probably just as well, since he'd tell her not to do what she fully intended to do anyway. She called again—he still didn't pick up—and said, "Pub says Anthony Doyle is down at Bull Island, and that Heather went after him. I'm heading that way. And don't worry, I'm being careful."

The island wasn't far from the pub as the crow flew, but there wasn't a good way to get there from where she was. She went up to Griffith Avenue, whose denizens claimed it was the longest tree-lined street in Europe, and turned east toward the water before driving around a bunch of little switchbacks at its far end to get down to the water. A business park sparkled across the bay as she drove north until she reached the wooden bridge and pulled over, trying to decide if she would take the bridge or the causeway, if she were Anthony Doyle.

After a minute she decided it didn't matter: the wooden bridge was closer, if he'd come the same way through Clontarf that she had. She pulled onto the bridge and

drove down its narrow length with a waning moon glim-
mering on the sea to her right.

The island barely existed in the night, its low profile
hardly more than a dark streak in the bay. Megan, feeling
like a trespasser, killed the car lights and drove as far as
she could before barriers forced her to park and leave the
car behind. Cold wind swept hair into her face, and she
regretted not having her chauffeur's cap and a warmer
coat, but she hadn't been planning to go island-walking
when she'd left the house. There were seals on the beach,
looking like shining lumps of driftwood until they lifted
their heads, curious about the late-night human. Without
any dogs or any noisy birds to comment, with only the
seals and the sound of surf, the island seemed remarkably
isolated, for all that the mainland lay only a kilometre or
so from where she stood. Humanity didn't feel welcome.
Megan wished there were shadows to keep herself hidden
in without sliding all the way down to the wall's leeward
side, onto the sand dunes. The moon did its part, slipping
behind clouds, but mostly she felt exposed to anyone who
might be looking for her. There were no hiding places
along the wall road, except in the two or three concrete
bathing areas for swimmers to enter and exit the sea from.
Megan stopped in one of those, shivering, and rubbed her
hands together before peeking out again.

At the far end of the wall, beneath the Réalt Na Mara,
Heather Walsh now stood on a precarious chunk of stone
with Anthony Doyle creeping toward her.

CHAPTER TWENTY-THREE

Megan darted to the side, hugging the concrete wall as best she could, so that *she* wouldn't stand out against the changeable moonlight. There was another bathing area well ahead of her, and then absolutely nothing to hide beside unless she wanted to crawl down onto the chunks of seawall, which she really didn't. Not only would it be precarious and cold from the bay water, but incredibly difficult to navigate. Teeth gritted, she stepped across the path so she was at least at an angle to Heather and Anthony Doyle instead of on their side of the wall. A staircase led into the water next to the high pile of stones Heather stood on, but Anto was farther back than that, standing near the edge of, but still inside, the circle beneath the Star of the Sea statue at the end of the wall. Megan looked once more for cover and, unable to find it, ran toward them, grateful that the surf drowned out the sounds of her footsteps.

Anto had a slender object—a golf club—in one hand, and though he held it competently, his broad shoulders sagged. The wind snatched words from him, carrying them to Megan: *idea, sorry, fault, money.* Some of what he said snapped with anger, the tone carried clearly even when Megan couldn't understand the words themselves. Then she was close enough, and Anto sounded anguished as he said, "You're going to have to jump, Heather."

"Anthony, you don't want to *kill* me!" Heather Walsh stood on a piece of grate affixed, somehow and for some reason, to the top of one of the enormous chunks of angled rock. Her feet were bare, which looked incredibly unsafe on the slippery, wet metal, although the high heels she'd worn earlier certainly wouldn't have been any safer. They might have kept her feet ever so slightly warmer, though. Megan's own toes curled at the imagined chill seeping through that grate into Heather's soles.

Heather was damp everywhere from sea spray, the black dress she'd bought earlier that day limp and wind-blown. Her hair had been pulled into a ruthless ponytail from which water-dark strands still escaped, thanks to the wind. She sounded baffled, and cold. "This afternoon—what you said on the course—you don't want to *kill* me," she repeated.

Anto howled, "Of course I don't, but now I've no choice, do I? If I don't, you'll tell everyone everything!"

"Tell them *what*? I wanted to talk to you about this afternoon, Anthony! That's why I came looking for you, that's all!"

"Don't lie to me!" Anthony Doyle's voice dropped into a deep roar of rage, and Heather Walsh's abdomen visibly tightened with alarm. "Just jump," Anto said a heartbeat later, weary now instead of enraged. "Go on and drown and leave me to my life."

Heather glanced over her shoulder. "People swim off here all the time, Anthony. You think I'm going to drown if you make me jump?"

"I know you can't swim." Even in the moonlight, Megan saw astonishment and sudden alarm crease Heather's face. "I know everything about you," Anto continued forlornly. "You'll drown. Everyone will hear about your affair with Lou and think you killed yourself. I told you, you shouldn't have thrown me off the course this afternoon. I just wanted to protect you from all of this."

"All of *what*?" Despite the flash of fear Megan had seen, Heather kept all trace of it from her voice. "You didn't kill Lou. Neither did Martin. You couldn't have. You were both on the course. Collins killed him, didn't he? For Martin. Did my bastard husband find out Lou and I were in love? I just don't understand why he killed Collins, and I sure as hell don't know where he got the money to pay him wi—"

The wind snatched her voice and threw it around, as if it might find more listening ears than Megan's, and it carried her sudden silence, too. "Shit, Anthony. Did *you* pay for it? Jesus, was this all *your* idea? Does Martin even know about me and Lou?"

Megan kept creeping forward, grateful for her dark clothes and hair, although Anto had his back mostly turned to her and she doubted he'd see her anyway. The big caddie gave a high, tragic laugh. "Mr. Walsh doesn't know about anything past the end of his own golf club. At least, I didn't think he did. But I didn't hire anybody to kill Lou. I hated him, I wanted what he had, but he made you happy, and I'd never have taken that away from you. Ah-ah-ah." He pointed the golf club at Heather, who had tried to sit down on the seawall. "On your feet, Mrs. Walsh."

Heather froze, half-crouched on the grate, and spread her hands. "Listen, Anthony, I will. I'll stand back up, if you want me to. But I'm trying to understand. This afternoon—Anthony, you surprised me out there, all right? I was trying to win a game. A game that would have let me leave Martin, if it all worked out. I wasn't ready to hear what you were trying to say. What you *were* saying." She crouched farther, even more slowly than she'd moved before. "Anthony, I didn't even know you *knew* me, not really, much less had feelings for me, okay? You've worked with Martin for so long, I thought your relationship was all with him. I didn't know it had anything to do with me." A smile flickered across her face, and her gaze darted, with unerring accuracy, toward Megan, before returning to Anthony.

Astonishment surged in Megan's chest, shooting cold thrills through her. Part of her was afraid Anto would realize Heather was looking at someone else, and part of her was bone-chillingly relieved that Heather knew she was there. As long as Heather did and Anto didn't, the two women had an advantage. Heather kept talking, passion filling her voice as she watched Anthony, ignoring Megan edging closer still. "I didn't even know you thought I was a good golfer until our car driver mentioned you'd praised me to her. So I wasn't ready, you know? Lou had just died, I was trying to win a game . . . I wasn't ready to hear what you had to say."

Anto gave a bitter laugh. "And you are now? You think I'm daft, Mrs. Walsh?"

"No." Heather Walsh sounded completely sincere. "No, I don't think you're daft, and I don't think I'm ready, either, honestly. But if—can I sit down, Anthony? My legs are going to sleep. It's cold up here."

"No!" Anto took a threatening step forward, the golf club lifted. Heather stood again, her hands raised in acquiescence.

"Okay, okay, all right. You're not daft." Heather's voice dropped, like she was making a confession. "You're obviously not. You're a hell of a caddie, and what a caddie has to know to keep his golfer playing his best game. . . ." She shook her head. "So I'm not trying to play you. That would be stupid, and I'm not stupid either. But you've got to give me a little time, Anthony." She looked over her shoulder at the white caps, then back at Anto, a little sadly. "If you make me jump we're not going to have any time at all."

"You're just trying to get off that wall."

"Maybe," Heather admitted, "but you'll never know if you make me jump, will you. Can I—can I sit? May I? I won't move past that. But it's easier to talk that way. I won't feel so scared. And my feet are freezing, Anthony. I can hardly feel them. If I sit, I can put them in my dress."

If Heather was genuinely afraid, Megan thought she should have gone into acting, not golfing. Anto nodded grudgingly, and Heather, moving slowly and gracefully, sat, then wrapped her arms around herself in a shiver that Megan suspected wasn't an act. "Thank you." Her gaze roved again, passing Anthony and locking on Megan for the length of a blink, as if saying it was safe to move in now that she was more stable. Megan dropped her chin in a nod so small she doubted Heather could see it, even if the other woman hadn't returned her attention to Anthony Doyle.

"I'm afraid," Heather said very quietly. "Not just of the water, but—two people have died and I hardly even know why. If Martin didn't have Lou killed, then who did? And why? And why get Oliver Collins to do it, for heaven's sake? And who *did* kill Oliver? This is all— what if someone comes after *me*?"

Megan swore the other woman's eyes filled with tears, shining in the moonlight. Anto jerked a couple of hard steps forward toward her, and although the rough stones of the seawall still separated them by several feet, Megan saw the tiny flinch of a woman trying to hide her fear of being attacked. Megan rushed forward a step or two, then stopped sharply as Anto cried, "Nobody will come after you! It wasn't about you at all! They only wanted Lou dead!"

"What?" Heather's voice went to nothing, the word little more than a shape on her lips. "Who?"

"That developer, the one who's been in hearings with wee Saoirse!"

Heather said, "What?" again, and this time rose, her toes visibly spreading and trying to get a grip on the freezing grate beneath her feet. Anto raised the golf club like a bat, and Heather edged backward, cords standing out in her neck as she reached the top angle of the grate and had nowhere left to go except the rocks piled beneath it. A genuinely frightened squeak escaped her and she crushed her eyes shut, looking as though she was struggling against tears before she forced herself to open them again. "What's the developer got to do with Lou?"

Anto howled, "I don't know! All I know is I saw him

paying off Collins, and next thing I knew, Lou was dead! And I knew it would break your own heart, so I went and took care of Collins my own self! And now everything's gone wrong! You weren't supposed to get mixed up in it at all! You shouldn't be here!" He brandished the club, and Heather shrieked for the first time. Megan finally bolted forward, keeping low, and didn't care if Anto heard her in the last few seconds.

He did, turning toward her, swinging wildly but high with the golf club, as if he expected an attack at shoulder height. Megan slammed into his knees, driving him over sideways. The club went flying. Heather screamed and a splash followed. Anto hit the asphalt with a scream of his own, and a terrible crack that said his arm had broken. Megan never stopped moving, no longer caring about him. She ran for the staircase, realizing as soon as she reached its top step why Anto had stayed away from it. It wasn't more than two metres nearer to the sea than he'd been, but the difference in the wind was incredible. It had the strength to push Megan around, even as she ran forward into it. She caught a glimpse of the jagged, rocky wall beside it, her gut clenching in relief as she realized Heather hadn't fallen on those stones. Still running, Megan sought the other woman with her gaze as she reached the lowest steps, kicked her shoes off, and dove into the sea.

Cold shocked the air from her lungs as she hit the salty water and surfaced again, gasping. She twisted, spitting salt from her mouth as she searched for Heather, who was very near the wall itself, lying on her back in the water and—even in the dim moonlight, even with the sounds of surf all around—obviously breathing through clenched teeth as she tried to stave off panic. Megan struck a few strokes over to her, shouting, "I'm here, I've got you."

She put an arm around the other woman's shoulder and neck in a swimmer's save hold. Although Heather was clearly trying not to give in to terror, she flailed at Megan's touch, trying to get herself farther out of the water. She dunked Megan, who tightened her arm around Heather's neck as she came back up and bellowed, "Knock it off! I've got you, just relax, you'll be fine! *Knock it off!*"

To her surprise, Heather, audibly crying now, stopped flailing. Megan allowed herself a single breath of relief, then spoke in Heather's ear. "I've got to swim out from the wall a little so I can see where we can get back on shore. *I have you*, okay? You're going to be fine. The waves are going to spill over us some. Just spit the water out I've got you. We're gonna be fine."

Heather wrapped her fingers around Megan's arm in an iron grip and nodded just a little, whispering, "Okay. Okay." Megan nodded too, then swam away from the wall with a powerful scissors kick, giving herself enough room to turn and search for the stairs. The ones she's dived off were too near to where Anthony Doyle would be. The bathing area where swimmers could exit and enter the bay was farther away, but felt safer.

The water got noticeably colder even a few metres out from the wall. Megan put the thought out of her mind as best she could. The swimmer's entrance was only about thirty metres away. They could make it. Megan spat out saltwater as another wave rolled across her face, promised, "Two minutes," and pulled Heather through the water. She was exhausted from cold when she pushed Heather onto the concrete steps a minute or so later. Heather grabbed her, pulled her up, and hugged her hard, muttering, "One and a half," through chattering teeth.

"One and a half what?"

Heather whispered, "Minutes," and Megan realized she'd been counting down the window of rescue time that Megan had promised. She laughed sharply and hugged back, both of them shivering from the bone. Heather's words slurred with cold and gratitude. "You saved me. You saved me. Oh, God, where's Anthony?"

"I think I broke his elbow." Megan, so cold she could hardly think, crawled up the steps to the open doorway in the concrete wall and looked down the road. The caddie wasn't visible in either direction, so he was either on the eastern beachfront or had made a break for the Royal Dublin's clubhouse. "The guards will get him. I'll call—" She felt for her phone, which had gone into the water with her and stayed there. Even if it had come back out with her, it would have been ruined. "I won't call. Come on. Can you walk? My car is down the road. We can warm up in it."

"I will do anything to be warm." Heather, gracelessly, got up and shivered her way down the road in a wobbling line. "Wh-whi-whoo." The last sound was just an exhalation, trying to get her breathing and jaw under control so she wouldn't stutter so much. "Lou. The developer. What . . ."

"Sean Ahern." A chill ran through Megan so hard it twisted her head of its own accord. She wrapped her arms around herself, rubbing her torso as they staggered toward her car, but it didn't seem to help much. "He wants t–to develop a park over there." She nodded toward the mainland. "I don't thi—*sheesh* I'm cold—I don't th– think Lou's death has anything t–to do with golf or you or M–Martin, Heather. I th–think it was about Saoirse. Okay, can you r–run? Let's run. I'm t–too cold to talk."

"I can do anything to be warm," Heather repeated. They broke into a shuffling run, which, while much faster than their walk, wasn't actually very fast at all. Still, Megan had warmed up a little by the time they arrived at the Volvo several minutes later. She got survival blankets out of the boot and, with the car's heaters on full blast, the two of them stripped down to their underwear, hung their clothes from the back windows to dry in the wind, snuggled together, and wrapped up in the blankets. Megan snaked a hand out to lock the doors, then tucked back in, and Heather blurted a shivering giggle. "This is going to be hard to explain."

It reduced Megan to unexpected tears of laughter. "Not really. Skin dries faster than cloth." It sounded very reasonable, and she whooped with laughter about it again, both of them dissolving until finally some of the stress had passed and they were able to control themselves. "Maybe a little hard," Megan admitted, wiping her eyes. "My boss is going to kill me for saltwater-staining these seats. I mean, they're treated against spills, but not against dripping wet people sitting in them."

"We're on the space blankets. They'll be fine." Heather gave her a bright, overemotional smile. "You saved my life."

"You saved your own life, holy moly, woman. You were so cool up there, keeping him talking. You got a confession!" Megan shivered again, but she could feel the warmth crawling through her, chasing away the cold.

"Yeah, but I was screwed when I went in the water."

"You were floating," Megan disagreed. "Saved yourself."

"Oh my God. I went to one of your movie theatres this summer and they had a cold-water shock ad, a thing to tell you what to do if you fell in. Like, it said the cold would basically make you panic and shut down your ability to think and you'd start flailing and you'd end up drowning, but if you could get past the first like twenty or thirty seconds of that you'd be able to think again, so even when I was talking to Anthony I was telling myself that was what I needed to do. It was still so hard." Heather choked off a sob.

"See," Megan said. "You saved yourself."

"With a little help."

"Right. Okay. With a little help." Megan closed her eyes, pulling the blanket around them more tightly. Heather put her head on top of Megan's, and for a few minutes they were silent, just warming up. Megan, tired enough that colors flashed behind her eyelids, blue and red, finally sighed. "Sean Ahern has a hearing to push forward his accelerated development plans tomorrow afternoon at the same time as Lou's funeral. Saoirse is the environmental expert for the community. Honestly, I think Ahern had Lou killed so Saoirse wouldn't be in any condition to make the community's case against development in front of the planning board."

"That's insane. Nobody would do that."

"It's hundreds of millions of euros."

"Why not just kill Saoirse?"

Megan slumped, stumped. "I don't know."

A hard knock sounded on the window. Megan and Heather both screamed, full-throated shrieks of terror. Outside the car, in the moonlight, Detective Paul Bourke jerked back from the window in surprise. Wheezing with the slightly demented laugh of dissipating fear, Megan rolled the window down about an inch. "Anthony Doyle killed Oliver Collins because Collins killed Lou Mac-

Donald. Doyle is somewhere on the island, probably with a broken arm, and we think Sean Ahern paid Collins to kill Lou so Saoirse couldn't interfere with his St. Anne's Park development plans." A little to keep the heat in, but mostly to see Bourke's expression, she rolled the window back up again. Heather burst into giggles.

Bourke stared at them both, then, stone-faced, took out his phone and started making calls.

CHAPTER TWENTY-FOUR

Not that I should be telling you this, but we arrested Sean Ahern at half twelve this morning. He was on the way out of his house, bags packed, when the gardaí arrived. Anthony Doyle had called, asking him for help, and Ahern took it as a warning. They'll both go on trial for murder.

New phone, Megan texted back. **Who dis?**

Paul Bourke sent a laughing emoji, and Megan sent a wink back. She'd gotten up early despite the late night, gone to the gym, then replaced her broken phone as soon as the shops opened. After some wheedling, she'd gotten her old number back even though she'd lost the SIM card, which meant people could get hold of her, at least, even if she didn't know who they were. She was waiting outside of Heather Walsh's hotel now, reinstalling apps and trying to figure out the new phone's idiosyncrasies.

At least texting was still texting. **Are you coming to the funeral?**

I don't think so. I've another arrest to make.

Megan, said, "What? Who?!" out loud before texting the same thing to Detective Bourke.

As if I could tell you, he replied a minute later.

Megan bounced out of the Continental, striding across the parking lot with suddenly high energy, and actually called him, but he didn't pick up. She let it ring until it went to voice mail, then texted an agitated **You can't do this to me!** to him.

I can so, Bourke texted back, and then, despite the series of increasingly frantic messages she sent him, he didn't respond again. Megan muttered a couple of good-natured curses in his general direction and got back in the car to await Heather.

The golfer looked about like Megan felt, honestly. Like she'd had a traumatic night, hadn't gotten enough sleep, and still had to be professional. Makeup hid a wealth of sins, but they exchanged a glance that admitted to the exhaustion beneath the professional veneer. "How are you doing, Mrs. Walsh? Do you really have to be there today?"

Heather made a face. "Martin doesn't need me, but with Anthony under arrest and Lou dead, I think I should be."

"For the optics," Megan said, and Heather, with a sigh, nodded.

"The media will have a field day no matter what, but if I'm *not* there, they'll hang me out to dry, and I'm going to need all the good will I can get, if I'm divorcing Martin when this tournament is over."

"I don't know," Megan said, not quite under her breath. "I think you might get more media sympathy than you expect. He may still be charming the masses, but after that showdown at the wake, everybody who actually knows him seems pretty fed up with him."

"I should be so lucky." Heather fell silent as Megan drove her out to the island under a clear blue sky. The wind seemed milder than the days before, but to make up for it, there was a media presence unlike anything Megan had ever seen. "They've caught wind of the arrests," Heather said grimly. "This has gotten bigger than golf, now. It's a *scandal*."

Megan kept in front of her, fending off reporters, as Heather made her way to the clubhouse. Inside, friends approached, and Megan backed away until the first competitors of the tournament were called. Martin Walsh was among them, and Heather, plastering on the smile of a dutiful wife, went out with the rest of his entourage. Megan followed in their wake and snatched her phone out of her pocket as it began to ring.

Saoirse's tone flooded with relief when Megan answered. "Megan, thank God. What's going on? The planning board called to say the meeting's being rescheduled after all, and it's just broken on the news that Sean Ahern's been arrested for Da's murder." Her voice rose in hurt confusion. "Why would he kill me da?"

Megan, trying to keep her voice quiet, shook her head. "I don't know. Or rather, I don't know why he didn't just have you killed, honestly." A high-pitched laugh broke her explanation and she winced. "I'm sorry. That was kind of abrupt."

"But it's true, though, why kill Da if I was the one in his way? I don't understand." Saoirse's voice broke and she clawed it back under control. "Will that police detective of yours tell you?"

Megan cast a shifty glance toward Dublin's city centre, as if Paul Bourke was out there somewhere and could somehow meet her gaze. "He might, but he said he's got another arrest to make this morning."

"*Who?*"

"I'll find out," Megan promised.

"Okay. You'll be here to bring me to the funeral?" the younger woman asked, her voice thin.

"I will," Megan promised, and Saoirse, reassured, hung up. Megan exhaled heavily and caught up with the golfing entourage just in time to watch Detective Bourke arrest Martin Walsh.

A wall of noise rose up around Martin's arrest. Reporters and photographers encircled Heather Walsh, whose shock was visible. Megan elbowed more than one well-known media personality out of the way as she got Heather from the crush into the car, where they followed the police vehicles off the island. Only then did Heather, on a broken laugh, say, "Accessory to murder. Did you hear? That's what he was arrested for."

Megan shook her head, trying to keep her voice low and calm. "I was too far away to hear. What . . . who?"

"Lou." Heather took a shuddering breath. "I'd like to go to the precinct and find out what happened, if I can, but do you know what I'm thinking now?" At Megan's negative headshake, Heather said, "That I can go to Lou's funeral now. I'd been stuck going to the game because I had to be the good wife, but I don't have to do that anymore. Not if Martin was involved."

"I'm driving Saoirse to the funeral," Megan said softly. "I'll see if she minds me bringing you, too." Questions absolutely bubbled inside her, but she kept a lid on them, concentrating very hard on driving.

It turned out following cop cars meant a smooth drive to the precinct. Heather went inside while Megan parked, and Megan followed her in a few minutes later. Heather was almost on her way back out again, face pale beneath her makeup.

"He's confessed. Apparently he started talking as soon as they put him in the police car." Her voice shook and she took a moment to gather herself. "I don't know all the details. I didn't—I didn't want to stay and hear them." Her eyes filled with tears as she met Megan's gaze. "Is that awful of me?"

"No." Megan opened her arms, offering a hug, and Heather Walsh stepped into it, clutching the back of Megan's coat and sobbing into her shoulder for a ragged half minute. "No," Megan said again, quietly. "You learned as much as you needed to. You don't have to take more on right now, Heather. It's okay."

"Thank you." Heather finally let go, wiping her face and fighting against more tears. "Somebody tipped him off last week that Lou got the wild card spot on the PGA Tour. He kept a lid on it—I didn't think he could act that well, Megan, I really didn't—and when Oliver Collins mentioned that Sean Ahern was looking to develop St. Anne's Park, but Saoirse was getting in the way, Martin saw a chance. He and Ahern went in on paying Collins off to kill Lou."

Megan, softly, said, "God. I'm sorry, Heather," and the golfing champion nodded, whispering, "Me too. Can we . . . can we go now? I just . . . I don't want to be here when the media shows up."

"Yeah. Come on. I'll take you to your hotel to change

for the funeral, and I'll call Saoirse. She needs to know this."

Gratitude filled Heather's face. "Thank you. She's been through so much." She left the building a few steps ahead of Megan, who cast one anticipatory glance over her shoulder, hoping she'd see Detective Bourke and get more answers. To her disappointment, he didn't magically appear just because she wanted him to, so, with a rueful smile, she followed Heather Walsh back to the car.

A whole load of Saoirse's friends—all the young men who had surrounded Martin at the wake—took it upon themselves to forgo actually attending the funeral. Instead they, along with Megan, blocked both the doors and the mourners from the arrival of pushy, curious media people who had gotten enough details of Martin Walsh's arrest to conclude something exciting might go down at Lou's funeral.

They weren't wrong either. Megan caught bits of Saoirse's eulogy, savage with rage and grief, and of Heather's slightly more measured words after. The voices of the mourners, afterward, were edged with anger, and when people exited to find busybody reporters hanging around for a story, a flash of outrage sparked through the crowd. Megan, driving Saoirse and Heather home later, thought it was lucky the funeral had ended without violence. She was shattered with exhaustion her own self, and couldn't imagine having to golf the next day, as Heather had to. Staying awake enough to be Heather's driver would be work enough.

Despite that, she stayed up late anyway, relating the details of the past few days to Jelena over dinner at a

Lebanese restaurant in the Temple Bar section of Dublin's city centre. "Driving people around is supposed to be boring," Jelena said, mystified. "It's not supposed to be an adventure."

"Well, if it wasn't, I wouldn't have *this*." Megan gestured to her gold pantsuit, and Jelena laughed.

"If we don't stop eating, you won't *fit* in that." They kept eating anyway, until Megan finally had to drag herself home and to bed. She was almost late driving Heather to the Howth golf course the next morning, and caught an earful from Orla when she skidded into the garage at the last possible moment.

Heather overcame a bad start to her game to take second, with Saoirse MacDonald caddying for her. It clearly just about killed Aibhilín Ní Gallachóir to not ask about her personal relationships in the aftermath of the game. Maybe as a reward for her restraint, at the end of the interview, Heather said, "Aibhilín? If you have half an hour for me tomorrow after the final game of the tournament, I'd be happy to talk to you."

The sportscaster nearly punched the air, promised the time slot, and went away trying not to wiggle like one of the puppies. Heather, watching her go, said, "No one will be surprised to hear I'm filing for divorce, but she'll be happy to break the news."

"File for it in America," Megan advised. "The Irish government won't even consider allowing a divorce until you've been formally separated for three years, even if you didn't get married here."

"We didn't, and I will," Heather promised. "Thank you for everything, Megan. I'm sorry we brought so much drama into your life."

Megan, thinking of Jelena's comment, smiled. "Well, at least it wasn't boring."

Heather laughed. "I guess not. Look, I'm going to go get changed, but I can get a taxi back to my hotel."

"No, it's fine, I'll drive you."

"Mmm. Well. You have a friend here, so you can decide while I'm changing." Heather sent a pointed look across the course, and Megan followed her gaze to see Paul Bourke, wearing jeans and a camel-colored sweater under a blue jacket and rather resplendent in a scarf matching the coat, coming across the green. "That," Heather said, "is not a detective here on business," and scooted off under the weight of Megan's bemusement.

"Ms. Malone," Bourke said as he reached her.

"Detective Bourke." Megan looked at his feet. "Your shoes match your sweater. How do you even do that?"

"Would you ask a woman that question?"

"Probably not," Megan admitted. "On the other hand, I'd probably ask where she got the shoes, if they were cute. Those aren't cute, they just match."

Bourke put a hand over his heart. "I'm wounded." He pointed with his chin after Heather. "How did she do? I wanted to get out here for the game, but I was too busy trying to match my jumper and shoes to be on time."

Megan laughed. "She came in second, which is better than anyone expected, with all the turmoil. What happened with Martin and—" She waved her hands in the air. "And everybody? Give me the dirt."

"You'll never believe it."

"Try me." Megan glanced in the general direction of the docks, a couple of miles away on the other side of the peninsula. "Heather's set me free for the afternoon. Want to go get some fish and chips at Dorans on the Pier and tell me all about it?"

"Only if I get to hear the entire story of how you ended up wet and naked with someone else's wife in the front seat of a hired car."

"We were not naked," Megan said primly. "We had our underwear on."

"And I heard it all anyway," Bourke pointed out. "Give me the salacious version."

"Not unless you adopt Mama Dog."

Bourke stuck out his hand. "Deal."

"Oh, well, crap." Megan laughed and shook his hand. "All right, fine, in that case, uh, let me see. Obviously, Heather and I have been carrying on a torrid but secret love affair for months."

"That's much too obvious. There must be a better story."

"I'll work on one," Megan promised. They struck off across the course, only pausing when a shrill whistle blasted behind them. They turned, and Heather Walsh, dressed in civilian clothes, waved vigorously from the clubhouse door.

Megan waved back, then pushed her hands into her pockets as Bourke said, "That woman has been through more than she knows. Once Walsh got started he wouldn't stop confessing. Sean Ahern had been looking for a way to stop Saoirse's interference with his development plans for weeks, but he was too queasy to take a hit out on the girl herself."

Megan barked a disbelieving laugh, and Bourke shrugged. "People are funny like that. So Walsh put it into his head that if Lou was killed, she'd be too broken-hearted to even realize the development was back underway. They hit on hiring Oliver Collins to do the deed when the both of them who had motive were able to produce impeachable alibis."

"Why Collins?"

"Partly because he'd do anything for a bit of flash, partly because he's such a snob they thought no one would imagine he'd get his hands dirty, and partly because he's got a deadly golf swing. He went out on the green after Lou and sliced a ball into the back of his skull. Even if the impact hadn't killed him, knocking him unconscious into the water hazard would finish him off. But it gets better."

"Better? How? Somebody else was involved?" Megan peered sideways at Bourke, whose thin smile told her she'd guessed correctly. "No! What? Who? When?"

"Do you know anything about Lou MacDonald's wife?"

"I know she got Lou into golfing and died in a hit-and-run."

"Martin Walsh confessed to driving that car."

Megan stopped dead, staring at the detective. "He never."

"Like he was dying to tell somebody," Bourke confirmed. "He hated Kimberly MacDonald."

"*Why?*"

Bourke shook his head. "For having more influence over Lou than Walsh himself did. For getting him into the game and proving Lou was better than Walsh. For living longer than Walsh's first wife. For existing, apparently. He took a junker car off a wrecking lot, fixed it up enough to drive, kept an eye on Mrs. MacDonald's schedule, and caught her on a blind bit of road one night."

"Jesus. Heather doesn't know yet?"

"Not yet. Neither does Saoirse, but it'll all come out. He's a piece of work, is Martin Walsh. Look, Megan, I want you to promise me something."

"What's that?"

"Don't get caught up in any more murders."

Megan turned a smile up at the blue afternoon sky. "Know what?"

"What?"

"I'm not going to promise *anything*."

*Keep reading for a special excerpt of the third book in
the* **Dublin Driver Mystery** *series . . .*

Death of an Irish Mummy
A Dublin Driver Mystery

CHAPTER ONE

The body lay in a coffin eighteen inches too small, its legs broken and folded under so it would fit.

Megan stood on her tip-toes, peering down at it in fascinated horror. Dust-grey and naturally mummified, the body in the box, nicknamed "The Crusader," must have been a giant—especially for his era—while he lived. Next to him, in a better-fitted coffin, lay someone missing both feet and his right hand. Megan didn't quite dare ask if he'd gone into the grave that way or if his parts had been . . . *misplaced* over the centuries. Given that there was a tiny woman called "The Nun" lying beside them both, Megan assumed nobody in ancient, Catholic Ireland would have had the nerve to divest the fellow of his limbs under her supervision. The fact that he was buried here, in the church, suggested he'd been a decent sort of fellow in life, although he was known, according to both the tour guide and the plaques in the crypt, as "The Thief." The final body, a woman, was referred to only as "The Unknown," which, Megan felt, just figured.

"Are any of these the Earl?" A brash American voice bounced harshly off the crypt's limestone walls and echoed unpleasantly in the small bones of Megan's ears. She, being Texas-born and not quite three years in Ireland, knew brash Americans. Cherise Williams fell squarely into that bracket. Megan had been driving Mrs. Williams around Dublin for two days and recognized the brief, teeth-baring grimace the young tour guide exhibited after knowing the woman for only ten minutes.

Like Megan had done dozens of times already, the guide turned his grimace into a smile as he shook his head. "No ma'am, the earls are interred here but not among the mummies on display. As you can imagine, the Church can hardly condone breaking open coffins to display the mummies, so those we see here are . . ."

He hesitated just briefly, and Megan, unable to help herself, suggested, "Free-range?"

The poor kid, who was probably twenty years Megan's junior, gave her a startled glance backed by horror. As he struggled to control his expression, Megan realized the horror was at the fear he might burst out laughing, although he managed to keep his voice mostly under control as he said, "Em, well, yes. Free-range would . . . yes, you could say that. *I* wouldn't," he said, like he was trying to convince himself, "but you could. Their coffins have slipped, decayed, or been damaged over the centuries, and in those cases we've chosen not to, em . . ." He shot Megan another moderately appalled look, but went along with her analogy. "Not to, em, re-cage them, as it were."

"But I need the *Earl's* DNA," Mrs. Williams said in stentorian tones.

"Yes ma'am, but you understand I can't just open a coffin at the behest of every visitor to the vault—"

"Well, what about one of these?" Mrs. Williams made an impatient gesture at the wall, where nooks and vaults held crumbling coffins of various sizes, and the floor, where a variety of wooden coffins had succumbed enough to age that mummified legs and arms poked out here or there.

"Yes ma'am, some of these *are* the Earls of Leitrim, but—"

"Well, let me have one, then! I only need a sample. It's not as if I'm going to carry an entire skeleton out of here in my handbag, young man, don't be absurd."

The kid cast Megan a despairing glance. She responded with a sigh, taking one step closer to Cherise Williams. "We'd better be leaving soon to get to your two p.m. appointment, Mrs. Williams. You're meant to be speaking with officials about this, not a tour guide. You know how difficult it is for young men to say no to the ladies. We wouldn't want to get him in trouble." She *wanted* to say it was difficult for young men to say no to women who remind them of their mothers, but Cherise Adelaide Williams wore her sixty-three years like a well-bandaged wound and seemed like the sort who could imagine no one thought her old enough to be a twenty-year-old's mom.

Just like that, the guide's gaze softened into a sparkle and he bestowed an absolutely winsome smile upon Mrs. Williams. His voice dropped into a confiding murmur as he offered her his arm, which she took without hesitation. "Sure and she's right, though, ma'am. It's breaking me own heart to see the distress in yer lovely blue eyes, but if I lose this job it's me whole future gone, yis know how it is. It's true university's not as dear in Ireland as I hear it is back in the States, but when you're a lad all alone, making his own way in the world, it's dear enough so. I'd be desperate altogether without the good faith of the brothers at St. Michan's and I know a darling woman like yourself would never want to see a lad lost at sea like." He escorted her toward and up the stairway, both of them ducking under the stone arch that led to the graveyard. He lay the Irish on so thick as they mounted the rough stone stairs that Megan lifted her feet unnecessarily high as she followed them, as if she might otherwise get some of the flattery stuck on her feet.

By the time she'd exited the steel cellar doors that led underground, the guide had jollied Mrs. Williams into smiles and fluttering eyelashes. "We have a minute, don't we?" she cooed at Megan. "Peter here wants to show me the church's interior. Maybe I can convince the pastor"— the tour guide bit his tongue to stop himself correcting Mrs. Williams on the topic of priests versus pastors, an act of restraint Megan commended him for—"to let me have a finger bone or something, instead of going through all this bothersome legal nonsense."

"Of course, Mrs. Williams." Megan could imagine no scenario in which that would happen, but she followed the flutterer and the flatterer into the church.

Parts of St. Michan's church looked magnificently old from the exterior. A tower and partial nave had survived since the 17th century and looked the part, all irregular grey stones and thick mortar. The rest of the nave had been repaired with concrete blocks that, to Megan's eye, could have been as recent as the 1970s, although apparently they dated back to the early 1800s. She had expected the interior to be equally old-fashioned, but its clean, cream walls and dark pews looked as modern as any church she'd ever seen. Arched stained glass windows let light spill in, and a pipe organ—one that Handel, composer of the *Messiah*, had evidently played on—dominated one end of the nave. Megan shook her head, astonished at the contrast with the narrow halls and sunken nooks of the crypts below.

But Dublin was like that, as she'd slowly discovered over the years she'd lived there. Modern constructions sat on top of ancient sites, and builders were forever digging up the remains of Viking settlements when they started new projects. Even this church, well over three hundred years old, was predated by the original chapel, built a thousand years ago. According to the literature, the ground had been consecrated five hundred years before *that*.

Any temples or building sites that old in the States had been razed to the ground, and all the people who'd used them, murdered, around about the same time St. Michan's had been built.

"Cheerful," Megan told herself, under her breath. Peter the tour guide had introduced Mrs. Williams to the priest, who currently had the look of a man weathering a storm. He actually leaned toward Mrs. Williams a little, as if bracing himself against the onslaught of her determination, and if he'd had more hair, Megan would have imagined she could see it waving in Mrs. Williams's breeze. He had to be in his seventies, with a slim build that had long ago gone wiry, and a short beard on a strong jaw that looked like it had held a line in many arguments more important than this one.

DEATH OF AN IRISH MUMMY   271

"—grandfather, the Earl of Leitrim—" Cherise Williams persisted in saying *Lye-trum*, though the Irish county was pronounced *Leetrim*. Megan—also a Texan—couldn't tell if Williams didn't know how it was said, or if her accent simply did things to the word that weren't meant to be done. Everyone who had encountered the *Lye-trum* pronunciation had repeated *Leetrim* back with increasing firmness and volume, while also somehow being slightly too polite to directly correct the error. So far the attempted corrections hadn't taken, leaving Megan to suspect her fellow Texan didn't hear a difference in what she said and what everyone else did.

The priest had interrupted with a genuinely startled, "Your *great-grandfather*?" and Mrs. Williams simpered, putting her hand out like she expected it to be kissed.

"That's right. I'm the heir to the Earldom of Lyetrum."

The tour guide and the priest both shot Megan glances of desperate incredulity while Mrs. Williams batted her eyelashes. Megan widened her eyes and shrugged in response. A week earlier she hadn't known Leitrim (or anywhere else in Ireland, for that matter) had ever had any earls. Then Mrs. Williams, styling herself *Countess* Williams, had called to book a car with Leprechaun Limos, the driving service Megan worked for. Megan's boss, who was perhaps the least gullible person Megan had ever met, had taken the self-styled countess at her word and charged her three times the usual going rate for a driver. Megan had looked up the Earls of Leitrim, and been subjected to Mrs. Williams's explanation more than once since she'd picked her up at the airport. In fact, Mrs. Williams had launched into it again, spinning a fairy tale that drew the priest and Peter's attention back to her.

"—never knew my great-grandfather, of course, and

my granddaddy died in the war, but his wife, my granny Elsie, she used to tell a few stories about Great-Granddaddy, because she knew him before he died. She said he always did sound Irish as the day was long, and he used to tell tall tales about being a nobleman's son. We'd play at being princesses and knights when we were little, because we believed we had the blood of kings." Mrs. Williams dipped a hand into a purse large enough to contain the Alamo and extracted a small book, its pages yellow with age and a faded blue floral print fabric cover held shut with a tarnished gold lock. The key dangled from a thin, pale-red ribbon tucked between the pages, and Mrs. Williams deftly slid it around to open the book. She opened it to a well-worn page and displayed it to a priest and a tour guide who clearly had no idea of, and less genuine interest in, what they were looking at.

"Granny Elsie never seemed to take it at all seriously, but after she died we found this in her belongings. It's all the stories Great-Granddaddy Patrick used to tell her, right down to the place he was the earl of, Lyetrum. She said he never wanted to go back because of all the troubles there, but that was then and this is now, isn't it? So all I need is a bit of bone from one of the old earls so I can prove I'm the heir, you see?"

As if against his will, the priest said, "But, em, your father?"

Creases fell into Cherise Williams' face, deep lines that cut through her makeup and drew the corners of her mouth down. "Daddy died a long time ago, and the Edgeworth name went with him. If I'd only known it meant something, of course, I'd have kept it, but when I got married I changed my name. Everyone did in those days.

But my girls and I, we're the last of the Edgeworth blood-line. My middle daughter, Raquel, is coming in this afternoon to be with me for all of this. We meant to fly together, but she had an emergency at work." She turned a tragic, blue-eyed gaze on Megan, who was surprised to be remembered. "Ms. Malone is going to get her at the airport while I speak with the people at Vital Statistics about getting an Edgeworth DNA sample from the mummies here, aren't you, Ms. Malone?"

"I am, ma'am." Megan was reasonably certain the Irish version of Vital Statistics was called something else, but neither she nor the two Irish-born men in the church seemed inclined to correct Cherise on the matter. "And I don't mean to pressure you, Mrs. Williams, but we really should be going. I'd hate to be late collecting Ms. Williams."

Cherise Williams gave the priest one last fluttering glance of shy hope, but he, sensing rescue, remained resolute. "I do dearly hope you find what you need at the CSO, Mrs. Williams."

"I'm sure I shall." Mrs. Williams sniffed and tossed her artistically greying hair. "I'm told the Irish love to be accommodating, and no one can resist the Williams charm." She swept out of the church, leaving Megan to exchange a weak, wry glance with two Irish people who had proven neither accommodating nor susceptible to the Williams charm. Then she hastened out in Mrs. Williams's wake, scurrying to reach the car quickly enough to open the door for her client. "I can't imagine why they couldn't just—" Mrs. Williams waved a hand as she settled into the vehicle. "Surely a little finger bone wouldn't be missed."

"Well," Megan said as gently as she could, as she got

into the Lincoln's front seat, "I suppose we'd have to think about how *we* would feel if someone wanted to just take a finger bone from *our* grandfather's hand."

"That's just it!" Mrs. Williams proclaimed. "He *is* my grandfather! Or one of them is. The last Earl was my great-grand-uncle, so it's his father who was my direct ancestor."

"But your immediate grandpa. The one who was married to Grandma Elsie." Megan pulled out into traffic, albeit not much of it. The River Liffey lay off to their right, beyond the light-rail Luas tracks, and she forbore any mention that Mrs. Williams would probably get to Rathmines, where her appointment with the vital statistics office was, faster on the tram than in Megan's car.

"No one would want Granddaddy's finger!" Mrs. Williams replied, shocked. "What a horrible idea, Ms. Malone. What on earth could you be thinking, suggesting somebody go and steal Granddaddy's finger?"

"My apologies, Mrs. Williams. I can't imagine what got into me." Megan crossed the tracks and pulled onto the quays (a word she still had trouble pronouncing *keys*), and offered bits of information about the scenery when Cherise Williams had to pause for breath while scolding her for the imaginary sin of violating the sanctity of her poor sainted grandfather's body. "Here's Ha'penny Bridge, it was the first bridge across the Liffey, and cost a ha'penny to cross—up there is Trinity College. I suppose it's possible the Earls of Leitrim were educated there—entering the old Georgian center of Dublin, made popular when the Duke of Leinster moved to the unfashionable southern side of the city—"

"To be a duchess," Mrs. Williams sighed. "Now wouldn't that be something?"

"Countess is more than most of us can hope to aspire to." Megan smiled at the woman in the rearview mirror, and Mrs. Williams, her anxiety evidently assuaged, listened to the rest of Megan's tour guide spiel in comparative silence. Half a block from the clunky-looking statistics office building, Megan broke off to say, "Now I just want to verify, Mrs. Williams, that I'll be bringing Ms. Williams back to your hotel, and you'll be meeting us there? You're certain you don't need me to collect you here at the office?"

"I'm sure, honey. You go get Raquel and I'll see you tomorrow morning when we drive up to Lyetrum."

Megan, wincing, said, "Leitrim," under her breath and pulled in under the ugly statistics building to let Mrs. Williams out. "You have the company's number if you decide you need a lift. Don't be afraid to use it."

"Thanks, honey. Oh! And you take my extra room key, so Ray-Ray can go right in." Mrs. Williams handed the key over, despite Megan's protestations, and disappeared inside the building. Megan, letting out a breath of relief, drove out to the airport in blissful silence, not even turning the radio on. Raquel Williams's flight was almost an hour late, so Megan got a passably decent coffee and a truly terrible croissant from one of the airport cafes, and sat beside Arrivals to wait for her client.

She would have known Raquel as Cherise's daughter even if Raquel hadn't waved when she saw Megan's placard. She was taller than her mother, with rich auburn hair that didn't match her eyebrows, but with the same strong facial shape that Cherise had. She wore her hair in a much looser, more modern style than Cherise's hair-sprayed football helmet, but otherwise she was her mother's younger doppelgänger, down to the pronunciation of Leitrim. She swept up to Megan, said, "Hi, I'm Raquel Williams, the heir apparent to Lyetrum, and I just can't wait to see this whole darn gorgeous Emerald Isle."

"Megan Malone. It's nice to meet you, Ms. Williams. I've dropped your mother off at—"

"Oh my gosh, you're American too! Are you from Texas?" Raquel leaned across the barrier to hug Megan, who stiffened in surprise and found an awkward smile for the other woman.

"I am, yes. From Austin. And here's your room key, from your mother."

"Oh, wasn't that nice of her? And woo-hoo! Keep Austin weird, honey! I live there now myself, but Mama's from El Paso. Who'd have ever thought an earl would settle in Texas, huh?" Raquel Williams tucked the key in a pocket and came around the barrier rolling a suitcase large enough to pack three-quarters of a household into, and wrangling a huge purse along with a carry-on. "Not that he did right away, of course. It was New York first, but when his son died in the war, he took sick and Gigi Elsie—that's his daughter-in-law, our great-great grandma Elsie—took him down to El Paso, where she'd always wanted to live, and heck fire, here we are. How's Mama?"

Megan smiled. "She's just fine. Visiting the statistics office now in hopes of getting permission to get a DNA test done on one of the mummies. I'll take this, if you like, ma'am." She nodded toward the enormous suitcase.

"Oh heck fire, sure thing, but you'd better call me Raquel or you'll have me feeling old as sin." Raquel swung the suitcase Megan's way and smiled. "I've never been out of Texas before, this is all a big old adventure for me. How did you end up here?"

"I had citizenship through my grandfather, so they couldn't keep me out." Megan smiled again and gestured for Raquel to walk along with her as they headed for the hired cars parking lot. "Not quite as fancy as a connection to the Earls of Leitrim, but it's worked for me."

"*Leetrim*? Oh my gosh, is that how they say it here? We've had it all wrong all this time! Won't Mama have a laugh!" Raquel chattered merrily, her Texan accent washing over Megan in a more familiar, friendly way than her mother's did, as they reached the car and drove back to Dublin. Raquel peppered her with questions about the scenery, Leitrim's history—Megan wasn't much help there—and whether the Irish were really as superstitious as she'd heard.

"It's not that they're superstitious," Megan said with a smile. "It's that you wouldn't *really* want to build a road through a fairy ring, would you?"

Laughter pealed from the back seat. "Gotcha, right. Look, I don't mean to be rude, but are we almost there? I forgot to use the ladies' before I left the airport."

"Just a few more minutes, and you can run right in to use the toilets while I get your luggage," Megan promised.

Raquel breathed, "Thank goodness," and, a few minutes later when they arrived, did just that. She met Megan in the lobby with an apologetic smile afterward. "Thank goodness for public restrooms. Would you mind helping me bring the luggage up? I hate to bother—" She nodded at the bustling lobby, full of people already doing jobs.

"I don't mind at all. It's room 403." They took the lifts up, Raquel in the lead as they entered a narrow hall with dark blue carpeting.

"Oh, isn't this terrific, it's so *atmospheric*, isn't it?"

"A lot of Dublin is. Old buildings, lots of history. It's one of the reasons I love Dublin."

"I can see why." Rachel slipped the key in the door, and, pushing it open, smashed the corner into her dead mother's hip.

Look for *Death of an Irish Mummy* on sale in 2021!